On Jerusalem Street

On Jerusalem Street

ANTHONY DEWS

RESOURCE *Publications* · Eugene, Oregon

ON JERUSALEM STREET

Resource Publications
An Imprint of Wipf and Stock Publishers
199 W. 8th Ave., Suite 3
Eugene, OR 97401

www.wipfandstock.com

PAPERBACK ISBN: 979-8-3852-6437-7
HARDCOVER ISBN: 979-8-3852-6438-4
EBOOK ISBN: 979-8-3852-6439-1

VERSION NUMBER 12/05/25

ONE

I N the remains of the dying city Jesus Contreras walked the streets
as if on a mission. It was November and it felt like July. "Shit," he
thought. "It always feels like fucking July." Pausing at the top of a rise
in the crumbling road he looked down on Los Angeles. It was his home
and he wasn't sure he'd ever be able to feel that way about anywhere other
than the collapsing skyscrapers and hunks of rusting cars he'd lived in
most of his life. Not for the first time he wondered, no he *knew* there was
more than this. This wasn't normal, nothing this hard could be. Someone
somewhere had started this and the truth the words contained gnawed
his entrails like a rabid rat.

The sound of a stone clattering off concrete sent him spinning, hand
on the pistol kept stuffed in the waistband of jeans that didn't reach his
ankles, the clank of extra ammunition in a pocket promising protection
from the dog packs, cougars, and wolves that roamed the collapsed city.
They hadn't come cheap, nothing did these days, and he wasn't about to
waste them. He squinted in the light, seeing nothing but a flitting shadow
moving swiftly out of view. He relaxed. A dog most likely, too skittish
to hang around. Jesus grinned suddenly, savagely, good thing it did, it
wouldn't be worth the bullet.

As well as the gun Jesus carried a slingshot and lead bearings in
a pocket. The slingshot kept all but the most persistent of predators
away. The weight of the shot along with the pistol was extra insurance.
Even though he knew they were lying low to avoid the heat of midday
he couldn't count on all them doing it if they were hungry. Until they
grew more active in the evening Jesus could make good time and distance
before they started to come out. By then he would be at his destination.
Or so he hoped.

Over his jeans and a torn t-shirt bearing a face no one recognized, Jesus wore a ragged greatcoat open for easy access to the weapons, flicking his hand to them out of a habit he no longer knew he had. On his feet were a pair of crocs to let the water run through so his feet didn't rot. A pair of gold sunglasses he'd found up in the hills where the Hollywood sign once stood kept the glare from his eyes. His face was gaunt, lined. Black hair hung in ragged, dirty dreadlocks past his shoulders. His eyes burned with a fevered intensity and a ragged beard, kept under control with whatever glass fragment he could find covered his chin and cheeks. People he met went away feeling something in his presence that lasted days.

He cast his eye up at the sky, seeing the clouds rolling in like a carpet fringed with angry reds and yellows. Another storm was coming. He hoped there wouldn't be tornadoes with it. There were few safe places to hole up when they happened, slamming through the streets and ripping buildings apart. He took a deep breath and headed out upping his pace driven by the urge to get to his destination before it hit—and hit hard from the way it looked. He kept going along the streets, senses on high alert, splashing across rivulets of water, leftovers from the last storm.

The heat of the sun on his back made him feel like an egg in a pan. Soon it would be hot enough to melt tarmac and blister feet if you were stupid enough to go barefoot. And the city had problems more than just the heat. The streets were a fetid carpet of concrete, rusted metal, shit, and broken glass. Jesus remembered watching as a friend died slowly of tetanus. It had been slow and ugly and he was helpless and scared for days after, his nights scorched by nightmares. Sometimes even now they would creep back bringing him awake with his heart pounding, his mind seeking refuge from unremembered pain.

Jesus watched the sky to see when the inevitable rain was imminent. He didn't like the rain. When it came it roared like a monsoon, sheets of water hiding the other side of the street from view. He hurried along relieved it would at least keep the predators off the streets. It rained a lot now and when it did there was no relief from the heat or disease. Sewers overflowed and he was in no mind to wade through what spewed from the ruined sewers.

The city changed from sauna to hot shower and back with the rain, sapping the minds and energy of those who still called it home. In the past people sat out the heat in cinemas, bars, and shopping malls drinking milkshakes, iced teas, and beer while waiting for the fogs to roll in bringing cool air with them. But they were all long gone. Only a few small bars remained with portable generators and the means to keep them running and it was to one of those he was heading to now. Theaters and malls had passed out of memory.

The city lay quiet. Even the air felt dead, the heat muting any sound as he kept going, ticking off the miles step by step. In the past the city blared a sound track of people, traffic, air-con units, radios, speakers, and sirens. Now the silence overwhelmed the senses helped by the enervating heat, smothering everything and turning life into death. Jesus walked along silent streets once home to cars and people in a hurry to get nowhere. Now wilderness was returning inch by remorseless inch, clothing concrete and rusted steel with green. Jesus remembered how the city had been as he strode on. Memories and stories he had heard mingled and mixed until he no longer knew which was which. When he closed his eyes he could see the old city shrouding the new like a specter. He remembered people leaving, fitfully at first until the last mass migration, the lights of the cars vanishing over the hills leaving behind a city they no longer wanted to see and those who couldn't or wouldn't leave. It was Westward Ho! in reverse.

For most of his life he had done nothing more than exist and he looked like it. He looked like all the others who still called LA home and asked for nothing more than seeing one more sunrise. The eyes and souls of the people who remained were dead and empty, their life beat out of them from fighting to survive from day to day with no chance of escape. The city drove the desire to survive out leaving a husk of flesh and the eyes of the people were as empty as their bodies. The thought there could be something and somewhere better had no meaning. He had been the same as all the others but no longer. Behind the gold sunglasses lay the eyes of a man who no longer waited to die but who desired survival. In the pit of his soul he knew there had to be something better. More than wanting shelter from the storm he was driven by the storm lying in him.

Jesus cast a glance over to the hills ringing the city. Behind him, over the first ring of hills, was the metal spire. He had come to hate that metal spire and what it meant. It gave notice to the people still living there they were going nowhere. It marked a boundary nobody dared pass. So far and no further was the unspoken message Jesus and all the others heard every day. It told the people the hills were home to more than four-legged predators. They were home to those who watched them day and night, waiting. He saw the fires they lit every night, everyone could see them and still avoided talking about them. As he looked he paused, seeing where they were from memory. He didn't know who they were but he knew what they were doing, had seen the results when some had tried to leave. The bodies strung up on power poles. The cars and trucks loaded with corpses left overnight as messages. Men, women, children, it didn't matter as long as it worked. Few tried after they saw them and fewer succeeded. Soon nobody was game to try.

Something told him the spire at the edge of the dead city's vision was the key. To why the people had no way out, barricaded into what bolt-holes they found. The desire to find out who was out there had lain in him as long as he remembered, for longer than he had been alone. Now it was growing stronger. LA wasn't much but it was the only home he had and needed protecting. In the back of his mind lay the small niggle he couldn't shake off. It whispered in his ear every day the certitude that he and all the others had to disappear. Out there in the hills and further someone wanted them gone. He heard movement on a nearby street and got moving again.

He relied on memory to find his way since the street signs were long gone. A few blocks further then he would be safe. He reached the corner of what used to be Wilshire and S Wilton and saw an open door. He was there. He didn't quicken his pace or blink when a block of masonry fell from the Wiltern Theater behind him. It had been famous once but now it was another ruined edifice in a city the angels had deserted.

Over the door of the bar hung a faded sign telling anyone who cared they had arrived at The Tentacled Den. Nobody knew why it was called that and the owner never said. The sign hung by wire so rusty it was a miracle it hadn't fallen; only nobody believed in miracles anymore. The Tentacled Den was the only bar for ten blocks and it had its regulars who had no idea why they came. The owner was proud he'd been able to hang on for so long after the city died. The bar was also dying but he refused to believe it. He continued to open everyday at the same time. He closed it when the last patron left or passed out on the floor. His called himself Wilton Muscatine but it wasn't his real name. He called himself that simply because he liked the sound of it; felt it gave him some gravitas so people would listen when he spoke. If they did nobody admitted it but then nobody argued with him either. He looked up as Jesus walked in.

Wilton was large and fleshy with a tendency toward roundness and philosophy. Above the rotundity sat a red face which sported blotches when he shaved. He had a preference for Hawaiian shirts not quite large enough to cover his stomach. Black hair tinged with white peeked over the top button and he wore Bermuda shorts tied with rope to keep them up. Flip-flops of different colors adorned his feet. He nodded as Jesus came in trailing a cloud of dust to add to what had already accumulated there. It was dingy. Wilton hadn't cleaned it for months and never would again if Jesus was any judge. Spider webs nested in the corners where the walls said hello to the ceiling. The lights were dim and it was a miracle they worked. Like the rest of the city they would soon give out when what power still got through stopped altogether. Until then Wilton would replace the bulbs and tape up the wiring to stop the place burning down around him.

Jesus took a seat at the bar, blowing dust from the stool and clearing a space from mouse shit and dead flies. He swatted at some bugs that had flown in when the door was open. He didn't look around. He didn't need to. He'd been here often enough to describe the place blindfold. The stools, once red, had faded to light pink, and cracks wrinkled the vinyl. On most of them, the stitching had frayed to the point of non-existence. The foam on the inside was so flattened it dare not peek out of the holes to chafe unwary legs. Windows grimed with dirt barred the sun and what light managed to find its way in was yellow. Pool tables lined one wall and a busted-down jukebox stood in a corner hoping nobody saw it.

Wilton wiped a few glasses. Jesus tried to imagine a reason to bother. He couldn't. They were dirty as soon as they put back on the rack. "What are you having today, Jesus?" Wilton Muscatine asked him.

Jesus puffed his cheeks like he was about to blow a trumpet. "Anything you can describe as drinkable my friend, which doesn't leave much to choose from," he said. "Most of your drinks are *muy mierda*. A roach wouldn't drink them."

"The roaches have better taste than you." Wilton put a glass with some liquid in it in front of his only customer so far today. "Best Mezcal in town."

"It's the only Mezcal in town," Jesus said.

"Pah, you are splitting hairs only. It is the same thing."

Jesus drank it in one gulp. "*Mierda*, as I thought it would be. You will go out of business selling garbage, *basura*."

Wilton laughed. "I already have my friend, I decided it was of no concern and so I carried on." He looked at the empty glass. "Another?"

"Yes, one more." Jesus Contreras looked over the bar to the mirror sitting loose against the wall. It was as dirty as the windows and he looked at himself. "Is this all there is to life?" he asked. He asked it of nobody. Wilton poured some more Mezcal. "Show me the bottle," Contreras asked. "As I thought. There is no worm. You are a cheat, Wilton Muscatine."

Wilton shrugged. "There was a worm in there earlier," he said, looking at the bottom of the bottle. He replaced the bottle behind the bar. It had few companions and each them contained Mezcal. "Is this all there is to life?" he asked returning to Jesus' earlier thought. "What brought on a desire for philosophy, and in you, of all people?"

Jesus smiled. "Is this is all life should be. Is this all there is to it? Sitting in a dump of a bar in a dead city that doesn't know enough to lie down and get buried? Because it will be. The sea comes in from one side and the trees from the other leaving the rest for the devil. And we sit here, drinking, surviving and waiting to die. Why?" He gulped down the drink and waved for another.

Wilton shrugged. He liked conversation as much as anyone but anything too deep was beyond him as a bar owner. He talked deep when he needed to, but depth was not what a bar required or needed. It was for getting drunk and bitching, *perra*. "For all I know you are right and it is so. I know nothing of these things."

A rumble of thunder outside told Jesus the storm he had seen building up earlier was almost on them. Rain spattered against the dirty windows. Rising wind blew in through the cracks in the wall and the gap in the door frame.

"How long have we known each other, Wilton?"

Wilton thought for a few seconds. "A long time *amigo*, fifteen years at least. Why do you ask?"

"I need to tell you something."

"Tell me something? You're not the talkative type as I recall. Getting you to talk is harder than getting a rock to do the same."

"Now it's different. You understand?"

"No, but tell me more."

"I will make sense I hope." Jesus tapped the glass. Wilton refilled it, taking the hint. "I arrived here over twenty years ago as best as I can recall. I arrived with my parents. We came from Oregon, near Portland. I can't remember why, I was a child then. I do not know if they were rumors about what was going to happen but anyhow we ended up here. And we lived here. And I am still here. Only I don't know how long the city will last or if we still be here to see."

He didn't want to tell Wilton everything. The reticence burned into him from years of struggle, of not appearing weak to others was too strong. He didn't talk about trekking along the coast with his parents, then finding their place here. Of finding the best places for food; what to avoid; what water and plants were safe. He didn't tell of his parents dying when fever swept through the city in weeks, taking most of the people with it. He was in his teens then, young, but he had to grow up fast.

Jesus' parents died ugly. He tried to care for them best he could as their bodies burned from the infection. The disease ruptured internal organs, leaving victims to drown on their own blood. It was not pretty, people died fast and dirty when they caught it. And a lot did helped along by malnutrition, no medicine, and less sanitation. But he stayed silent on what he felt then and still felt now.

"So do a lot of people." Wilton sat down.

"We are only here because we didn't get out when we could, as the others did. We are trapped, Wilton. And something is in the wind, and it will end this city. I can feel it in my bones. My parents were right to get out of Oregon when they did or I wouldn't be here now. Something is coming from beyond the fires in the hills. They won't leave us in peace. They think they are like Gods watching us suffer like beasts. They have caused all this, I know it and they have been patient so far. But no longer." Contreras tossed the drink down. "Another drink, Wilton. The ones who watch will loose the hell-hounds. They will rampage over the hills, bring the apocalypse and put LA to the sword."

Silence drew close in the dust of the bar. "Very philosophical but I never thought of you as someone who would let fate happen to them," Wilton said.

"I had a dream last night Wilton. The end will be soon and if I don't do anything we will all die when it does." He took off his sunglasses and in the yellow dimness his eyes burned. "I am going to stop them, Wilton. Or at least try. I can't let what drove my parents away happen here. This is my home, I want to protect it. When I was young I couldn't do anything. Now I can."

Wilton Muscatine didn't believe the words. "To fight is impossible, a dream only." He looked at Jesus, seeing a man who carried fire in his eyes where once there'd only been dull resignation. "The only thing coming is another fucking storm." He looked at Jesus Contreras. Saw his eyes flash as he was speaking. Wilton crossed himself. It wasn't the first time Wilton had heard words like those many times when the heat got beyond bearing. People would imagine anything to cling to. Fighting for what? Hope was a good thing when deserved but what good is hope here? It had abandoned them, vanished over the hills with all the others. Jesus wanted it where it neither existed nor belonged. And when nothing happened and nothing changed? Wilton didn't care to think what the answer would be. Hope was futile, a chimera. Life had taught him that much.

Wilton poured Jesus another drink since he could think of nothing else to do. He hoped this would pass like all the other dreams. Jesus forgot a lot of his rants the next day, but this time? He didn't know. Wilton shivered. He hoped it wasn't a foreboding. But he knew in his soul one deep truth, whatever was coming wouldn't end well for the man sitting at the bar. 'Father, make it different for this man, whatever your plan is, let it end well for him.' He knew it was a slim chance only, bordering on none. God let his son die, what chance was there for he who shared his name? Wilton poured a drink for himself and the storm blew past to dash itself out in the desert to the east.

TWO

I N the barrios around a day's walk from where Jesus walked in the pan-hot sun a building stood like most of the other buildings hemming it in. Nondescript and forgotten it leaned to one side. Most of the windows and doors were missing, crumbling into sand and debris on the street. Holes dotted the walls and the roof, drenching rooms when it rained. An old man called Ishmael lived there in the only apartment where the windows weren't broken. He said he liked it that way, it made it easy to tell which room was his from the outside. He shared the apartment with a small generator that coughed and wheezed like an asthmatic. He kept it going by whatever gas he could scrounge. Every time it stopped he bashed it with a hammer, pulled a few levers, and cranked it back into life. It was an everyday occurrence and Ishmael worried it would soon quit altogether. Elsewhere in the apartment some furniture, a table, a chair without legs, a bookcase devoid of its reason for existence save for an old bible and a battered copy of Moby Dick, a hammock, all stood as if waiting for the end of days. Ishmael was gaunt, deep lines from age and worry creased his face. His hair tufted in small clumps as white as the smile that lit his face when people never expected it.

His skin was deep black, almost blue and most of the time covered in dust from what breeze blew across the ground and through the holes in the building. He looked like a wraith. He wore ragged pants and a threadbare shirt of indeterminate color. He'd tried to keep them stitched but it hadn't helped for long and now he let them fray as much as they wanted to. He would find something to replace them when they fell apart and challenged his modesty. His feet were shod in flip-flops worn almost flat. He kept them on his feet using pieces of string. The string irritated his skin but he preferred it to walking in wet shoes.

9

He was good at making things last, keeping things going. It was a valuable talent in a city where things had fallen apart. He lived among people who depended on him even if they thought he was a bit crazy. He spoke to himself, heard voices and acted on them. He wasn't dangerous and people left him alone until they needed him. His father had given him the name Ishmael. He'd read Moby Dick so often he could and did quote it line and verse. Ishmael liked to throw them into conversations every time he had the chance. The main result was most people wondered what the fuck he was talking about.

Now wasn't one of those times. Something needed to be done and only by him. Time was getting short. He scrambled over the wasteland stretching from Compton to Paramount. The last earthquake had demolished most of the buildings and debris lay where riots once stopped a nation in its tracks. He knew about them well, had learned of them at his grandma's knee. Now she was dead. Only Ishmael was left of his family, trying to survive as best he could in a world where no one belonged. Survival drove him and it wasn't his.

He scrambled across broken brick, busted pipes, distorted concrete, and weeds. He tasted dust in his mouth and under that the sea washing up in the streets where Torrance and Gardena had been. Piers once lined the beachfront. Now only a few pillars remained standing above the water like sentinels. He knew the area well. He used to be a preacher here, standing on street corners urging people to repent as God's wrath was on the way. Now he stood in the water on the same corners waiting to baptize people. Few came and he was happy to help them find some comfort. It wasn't easy; Lord no it wasn't, it was hard but necessary. It looked like the end of the world to man but it was the passing of the old and the coming of the new. Only the Lord knew what the outcome would be. Now he sensed God sending him on again. He followed the call up the old streets to the shattered ruin of the 605 freeway.

People lived under there in old boxes and cars in the rubble. He waved as he passed those eking out an existence and those who knew him raised desultory hands in return. He found Alondra Boulevard and the going became easier. The road was wide and smooth enough to find an easy path. Up ahead the broken freeway lay like the great white whale, it had escaped Ahab's harpoon only to die here, stranded in the rubble. "Thank You, Lord, for making my path straight," he whispered to himself. "But not easy, Lord no, not easy. Help me with the woman Lord, she needs all you can give her."

He scrambled on watching out for dog packs, wolves, and wildcats looking for an easy meal. He'd seen dangerous predators more times than he cared to know. They preferred deer to humans but like everyone he wasn't about to press his luck. "Keep me safe Lord for a little while longer." He walked and ran between the collapsed buildings and rotted down vehicles. He didn't look into them. He hated seeing the skeletons left behind by scavengers. Every so often he looked up and crossed himself. He checked his water bottle, the water sloshed inside. He prayed he wouldn't be too late.

Ishmael muttered to himself as he walked. "Do I myself still forever centrally disport in mute calm; and while ponderous planets of unwaning woe revolve round me, deep down and deep inland there I still bathe me in eternal mildness of joy." Even fiction has truth in it he thought to himself. He arrived at the wreckage of the freeway and looked about. Over there, he remembered the directions the panicked woman had given him. The woman had been frantic, crying and screaming, and needed calming when she came to him in the apartment. He remembered how the Lord had moved through him and settled her so she could tell him what he needed to do. He scrabbled up the piles of rubble using what handholds he could find. It seemed to take forever until he reached the top. Below him lay the car, wedged in place, more stable than any building he could think of.

He looked in the window at the small Mexican woman laying there, a baby wrapped in her arms. Dirt grimed her face but she smiled at him. "He came last night," she whispered. She had no strength left to speak louder. It had been a hard pregnancy; he could see it in the way the pain shone in her eyes. Lines carved her face as if left there by a sculptor's chisel. He could see her ribs where her top had ridden up. She was too thin, her breasts flat against her chest. She would have no milk. Her breathing was shallow and it rasped in her throat. He held her hand and felt for a pulse, it was shallow, almost indiscernible, and he knew she wasn't long for the world. Ishmael wondered why God had permitted it to go on when He could have spared her so much pain. At least she would be with him soon and this would all be over. "Please?" She offered him the baby.

Ishmael took the child and opened his water bottle. Someone better than him should have done this. But there wasn't anyone better. He sprinkled the water from the beaches of Torrance over the forehead of the baby and welcomed him to Jesus. When he looked back into the car the mother was gone. Her eyes were open and lifeless and her body was limp.

Her pain was over but he still grieved for the woman he didn't know. Reaching in, he closed her eyes and prayed for her deliverance into His hands. It was a vain hope and he knew it. He wrestled rubble against the windows of the car. Scavengers wouldn't find her body easy to get. The baby gurgled. It would need milk soon or death would take the child this day and damned if he was going to let it happen. Wrapping the baby as tight as he could in rags he placed it under his ragged coat and left the mother where she was. She was in God's hands now. He thought for a moment and then he knew where to go. He smiled for the first time since he woke up. "Let us all squeeze ourselves into each other," he said to himself.

In yet another area of LA Maria Carranza lay on her bunk on the second floor of what had been the Best Western San Dimas plucking her t-shirt to bring what cool air there was closer to her skin. North lay the hills. She'd read once in a tattered, decades old paper they'd filmed TV shows and films in those hills but it was all so long ago. Not even a memory lingered from the past. Her room was open, the windows had vanished but she didn't mind. If the wind blew in bringing the rain it was cool enough to sleep. Only now there was no wind, only stifling heat. She didn't expect that to change until the evening and she would be out by then.

Maria was tall, near on six feet, her hair lopped short. Washing hair wasted water and there was precious little left. Roof top tanks had helped once but they were mostly rotted away these days and the ones that weren't had so many dead critters in them you wouldn't use the water even if you were desperate. Her eyes were blue and hardened by years of what passed for life. She was alone, her parents long gone. She rose from her bunk and got ready for the day. She dressed quick in cut-off jeans for ease of movement, loose t-shirt and a leather vest. Her feet were shod in desert boots. She had three pairs left and would need more soon. She was used to living her way without having to worry about anyone else. She was lean but not weak. She had a hidden strength inside and it kept her going when others gave up. She had bigger plans.

She looked out over the city over to the hills. At night she could see the glow of fires in the hills. She knew who they were, had thought about them and heard the stories the people told. The fires last night were small and scattered. Other nights they were lined up like strings of red pearls almost touching each other. They were a ring around the city to stop anyone trying to get out. People tried to escape the dying city once but nobody tried to escape anymore. It had become a mausoleum filled with the bodies of the walking dead. She wasn't going to be one of them. One day she would get out.

Through the window came a rapid pop-pop-pop. Probably some asshole shooting dogs or rats for target practice. At least she hoped it was dogs or rats. The city had died but people still liked shooting things. Sometimes the things were people. Dead bodies were here and there, she'd seen them often even though they were never around for long. Scavengers took care of them. She was glad something was around to take care of the carrion; another epidemic was the last thing they needed.

Gunfire echoed through the streets where she lived most nights and often during the day. There were not enough buildings to deaden it. She wondered if it was psychological, the need to fire at something. Just relieving the tension. The popping started up again and a thin wail came to her ears. She ignored it. It wasn't good to think about who it could have been in case you knew who it was. It wasn't worth it to interfere. You could end up dead yourself.

The popping had been rapid, an automatic. They were still fucking easy to get in LA. People brought things in and took things out for a price. A steep one. Looking out to Mt Baldy she could see it in the distance. A metallic spire stretching into the sky, vanishing at a point her mind shrank from. From her vantage point it was a thin thread, small and fragile. At night light glowed around it in the air and on the ground. Glinting off the metal the lights looked like they were trying to climb it. All who lived here knew it was there, knew someone who said they'd seen it built many years ago. Maria called BS on the claim.

She turned away from the spire and the hills and finished readying herself to go out into the city. She was running short on food, little was grown here and still less came in from outside. She foraged most days, she knew the edible plants well and where the fruit trees grew. It would be a long day and she made ready. She picked up a rucksack and an old 38 revolver. She spun it to make sure the action was smooth and then stuffed it into a side pocket of the rucksack along with what bullets she could spare. Into the main compartment of she put a knife and enough water and jerky to last the day. She threw the rucksack over her shoulders and left the building. She took a zigzag course through the streets toward the hills to hide her intent. She went to the hills a lot. She told people it was because food was easier to find there but she liked to keep tabs on the camps. It was risky but she was careful.

THREE

THE ring around the city was there night and day. It was no secret. No one doubted it was there to keep them in the city like exhibits in a zoo, watched and ignored until they died. Those inside couldn't get out and those outside didn't want to get in. The ring was death. Beyond, where the city couldn't see, lay razor wire, tanks, spotlights, and mines. Men with rifles and dead eyes tended the fires, waiting. Thermal imaging cameras lined the trails and motion sensors dotted the landscape. Drones patrolled the sky, streaming vidfeeds back to faceless men and women in rooms filled with computer screens. Whoever was in LA was going to stay there until it died. Except it hadn't.

Behind the camps and the fires lay a fiefdom. There was more than one and the rulers called them that. It fitted. The regent of this fiefdom wasn't about to let LA's beating corpse spoil the image he'd made of it. If it meant sacrifice and slaughter, so be it. It was on their heads not his. They had no right to be there and soon wouldn't be. There would be no comeback on him. No one living in the fiefdom knew it was still there, it was long gone, vanished like Atlantis. It was where parents threatened to send their kids if they didn't behave. Because it wasn't there, no one went to see it. No one cared. Disneyland was a fable, Hollywood a myth.

The center of the fiefdom was Las Vegas, the city of broken dreams, and bad Elvis impersonators. They were still there. So were the casinos and the losers. The city was bigger than ever despite the desiccating wind that blew hot no matter the time of year.

In the middle, off the strip where the Arts District had once been sat a building ten floors high. Wider at the bottom than the top, with four concrete pillars at each corner it looked like a turtle. Atop the convex roof was a glass ceiling. The glass was green and filtered out a lot of the sun and heat. Under it, bathing in the green light, in a leather chair behind an oak desk sat Rantall Heyusser. He was one of the few in the city who knew about LA and the people who still lived there. Its lack of a future lay in his hands.

Heyusser was thin with the looseness you see in people who once were fat. His hair was going gray, he preferred to call it silver, and he fooled no one on the occasions he dyed it to make himself look younger. He walked like he had pins in his feet giving his stride a slight bounce. He'd worked hard to get where he was, doing favors when necessary and he wasn't averse to blackmail. He claimed to have perfect eyesight but used contacts. As if to counter this, his hearing was perfect.

He loved classical music, opera, drank good red wine, and smoked Cuban cigars. He thought it gave him a certain style. He closed his eyes as Chopin breathed out of hidden speakers and cosseted his ears. Heyusser had LA exactly where he wanted it until he let loose the apocalypse. He hated unnecessary deaths, it offended his sense of propriety but he accepted them when necessary. Death was inevitable; it came to all in time. He told himself each day when it came to LA the time would be of his choosing. He liked the power of life and death and wielded it without concern or mercy.

He poured some cabernet into a glass. While raising it to his lips, the buzzer on his desk stopped him. He breathed a curse. The door opened and a man came in with a military bearing, no smile, no soul, and less imagination. "The situation at the border with LA is normal. Nothing to report." He stood at attention. Heyusser wondered if he ever relaxed.

"Dismissed," he said. The man about-faced, walked out and closed the door behind him, it made little sound. Heyusser admired the craftsmanship of who had made the door. He'd forgotten his name. Not that it mattered. He'd had him executed a little later since he didn't want anyone else to have a door like his. It also generated a little frisson of fear to help keep the population quiet and know their place. Heyusser knew the trick was not to go so far to cause problems when his subjects got restless. A life in politics and an interest in psychology and history helped him to draw the line where others hadn't. They paid the price for not knowing. He wouldn't.

Heyusser wanted the end of LA. It was the burr in his ass that would never go away until he did something about it. The city and the people were nothing but the playthings of the rulers, who had long ago divided the planet between them. Heyusser knew about where he was in the pecking order. He had missed out on running the most powerful country in the world and in his dreams he was. The knowledge of what he had missed irritated him but he made up for that here.

He closed his eyes to what had never been and cursed the fates for being born too late. Then he turned his thoughts back to LA. The end was inevitable. The time left for the city had to be short. His bosses weren't going to wait forever and he wanted to roll over the top of it tomorrow. Or the next day. It didn't matter which, the end was going to be the same. It bugged him how the people still clung to their existence like lichen on a rock. They couldn't know what was happening, what had happened, but carried on living anyway. They had no understanding of the inevitability of change. No sense of reality was their problem. He huffed a breath, they would soon learn all about it like many who'd stood in his way. He pressed a button on his desk and a face appeared on the computer. "Yes?" said the face.

"No change," Heyusser replied. "All is in place. We are ready to move as soon as I get the order."

"Good, we will let you know." The face never changed its expression.

The screen went black and Heyusser tapped his fingers on the desk. It wasn't his boss, Woodhull Fleming, it was his lackey. It always was. Fleming must think I'm not worth the effort, thought Heyusser. He pressed another button. "Keep the defenses on alert. More than ever, let no one out." A squawk confirmed the order.

The next morning saw Jesus striding the same streets and he wasn't feeling well. It had been a long night, ending only when he passed out. He'd drunk more than he expected or wanted to. After his seventh it got foggy, indistinct. Then he remembered nothing. His body was paying him back. Nice try buddy it told him, you ought to know better than to try that shit with me. It was around ten by the time he woke up stretched along the bar like a towel and the sun was searing through the windows. His head ached. His mouth was dryer than the Mojave Desert and it tasted like seagull shit. He'd brewed what passed for coffee before leaving but it hadn't helped. Neither had walking. His legs felt like they wanted to go in different directions. His head throbbed each time his feet slapped the pavement.

The sun beating down didn't help his mood and there was too little shade to get much comfort. He walked on, the smell of the sea in his nostrils. It seemed as good a place as any to go right now. A splash of sea water might help him feel a little better. At least it couldn't hurt. He headed down S Wilton until it became Arlington and then morphed into Van Ness.

He crossed the Columbus Transcont and kept going over 105. Sharp concrete sliced cuts into his hands as he scrambled up and down. The water covering Gardena and Hawthorne glistened in the near distance. It would be a blessed relief. God, he wanted to lie in the water while the flotsam and jetsam floated around him. He was hung over, thirsty, and tired. His feet hurt and even though he didn't know it his skin had burned and blisters had started to rise. In a day they would burst but they were of no concern.

He kept on, kicking a rock out of his way as he turned a corner. Not far off a man in rags was holding his hands up, exhorting a crowd gathered around him. Jesus saw people old and young, sitting and standing, listening with an intent he could feel. The words were loud but indistinct, but they drew the faces of the people. The ragged man was in his element, feeding off the crowd. Several looked soaked. As Jesus stood back from the crowd and watched, the man in rags gestured to another who rose and walked towards him. The ragged man spoke and pushed him under the water. Jesus realized he was watching a group baptism. He smiled. Human nature was always the same. People sought help where they could find it, whether it worked or not. He doubted they would find any from the man who held them enraptured but he didn't want to stop them hoping. They needed it.

Jesus watched knowing in his heart getting their heads wet wouldn't help them. His thoughts went back to Wilton's bar. He told everyone who had come in something big was coming and it was close without saying it was him. He feared the ridicule then but the heat burned the fear away as he walked. The idea came to him like a worm that he needed to tell the ragged man ahead of him. The ragged man saw him and beckoned. Jesus had wondered if he would see him. Now the beginning had come.

Ishmael had seen better days. The baby the woman had given up before she died had been born hard. In the past there would have been hospitals and doctors, nurses and paramedics. But not now. He'd held little hope for the child. He'd seen in her face and body the mother hadn't eaten for days and the child was born starving. He had tried his best God knew, but there was little he could do. In the ruins there was nothing to feed it. He fretted the rest of the day and the baby squalled from hunger, not ceasing until the night drew close. He slept little during the night and went to search again for food in the morning when the sky began to lighten. It took a few hours until he found some old powdered milk in the ruin of a chemist shop near Rosecrans. He'd brought it back and boiled a little water on a butane stove. He found an old bottle and cleaned it as best he could, cut a finger off a rubber glove and hoped it would work.

For a while it seemed to. The baby moved as if drugged, waving its arms and legs without energy. Ishmael frowned. It was too late. The baby gurgled and spat what it had drunk back up onto its clothes. Then he watched the child grew still and calm and it looked at him. Ishmael trembled, seeing in those eyes an ancient wisdom beyond reckoning. He'd heard of it but never seen it himself. He realized at some innate level the baby knew what was happening. He saw a soul aware it was going to die and knew Ishmael could do nothing to stop it. In that small body was a soul ready to forgive him for failing yet thankful he had tried. He saw acceptance. He watched the baby for an hour until it stopped moving and closed its eyes. He waited a little more until the baby stopped breathing. The time was 9:30 in the morning. Something told him he needed to mark the moment and he wrote it down in an old moth-chewed journal. He wrapped the dead infant in a towel and took it outside. He found a place in a vacant lot where the weeds were thin, dug a deep hole and buried the pitiful corpse there. Then he marked the grave with a cross of old window slats. He cried at the waste and the loss. In his soul he felt a deep, abiding loathing for the city and what had happened to the people who tried to survive in it.

He prayed then, for the mother and the baby. "Lord, help bring this baby and its mother together in Paradise. Let the mother know I tried my best Lord, you know I always do but I'm afraid it isn't enough most of the time. I pray she will forgive me too. And Lord help me to forgive myself because I don't know if I can do it right now. Forgive me for my feelings about this city. A sign you're here Lord is all I want to see. Let me see it before I pass from this place and return home to glory. Ashes to ashes, Lord, dust to dust." He packed down the dirt and dragged cement blocks over the grave so scavengers wouldn't dig it up and left. He didn't know the baby's name. He didn't even know if it was a boy or a girl.

He walked down toward Gardena, calling to the city as he went. He wasn't sure why unless it was to mark the end of the child by doing something right. He felt he needed to give the child's death the meaning it lacked it in life. The sense drove him out into the streets to where the sea washed the bottom of the buildings. He opened his mouth and the words came unsought and unbidden. "Come all you people, there's a storm coming soon, a storm He will bring! The Lord will come and judge all and you don't want Him to leave you behind!" He called out to anyone who would hear him among the shattered buildings, weeds, and dirt. Whether they listened and followed his voice or not out was in the hands of greater than he. He found heart in agnosticism as he marched to Gardena. Behind him a people blinked themselves into the morning and came out to hear him. "Come! Be baptized in the spirit of the Lord. You all won't know when He will come but know he will. Yea come He will and you should be ready and repent as His day is coming!"

He came to the new beachfront and sat down to wait. A few people came, then a few more and when he saw Jesus standing there he had baptized over a dozen people. More were waiting, he couldn't count how many. Many had left wondering what the fuss had been about and went back to waiting for the death throes to end. "Behold the oncoming storm," he said. "I can baptize you all but one is coming who will lead us all further from the abyss than I can. He will call many but few will go the whole way. Some will leave and some will fall, nothing is assured to any of us but God will be with us in the middle of death. Do not fear. I have seen much and I will see more. But what will I see even God will not let me know." His voice carried in the afternoon heat. Jesus heard him as if he was standing next to him. His voice rang like a bell in his mind. He came forward. "Choose me," he told the ragged man.

Ishmael waved him forward. "Do you repent?"

"Yes."

"Then in the name of the father, the son and the spirit of God I wash away your sins." Ishmael pushed Jesus backward and after a few seconds pulled him back out.

"Thank you," Jesus said. He wanted to sputter and the taste of the sea was salty and foul with death.

"You are with Him now," Ishmael said. Then he bent closer. "Wait for me, my friend. We have things to discuss." Ishmael raised his voice once more. "Wait for his call my friends. Go or not, it will be your decision alone to make, God will not punish you for following your heart. Go in peace and go with God in all you do."

The last of the baptized left to think on their own course, scattering back to the shelter and shade they craved. In the afternoon sun Jesus and Ishmael sat on an upturned VW. The current swirled the shit of LA around their feet. "You've seen death recently, Ishmael," Jesus said. "Or you could not have spoken as you did today." In the distance the hulk of the Queen Mary looked like a beached whale, washed up by storm surges, ribs bare.

"Very true Jesus," Ishmael agreed. "It has a way of concentrating our thoughts when we see it up close." He looked over towards the old harbor. Rusted hulks lay on their sides, fish filling their empty holds. "It was this morning I saw death come and take a life. A baby left to me by her mother. I did what I could." He looked out over the water and the debris and buildings. "She died yesterday as soon as she gave me the child. I didn't know their names, either of them. I don't even know if the child was a boy or a girl. I buried the child in an empty lot and I hated this city more than I thought possible. How did you know?"

"Your eyes; there is nothing behind them. You look dead inside. Like the rest of us I don't doubt."

"If I am why shouldn't I be? I tried to save a life I had no chance to save. I am tired of life my friend and I am tired of seeing death." He closed his eyes and pain seeped from him. "But I will recover, the process has started already. And where have you been hiding? I haven't seen you for months. Did you like the words? 'Behold the oncoming storm'?'" Ishmael grinned and his face lit up amid the whiskers and dust. "They came to me when I saw you standing there."

"They were pretty good Ishmael, some of your best. But there is a storm coming old friend. You were closer to the truth than you thought." Jesus kicked at a dead rat floating too close for his comfort. It jigged and then disappeared, pulled under by a fish.

"A storm huh?" asked Ishmael. "Not exactly a new metaphor for change. Not much of an insight either. It's not that new a concept you know. People have been saying the same thing for longer than I can remember. Wrath of God stuff to try and get sinners to repent for the end of the world is nigh and all that crap. Want a drink?"

"I thought you preachers were against drinking and all for repenting, wrath of God or not."

"Jesus turned water into wine and who said I was a preacher?" Ishmael lobbed a rock into the water. "Besides, I'm too old to get judgmental and you're too young for a hangover."

Jesus nodded in the direction of the departing people. "They seem to think you can preach pretty well my friend."

"It's not the words; it's how you make them sound. Anyway let's go; there are better places to be than sitting here getting our feet wet." Ishmael rose and led them away from one death zone to another. They were all death zones here; all that differed was the manner of death.

FOUR

ARIA had spent the night holed up in a cave under the Columbus Transcont. She'd needed to. She was lucky and berated herself for getting into trouble in the first place. "Stupid bitch, stupid bitch." The afternoon had not ended well. Her reliable alarm had failed to buzz and she hadn't noticed the passing time. The dogs and the night hunters had started to search for prey when she realized her predicament. "Fuck," she snarled to herself when she heard the first howls of the wolves. They were getting bolder. They didn't fear the dogs, and with the bears and the pumas, they were coming further and further in. Finding herself a wolf pack's choice for dinner was not her preferred option.

She saw the hulking Transcont up ahead. The day was starting to lose light and the Transcont was at least two miles off. She checked her pack. She hadn't brought a weapon apart from the gun and tools she used to dig up the weeds and flowers she wanted. They wouldn't do much good if the wolves caught her scent. If? More like when. She left the gun where it rested in the rucksack. If a pack picked up her scent, and the howls told her it was, it would be useless; they would be on her too fast. Maria thought fast. Shots might bring other hunters in, not a comforting thought and a complication to avoid. All her life she avoided fights she couldn't win and wasn't about to change her tactics now. She chose flight, to move and move fast. She started to jog towards her destination. Adrenaline flooded her system and it was difficult to hold her speed back. Not too fast, they could smell the fear coming from a panicked animal and if she ran she might draw them to her. She kept a steady pace, running smooth so the rucksack would stay balanced. Running steady also made her seem healthy. Enough for the pack to go after something else. 'As if,' she thought. She listened for the sounds of pursuit and heard nothing. There was only the sound of her breathing.

As she jogged on she scanned the ground for something she could use as a weapon. She found what she wanted; a piece of rebar two feet long jagged at one end and rusted. But it might be enough and worth the time it took to retrieve it. She weighed up the options. Take it and risk it slowing her up or leave it. She decided on the first. She hefted it to find the right balance point and kept on jogging. The Transcont was getting closer. She felt she could almost touch it. The howls kicked up again. They were calling, they hadn't spotted her yet but they had her scent. She picked up her pace and she thought for a moment she'd lucked out and the pack had gone after something easier.

She was wrong. There was a howl, it sounded like it was a block away. They were closer now and one of them had found her and judged her worthy of a chase. The Transcont seemed a lot further away. She kept going, upping her pace. The howl came again, closer, to her left and behind. She chanced a quick look. The wolf was pacing her, keeping in contact with the pack to let them know where it was, that prey was close and it needed help to bring it down. She picked her pace up again, sweat and the Transcont shimmered in her eyes. She knew it would pace her with ease, able to run all day when she couldn't. The wolf knew it didn't need to be closer since the pack would arrive soon so she could be taken down easily. She hoped she would reach the Transcont before she flagged. 'Over my dead body' she thought to herself then winced at the reality behind the bluster. She hoped it wasn't going to be the case.

The Transcont swam in her eyes. The wolf stayed where it was. She wanted to look all the time but the road had debris scattered across its length. Twisting her ankle or worse would see the pack on her before she could make twenty yards. She hoped her pursuer would pace her for a while longer. The longer it did, the more likely the pack was far enough away and might give her the time she needed to get to safety. She focused her mind on the Transcont and looked around to see if there was a place to hide. Nothing. The buildings were too open to give her any safety and the pack would catch her if she went into one. The ruined freeway had holes and caves she could crawl into to keep the pack off her until they gave up.

The pack bayed a response to the one animal following her. They were several blocks away and the Transcont loomed larger. It was closer than the pack and she might win the contest. She heard a snarl as if the

wolf knew her intention. Maria's feet pounded the pavement like a sprint-
er. Her breathing was starting to come hard but she couldn't let it slow
her down. Her legs were starting to tire and her muscles burned with the
continued effort to stay ahead of the pack. Her breath rasped in her throat
and rucksack was wearing gouges into her shoulders. She felt a pain in
her side but she kept the pace. 'Damn fine place for a stitch,' she thought.

She pressed on; safety was mere yards away. A gap loomed in the
shattered concrete of the overpass where it crossed the road ahead.
Several stories had collapsed years ago. Squashed cars and trucks poked
out of the wreckage like ass-backward decorations. She didn't care; she'd
used them before when eluding human predators and it would work just
as well with the wolves. See saw the hole she needed. It was a couple feet
wide. Inside was a safe haven. The wolf howled again, louder, with an
edge, it was telling the pack to hurry. The pack responded. She spared a
moment for a look behind, the pack was less than a block away and they
were running hard. It was going to be close. Very close.

She sprinted forward, taking her pack off for the last few yards. The
growls and snaps from the chasing pack all she needed to put the extra
effort into her sprint. 'Nothing like incentive,' she thought as she swung
the pack through the hole and dived after it. Teeth snatched at her desert
boots but failed to hold on and she slithered inside. Turning, she swung
the rebar hard, smashing it into the skull of the wolf that followed her in
behind the eyes. It snapped at her, intent on the kill despite the pain. She
swung twice more, feeling the skull splinter, pieces of bone penetrating its
brain. The wolf died hard and ugly, its blood splattering her as it spasmed
in its death throes. She took a deep breath and after it had died she pushed
it outside with her feet. It fell out onto the rocks and rubble and the pack
turned on it, squabbling and snarling over the carcass. There was no pack
mentality here. No sentiment to waste for a dead wolf that was food. After
they had eaten they left, leaving the carcass for any scavenger hungry
enough to want it. Maria didn't want scavengers so close so when she
felt safe she dragged it away. She dumped it half a block from her refuge,
returned and settled in for the night. Resting her head on her rucksack
she fell asleep.

In the morning she woke and uncurled. Pain in muscles she didn't
know she had shot her through with pain. After the pain eased she
scrambled out of her bolt-hole and stretched in the sun beating down on
the streets before getting the last of yesterday's jerky out of the rucksack.
She walked past where the carcass of the wolf had been, nothing more

than a smear of blood on the ground remained. Tracks told her a bear had been there. A big one. She was glad she'd moved it. "Sorry buddy, it was you or me." Maria walked off, stretching the kinks in her body and eating the jerky as she went. Without a backward look she headed south and west to where the sea came in. It would be high tide in a few hours and she could do with a bath. Dried wolf blood didn't smell too good and might bring unwanted attention. She wrinkled her nose. "I smell like a cheap date's cologne."

She didn't run but she didn't take her time either. She knew the smell of the wolf's blood would deter dogs unless there were too hungry to care. A dog pack might be different but they would be heading for cover to wait for the cool of the evening. So would any other predator out there. She hefted the rebar, confident she could handle anything now it was getting too hot for anything to move. As she headed to the sea she saw the furtive shadows of wary dogs. They would follow her, confused about the wolf smell, then slink away to look for something easier. Over an hour later she caught the smell of seaweed and salt. She was getting close. God it would be a relief to feel the salt-tang water wash over her. A cat, it must be the last one in LA, sprang out of a bed of weeds, a mouse in its jaws. "Good luck buddy," she said as it vanished. "You'll need it."

She headed down to Compton and Gardena, the brine smell getting stronger like ozone as she walked. She ducked down a side street and hunkered down behind a wall to avoid a droning mass of people. They were too intent on what they had done or seen to pay her attention. Some dripped water as they passed. 'It's a good day for a swim,' she thought. 'Even in clothes.' After they passed she walked on to the water, following the direction they came from. She saw the water glistening with oil that hid shit, dead rats, tennis shoes, and plastic. She saw two men talking and sitting on a wall. Both looked like scarecrows. One looked familiar, but she couldn't place him. He was like one of those faces you could never put a name or a place to where you saw it. She shrugged, it didn't matter who he was when there was nothing else left.

They knew each other, she could tell from the easy familiarity they shared. After a few minutes they stood and walked off. They didn't see her behind the door, only her head poking above the wood and she was happy about that. She didn't feel like talking to anyone, she rarely did. She preferred to keep to herself unless she needed something. If someone needed something from her she dissuaded them with a glance. She walked to the water and lay down in it, feeling the sensation of the blood and dust and shit wash away. The current flowed around her and the sunburn from yesterday eased in the cool. She knew she had to do this more often it felt so good but walking so far was dangerous. She decided to enjoy it while she could. Fish came up to her feet and nibbled at them. Plastic bottles bumped her hips and shoulders. The water around her flowed red with blood and dark with dirt and the sea took it away from her and she closed her eyes.

When she got out the sun was lowering in the west. "Crap, another night in the open." After last night she wasn't about to let that happen. She'd ridden her luck then and two nights in a row wasn't the smartest option. Standing up she let the water drip from her onto the ground. Soon she would be dry. She looked at the sun and judged there were three hours until it disappeared. At least she had time to find shelter for the night and it wasn't as if her room needed her to make sure no one broke in. There was little chance of wolves or mountain lions this close to the sea. The Transcont was about as far as they got, along with the bears. Dogs were her major worry but she could handle them. Over the last years she had crossed the whole of LA in each direction. There wasn't anywhere she knew where finding shelter would be a problem. There hadn't been much else to do but learn the city while she grew up, more so after her parents left. She had stored in her mind all the places to hide, where to find food, where her allies and friends were and who to avoid. She had learned enough to survive and learned it better than many others. She needed to, women were often easy prey here.

A sign she remembered came to her thoughts. There would be good enough. The owner wouldn't care who stayed as long as they didn't wreck the place. It was close enough to make while daylight lasted. Hunters were far too common to be safe outside when night cast itself through the city. She hadn't been there for some time, last year maybe, or maybe the year before. She hoped it would still be there and hadn't collapsed like so many other buildings. She grinned at the thought. If she knew the owner as well as she thought she did he wouldn't let a collapsed building stop him. He'd be serving bad alcohol amid the detritus without even noticing what had happened. She stood for a moment to get her bearings. A gull swooped low, the eternal optimist wanting a scrap of food. If she had a scrap she'd eat it first. "Sorry gull, you're SOL."

She headed away from the flotsam and jetsam toward drier ground. The sign in her mind was calling her like a siren. She bent her steps to the north, following her mental directions. It was like a voice was in her head and she followed it. *It's still there. Follow me and go there. See who's there and what an adventure we will have.* 'Damn voices,' she thought. 'Leave me the fuck alone.' The buildings around her watched as silent as tombs as she strode on. The idea that they were tombs stuck with her, but it wasn't the buildings. The whole city was a tomb and they would all end up buried in it. In death they would all be together, entombed in concrete and cement. She raged against death in every fiber. She found it offensive, not in its finality; she knew it came to all, but in the passivity of waiting. 'Not me, not me.' It would not happen to her. She looked up at the hills where the fires burned at night and saw smoke rising into the sky. She would go past those fires into the east over the mountains. She might die trying she knew, but it would be better than dying whimpering like a cowed dog.

She turned left, walked two more blocks, firing at a dog who had strayed too close than she liked on the way. The bullet chipped stone close to the animal and it disappeared with a yelp down an alley. Then she turned right, saw the Santa Monica ahead. She was close. A few more dogs came out of alleys and side streets. She grabbed a few rocks from the road and held them ready, not wanting to waste bullets. She was a damn good aim and it would need to be a quick dog to avoid getting hit on the head when her eye was in. Most weren't. In the distance a few people saw her and ducked out of sight, not wanting trouble. She stuck to the middle of the road, eyeing escape routes in case of human trouble.

In an alley a group of men huddled around a bin cooking something. It was hard to tell what it was and she didn't go and ask. They looked up as she walked past, waited until she was far enough past then returned to the fire. Paper bags sat on the floor between feet almost covered by patchwork shoes. She walked on, reached Wilshire, the sun low on her left. Shadows cast by the buildings stretched half across the road. A semi lay on its side, trailer open and collapsed in on itself, the wooden floor rotted away. She went right, turned onto Wiltern and saw the sign on the wall. Opening the door she stepped into the shaded interior of the Tentacled Den.

FIVE

INSIDE it was dustier than she remembered. Maybe more had had collected in the corners since she was last there. Wilton Muscatine was cleaning the counter with the same rag he always used. Gray, grease-spattered, it left streaks of dust. It wouldn't have made much difference if the rag was clean. The dust was never-ending, blown in through the still broken windows. The light oozing through the windows was still yellow. It made everything look jaundiced. It hadn't changed.

Wilton looked up from his futile work as the door opened. He grinned, grateful for the excuse to stop. "Well if it isn't Maria Carranza, come back at last." He opened his arms wide in welcome. "How long has it been? A year at least. I sometimes wondered if you had left the city for greener pastures."

He still knew her name. It surprised her but she didn't show it. "Keep your hands to yourself or I'll leave sooner than you think old man. And the pastures are no greener outside this place." She sat down on a stool after wiping the worst of the dust off with her hand. Then she grimaced at it, wiped it on her shirt where no one would notice. Over a year, that answered her question. She slapped her hands on the bar. "Give me what you have you old creeper." She looked around. The bar was the same as she remembered it except the dirt on the mirror was even thicker. "You have anything edible?"

Wilton shrugged. "I don't know, maybe." He still wore a Hawaiian shirt. He always had the times she'd been there before. This one bore large prints of hibiscus. They seemed to her to be his favorite, the number of times she'd seen him in one in the past. He must have a supply out back. He didn't look good in them, he never had, but telling him wouldn't stop him assaulting the eyes of all who saw him. "I'll look in back, wait here."

28

He was gone for ten minutes and when he got back she had poured a glass of Mezcal, the only drink she could find. "I hope it's just the one?" he said. "It is not good for me if people drink my profits."

"How can you make a profit when no one pays? It's only the one," she replied. "As if I'd try to steal more of this *escoria*."

Wilton acted as though she hadn't said anything. He placed some food on the counter. "Salad, all I have since I ran out of rat filets." She looked at the plate of what weeds he could find that wouldn't poison anyone who ate them. She picked at it. It tasted okay, maybe it wouldn't kill her. "What's the dressing on this?" She looked at some liquid in the bottom of the bowl. At least it wasn't green. She sniffed it and still didn't know what it was.

"My own recipe," replied Wilton. "I could tell you what it is but then I'd have to kill you."

Maria laughed. He hadn't changed since she was last there. She thought it helped him to stay sane amid the insanity. "I'd like to see you try *cabron*. You will get to know your ass more than you ever thought possible."

Wilton gestured a prayer. "Why do the young people doubt me so?"

"Because we're young, you're not and senile on top of it."

"Maybe so," said Wilton. "I make no apologies."

She didn't believe Wilton would apologize for anything unless it had to do with money. "How has business been? With all the dust in the place not good, right?"

"I keep on top of it but I survive," Wilton said. "Not so many come in these days but I stay because everyone needs somewhere to get away from things. Whether they know it or they don't." He looked at the door. "Of course there isn't anything left to get away from or many people trying."

"Even nothing needs forgetting sometimes Wilton."

He laughed. "You remember my name, Maria. I am impressed considering how long it's been. You must have another Mezcal in celebration. I will also, a celebration cannot occur if only one is drinking."

Maria nodded. He poured one into a less dirty glass. He poured more than he poured for her she noted. 'Mean bastard.' She raised hers, draining it at a gulp. "I swear this Mezcal is *pinche*, shit."

Wilton leaned on the counter, his glass in his hand. He sniffed at the liquid. "You drank it fast enough."

"Only so I can avoid tasting it."

"If you can get better somewhere else you are welcome to go there."

Maria shook her head. There was nothing better anywhere, they both knew it. "I think I'll hang around. It's too far to get home tonight so I'll need a place to sleep and here is as good a place as any." She looked around the booths lining the walls and wondered if that was the case. "I've had enough of wolves to last me at least for tonight."

Wilton agreed and the door opened behind his sole customer. In came two men. Maria swung around as the door closed and saw they were the same men she'd seen earlier by the water. She turned, got off the stool and walked over to where they were sitting. Anyone other than Wilton would be better to talk to. She remembered where she had seen the one she had wondered about. It was in here when she had been here last. They had shared what Wilton passed off for drinks. He was at least a head taller than her with ragged dreads, a beaten face, and a quick smile. The other she didn't know. He was as tall as the other with clothes so patched it was hard to know what they had looked like when new. He looked at her with shining eyes betraying a tired face. He looked like a storm in summer.

Wilton followed to give them some Mezcal. He knew Jesus would order it, Maria too, the other man was unknown to him. He hadn't seen him before but since Mezcal was all he had he gave him a glass. He didn't say it was all he had, Jesus and Mary knew it and if the stranger wanted something else he'd be in for a shock. The man was wary of the drink and the glass but he drank it anyway, wincing at the burn in his throat. Wilton sensed an air about him. Something wild glimmered behind his eyes and Wilton felt a crackle in the air like the ozone before a storm but where it came from he didn't know. He remembered the old stories of John the Baptist, he wasn't going to be the storm but he would tell of who would be.

He had sensed the feeling once before and only once. It was before the last big quake shattered the city leaving much of it strewn on the ground. It was after the quake when the fires were first seen ringing the city. With them came the slow death of the city and the people. He felt afraid and at the center of things and didn't want to be there. He knew in his bones that if he didn't feel afraid he would have felt alive for the first time in years.

Jesus and Ishmael had seen the woman sitting at the bar. Jesus knew her in a vague way, had seen her here before, maybe even shared a drink if nothing else but Ishmael didn't know her. He never ventured this far, staying close to Compton when he could. They watched her come up to their booth. Their stares were open, devoid of mistrust and hostility. If they needed either it would come in their own time. Wilton trailed her with glasses and a bottle and wondered what she was doing. She sat down opposite, giving off an aloofness like perfume. Jesus remembered she was aloof the first time he saw her. Not impossible to know, but hard as if she didn't want to let anyone close. She didn't let her guard down easy. "You guys mind if I sit here?"

They looked at each other. "I can't see why not," Ishmael said. "Unless you have a reason we shouldn't let you."

"If there was I wouldn't tell you, would I?" Maria pulled up a stool and sat down.

"I wouldn't either," Jesus said. "But then who would around here. He regarded her with cool eyes. "I've seen you in here before. A year ago."

"Yeah I was here then, surprised you can remember me, I thought I kept a low profile. We did drink together, I remember that much." Maria downed the Mezcal. Jesus followed her lead and waved at Wilton for another.

"You bring that memory back to me. But there's not a lot of people coming in here every day to make me forget a face. And I never do, names however, they are another matter."

Maria had to acknowledge he was right. "Do you remember my name?" Maria asked Jesus.

"Do you remember mine?" Jesus replied.

"Answering a question with a question is no answer," Maria countered.

Jesus went into his mind and dredged up a name. Yes, he knew it now, he remembered her. "Maria. I needed a time to think, you understand? But do you know mine? A woman like you might not, with so many men chasing you."

Maria made as if to spit on the floor. "A man chase me he better hope he doesn't catch me."

Jesus only smiled. Ishmael preferred to remain quiet. This seemed to be something between the two of them, whatever it was. He was waiting to see where it would lead. It looked like Jesus had started the chase and Maria hadn't done much to stop him. He wondered about the ways of the young, even if the city had a way of making the young older than they should be. It saddened him. He reached for the drinks and picked one up, keeping pace with Maria and Jesus would be foolish.

It looked like it was going to be a long night and he didn't want to miss anything. The oncoming storm might be on its way. Wilton had returned to his place at the bar, wiping it yet again as much out of boredom as anything. He hid his interest behind the aimlessness of habit. He watched and listened with the barman's air of not paying attention yet missing nothing.

Jesus looked at Maria again. She looked tough, wiry. She had an inner strength that flashed in the depths of her eyes. Here was a woman who wouldn't take crap from anyone. She was a survivor, but she had to be more. Women had it tough here. Too often picked off, used up, and thrown aside like the woman who had died after giving Ishmael her baby. Something told Jesus this one would not go easy. She would extract a cost on anyone who thought she would. Jesus saw it not from her words but how she carried herself. She looked like she owned the streets. It was a good strategy. He told her his name. "Jesus, Jesus Contreras. This is Ishmael." He nodded to his old friend. "He's a preacher, but he says he isn't. He doubts himself too much." He said, smiling.

"Hi." Maria shook their hands, her grip was strong. "I saw you both earlier, down by the water in Gardena. You were talking, and then you left. I didn't think I'd see you again and not in here."

"Hey, Maria, you want to drive my customers out and me out of business?" Wilton complained. "I'll kick your *fresca* ass back into the street if you do. You think I have people beating my door down to get in? *Muy irrespetuoso.*"

Jesus laughed. "You can barely manage to throw a trash can out without hurting your back. How are you going to manage to toss her into the street? You try and she take your balls and make castanets out of them."

"You too," said Wilton. "Both of you out like a pair of old *botinas.*" He waved the dirty rag in their direction in mock anger, his eyes laughing at the absurdity of his statement. Then he went back to his habitual wiping.

"You might think this sounds weird." She paused. It did sound weird. Maria took a deep breath. "I need to be here, I don't know why but here was where I wanted to be tonight out of any other place I could be. I can't say what but I know it in my bones, my *agallas.*" She picked up a glass of Mezcal and toyed with it, watching the yellow light glitter in the liquid. "Something guided my steps to this place after so long, it was a voice. There is a reason I am here, why you both are here, even Wilton who is pretending to ignore what we are saying." Wilton muttered a protest. "Nothing happens by chance." She smiled. "Besides I need a place to sleep tonight."

"A place to sleep in safety is not a bad thing," Jesus said. "Sounds like you believe in fate Maria."

"Not fate, fate is something you can't stop. We can all leave if we like, but we won't, it's our choice to stay or not. Fate doesn't work like that." Maria was scornful.

"I don't need fate to be, only Mezcal. Here it is shit but at least it's here." Jesus answered. Ishmael was still silent. "Any guidance I want will be out of here. Not to stay." Wilton snorted from behind the bar. "Old man the only thing you need would tell you how to clean the glasses." Jesus said with a smile. "And you've never heeded it have you?"

"If I did you wouldn't have anything to complain about." Wilton turned his back on them in dismissal.

Jesus and Ishmael looked at Maria. "In the year since I saw you in here," Jesus said. "Where did you go?"

"I've been out by San Dimas; it got too crowded and dangerous around here. Seems more peaceful there, even if there are no bars to go to. And I like being close to the mountains. At night I look out at them and see the fires." She shrugged. "They are always there, sometimes more, sometimes less. But they are not so nice up close."

"We've seen the smoke when the weather is good during the day," Ishmael said. "What are these fires? I've seen them too, we all have."

"They are campfires. Sometimes I've gone out there and watched men sitting around with guns. I don't know what they're doing but they are watching the city. They have dead eyes."

Jesus nodded. "I've heard of them and we've seen what they are capable of. You remember the semi years ago, filled with dead bodies and the crucified ones. They want us all to die here, I am sure of it. Die like the *cochinos* they think we are. I told Wilton yesterday, Ishmael today and now you. There is a storm coming." He played with his glass of Mezcal, circling his fingers on the rim. "Fate may have brought us here I don't know. But something is coming. It is the storm and we are inside it, a part of it." Jesus paused and his eyes clouded over. "We are the storm."

Wilton guffawed. "I'd prefer to be well away from any storm Jesus, it's more peaceful there than in the wind."

"Peaceful, but boring." Ishmael pointed out. "It's much better to be at the center of great things, to bring them about than sit and do nothing while they pass you by. It makes you glad to be alive when you do. Better to be part of whatever is coming. What it will be I know as little or as much any of us but I'll welcome it. Time for me to practice what I preach."

"That is your choice." Jesus waved for more drinks. "By the water you pointed to me and said behold the oncoming storm, what did you mean? How could you have known I had said much the same to Wilton?"

"Oncoming storm?" asked Maria.

Ishmael sat back and folded his arms. "I have no idea; it was like I was John the Baptist and saw Jesus Christ himself for the first time. So it was with you. You were different, I saw lightning and thunder about you, how or why I cannot say. I don't know what the future will bring, none of us can, but something is going to happen and things will change. Great things are upon us all." Ishmael looked very old then, older than Jesus had ever seen him. Lines drew down his brow and clouds gathered behind his eyes. His white hair looked like wire and his skin shone. He glowed as if something transcended him, hiding his ragged clothes. The bar grew chill and they reached for their drinks as one. They passed the night drinking Mezcal and talking of inconsequential things. For that night only they hid behind the façade there was nothing else they could do.

SIX

"So what do we do?" Jesus asked the next morning. It had been a good night and he felt better than he did the previous morning. Enough to know talking about oncoming storms and fires in the mountains wasn't enough.

"Your namesake had it worked out." Wilton said. "He said follow me and people did until the poor bastard had to run up into the mountains to get some peace."

"Knowing what he was doing helped, Wilton," Ishmael pointed out. "We don't know what to do or how to do it."

"What if we aren't going to be part of change but bring it," Maria said. "And if we are going to do anything we need to know what's happening, right?"

"And how do we find the answer and where? And where do we start?" asked Ishmael.

"The place to start will be finding out who exactly is out there and what they want from us." Despite the words Jesus felt less sure of himself than he did yesterday. Things were looking far more complicated than he would like. Lows always followed highs and last night they had been higher than they had known all their lives.

"Which will mean getting through the ring around the city, and I'd like to know the purpose of the spire out in the hills." Maria felt sure it was a key to the future.

"I have seen it too, as we all have, yes?" Jesus said. "When the sun is out the light glints off the tower and it looks like silver, we all know this. It's high, I know only that."

"So there's the first step," Ishmael said. "Know your enemy, a good saying for these times. But how do we find out?"

"I know someone who might be able to help," Maria said. "He lives near me in the same building and pretty decent when it comes to tech shit. Spends his time watching the feeds he gets from the outside as much as he can. I've used him a lot when I go into the mountains. He can help find a way through the worst of the ring out there. Must be worth trying, huh?"

Jesus scratched his head. "We have to start somewhere and there's as good a place as any I can think of."

Ishmael agreed. Wilton wasn't so keen. "I know you said we are all here for a reason, to be part of something big enough to change our world. Hell for the better or not I don't know. You don't either and you know it but can't I be part of things and stay here? I've lived here all my life and I'm happy, why fuck with it?" He looked wistful for a moment. He wanted to cling on to the past and still keep the promise of the future. He knew he couldn't do both. "I have this business, it's not the best I know but at least it's something. And I remember the past better than most. I remember seeing the Hollywood sign up on the mountains and looking at the handprints in front of Grauman's. I remember the gangs running the show but where are they? Gone for somewhere better while the rest of us wait for the end, you know what I'm saying? "

They did. "You're older than me old man," Jesus said. "It was already gone to shit when I got here. The only difference is the level has gone up."

"And you lived," Ishmael pointed out. "I watched a baby die not two days ago and it still tears at me and it will for a long time. I buried it in an empty block of land. There was no one and nowhere to take it and no one to mourn it. In the past it would have a chance, now it did not but I took it anyway even though I could do nothing but let it die. This is the way of things here now, life is cheap and death is easy. In the past they would have lived. But not here and not now. There has to be better than this and over the mountains is where it is."

"You gave the woman hope, Ishmael," said Jesus.

"What good is hope in a city where hopelessness is normal?"

They were silent for a while. The baby had intruded. Dismissing it was impossible. Maria broke the silence. "Even if we can find out something about who is out there watching us, getting there will be the hard part. Getting past the camps and whatever else they have up there won't be easy. We're rats in a trap. We know it, they know it and they don't give a fuck about us." Maria slammed her fist on the bar. "But I do."

"We all give a fuck," Jesus said. "But let's not get ahead of ourselves. We'll take the first step by seeing Maria's friend. Then we can decide more after we learn what we can about where to go, how to get there, and what to take with us." Jesus left the point unsaid. "But no guns. We couldn't carry enough and if we do they might shoot first and ask questions after. Dying out there won't get us anywhere."

"What do you want to do, go ride up to the camps on an ass?" Wilton laughed at his suggestion.

"It sounds better than carrying you on my back or vice versa." Jesus' eyes sparkled with humor. "Neither of us would get far."

Wilton managed to look abashed. "I walked into that, didn't I?"

"Low profile sounds the best," Jesus affirmed his point. The others nodded agreement, even Maria who never went anywhere without a weapon of some kind. Something in Jesus made her think how his was the right way to do it. Like Ishmael there was something behind his eyes she hadn't seen before. A flame of will flared for a moment and she knew she would do what she could to help.

Jesus stood and wiped his hands on his pants. Dust spread from them through the air. "I say we get started, go see the *tipo* Maria told us about and see what he can do. We must get word out, build our numbers, make people to listen to us." He dared the others to stay in the bar by his stare. They followed him out the door into once-was LA. and walked into the future.

Rantall Heyusser was sitting in front of a computer screen. On the screen was a graph showing a line sloping down to zero, left to right. Years ran down the screen, oldest at the top down to the present. This year the projection for LA read zero. But there they were despite the predictions, scratching out their pitiful and useless lives. It was wrong, it went against all Heyusser liked; safe, predictable outcomes you could count on. This was worse than predicting the weather and getting rain instead of sun. How could you do anything without knowing if you need sunscreen or an umbrella.

LA remained the thorn in his side, festering, ready for lancing with no pain relief. And he had the equipment to achieve it. The force waiting at his call was ready. Cometh the hour cometh the man, it was the reason he was here, why he lived. Heyusser liked the idea. Natural attrition had failed and he was to bring the end. Force and death were part of man, as natural as eating. All he was doing was giving the natural order a gentle nudge. He flicked a switch on the desk and a shimmering 3D mirage of the LA to come lit up his face. Even the sea wasn't going to stop it. It was beautiful, beautiful.

Then the computer beeped, interrupting his reverie. He had an incoming video call. He accepted the call and the screen came into focus. He pressed the button on his intercom and the screen jiggled and waved into focus. A face looked at him, arrogant and confident of its place over Heyusser. He was African and he knew Heyusser well and didn't like him. And he didn't look too happy. "Yes?" asked Heyusser.

"LA is not behaving according to predicted status. It was to be an empty city by now."

"Some things defy predictions," replied Heyusser.

"Why are there still people living there?" asked the face.

Heyusser sighed. "You might want to ask them yourself, I have no idea. I could send in people with questionnaires, if it will help to find out?" Heyusser smiled inside, he always liked to irritate the man on the other side of the connection. His comment had struck a nerve, the man's nostrils flared in response.

"Take preemptive action as soon as practicable," said the man. "But be swift Heyusser, questions are being asked and when they are I do not like it, neither does Mr. Fleming. You have one week to report an improvement in the situation." The face motioned to cut the connection then halted. "One more thing, we have need of new staff, send suitable people within forty-eight hours." The screen went blank.

"As you wish," Heyusser said and gave the blank screen the bird. He sat back in his leather chair and it creaked under his weight. It had gone a little better than he had expected. At least he could do something and get things done. He'd been sitting on his thumbs waiting for something to happen but he could finally get things moving. Time to flush out the pus-filled sore in the west. He picked up the phone. "Get the chief of security in here. We have something to discuss."

He only waited ten minutes before a stern man wearing a Marine haircut and military fatigues arrived. He wore no badges and no one knew what he was by looking. He was serious, never smiled, and obeyed orders like a pro. He had a deserved reputation for finishing everything he started with extreme efficiency. There was a reason he was the chief of security and it wasn't his sense of humor. "General Moore, you were prompt." Heyusser waved him to take a seat.

"I was in the building on another matter Sir," General Moore said as he sat. Heyusser offered him a bourbon. "No thank you, it's too early for me."

Heyusser poured himself one. "General, you should know it's always time for a drink somewhere in the world." Heyusser smiled. "I want to go over something with you," he said, steepling his fingers under his nose. "How soon can you give me a plan to go into LA and start action to remove the last of the inhabitants?"

General Moore didn't shift his expression and his eyes said nothing. "Have we received the order to go ahead?"

Heyusser knew Moore would be itching to get started, as much to give his men something to do as anything. "Indeed we have General. We have a week to clear up the matter at hand and sweep LA away like a sandcastle."

General Moore knew when Heyusser said 'we' it didn't include himself. It didn't matter. Moore had his ideas on how he would work it to his advantage. But he was a professional and he liked what he did and his face didn't change. "I'll have a plan on your desk in twenty-four hours. Will that be all sir?" Heyusser nodded over his fingers. He knew that Moore wanted his job, had done for years. It was time to get him out of the picture for a while. "Good afternoon, sir," said Moore. "I have work to do, with your permission."

Good tone, thought Heyusser, obedience without sounding too servile. "Permission granted General, I can't wait to see your plan."

Moore left, closing the door behind him. Heyusser sipped his bourbon, things were looking up and it was about time.

Maria took them to a room in her building on the fourth floor. Wilton found the climb hard and was puffing hard. His face looked liked one of the flowers on his shirt. Maria pushed open the door and almost called out as a man loomed out of the dim interior. "Holy shit Maria!" The voice spoke. "You almost scared me to death, what the hell you do barge in here for, ever heard of knocking? It's what civilized people do."

Maria put her hands in the air. "I am so sorry Jeremiah. I forgot. I get so used to pushing mine open." The man looked pained. "We need you. You might be able to help us."

As their eyes got used to the light level Jeremiah emerged like a ragged scarecrow. His eyes were alert, wary, unsure of the newcomers. Without Maria, Jesus sensed they wouldn't get far asking for help.

Inside the room it was dark and cluttered. Curtains covered the windows to prevent anyone from looking in. Two small lamps on the walls provided almost enough light for them to see. Jeremiah shoved aside some trash to clear a space for the four to sit and then returned to an ancient computer. Wires ran everywhere, connecting his equipment to an old generator. It sat on the balcony outside, shaking it when it ran. Jeremiah had rigged it to run on whatever he could find to fuel it. Usually it was shit. The screen was dusty and crazed with fine cracks. On the desk sat two routers, lights flickering. Maria turned to Jesus. "Don't ask how it works, Jeremiah knows. I don't and I never asked." She looked back at the ancient machines. "If anyone can show us what's happening out there, he can."

Jesus looked at Jeremiah's ancient wire-strewn setup. "If he can get anything out of this *mierda* I'll give him a medal."

Jeremiah spun on his chair. It threw up a cloud of dust. Jeremiah didn't notice it. Jesus saw a thin man, bony, a pair of cracked glasses rested on short hair. His skin was dark and stretched over his frame like cling-wrap. He wore gold rings on six fingers, a red bandana, and a gold chain rested on a threadbare purple shirt. His pants hung off him and he wore battered keds. "What do you want me to do?" he asked Maria.

"We want to know what's happening out there." Maria waved her hand towards the hills. "What are they doing and what are they planning."

"I can tell you what they're doing easy. But planning, sorry man, no can do." Jeremiah asked. "I may be a genius but I can't hack into those systems, I've tried but it's impossible. No one can do it, trust me I've tried and so have a lot of people out there."

"Why?" Jesus asked.

Jeremiah looked like he was about to tell a child about the world. "Quantum shit, man. They got the latest quantum encryption out there, all I have is digital. Upshot is there's no way in seven hells for me to penetrate their systems. Well I could but it would take years to bust the codes. As long as they don't change them regular and if they do," he threw his hands up in the air, "I won't even be able to get to first base. Trust me, there's only so much a guy like me can do with what I have."

"Is there anything you can tell us?" Maria wanted to know.

"I can track their movements, get intel from other hackers but it won't be much use. You can find that shit out with your eyes and a working cell phone." Jeremiah left out the obvious; there weren't any in the city. "What are you *gueys* up to that you need my help?"

"We want to change things Jeremiah." Ishmael spoke for the first time. "Real talk now man, things are going to be happening soon, too soon for many folks. You know we are dying here and out there they want it to happen sooner rather than later. They're not going to let things ride forever. They'll do something to bring it down sooner. I don't know what but I want to find out, we all do. You want to as well, why else would you be so interested in seeing what's happening out there. We've had enough of sitting and waiting. Have you?"

"This situation is not good, we want to change it like Ishmael say," Jesus said. "Or try at least. I've had enough wandering round the streets, looking for wolves and bears and worse. So has everyone else only they lie like dogs waiting for the farmer to shoot them dead. And you? Don't you think there's something better than hiding in here in shit and dirt? *Mierda.* You want to help or sit behind your screen while the world ends while maybe you think it will pass you by. *Ay* we don't know if we can do anything but it's no reason not to try, *compadre.*"

Wilton rubbed his feet. "*Ay* my feet hurt. Look at me Jeremiah, this morning I was an old fat man running a bar and now I'm with these crazy people on a fool's quest. Yes it's so," he said to the others, "whether it's worth it or not doesn't change anything. Me? I'm like Sancho Panza following Don Quixote. But I am here and I will see it through whatever the end might be. Like me you could face the end sitting on your *asno*, comfortable and ignorant or face it standing up." He grinned. "You see my point, Jeremiah. Anyway this is what I decided to do, you can also or not. It is up to you and we won't blame you if you stay here. And I'm still fat and lazy." Wilton sat back, speech over.

"It's alright if you want to stay here Jeremiah," Jesus said. "Wilton is right, we won't think less of you if you want to stay. It's your choice, not ours."

"Okay, I didn't want you all to think you were being moded here. I wanted to be straight about what I can do," Jeremiah said.

"We know, Jeremiah," Maria said. "Is there anything you can show us we can use to help?"

Jeremiah thought for a moment. "There might be, I get images from the older satellites that still function in orbit as well as vids from the drones I send out. What I have left anyway." He nodded at a box half-hidden in the detritus. Drones filled it to the top, scavenged for parts to keep others running. "Only it won't be in real time, I don't have the tech. I run my own software, better than most, no ghetto shit, kinda like them old map applications from decades ago. I get the download from the satellites and transfer them into the program. You get movement like stop-motion. I use the vids to help fill in the gaps. It's weird, it's like they don't mind being watched, coz there's nothing we do to stop them and they know it. Sometimes they'll take potshots at them for kicks but most of the time they don't notice them nowadays. Like I said the fuckers out there don't care." He tapped on a few keys. "It ain't perfect, heaps of lag, but it's the best I can do and it might help you get a handle on things."

"I thought you said they had quantum systems. How can you see to get this?"

"Older satellites, they be digital. Left up there when they launched newer. Made no sense to do anything but let them burn up on re-entry when their power failed. Guess whoever is in charge didn't figure they were any use to anyone else. Getting into the feeds is easy. Little or no encryption and firewalls a kid could get past. The images are good but at hi-res they're blurry as hell so I have to stay at a meter resolution. Back then they could even see us walking around or having a piss. Hell, even see how long our dicks were." Jeremiah was enjoying showing off what he knew and Jesus wanted him on their side more than ever. "Those over the mountains have stuff I can't get into like I said. I wish I could. Quantum man; sucks not to have it." In front of them the screen came into focus, the center of the screen showed LA. Jeremiah swapped to terrain view and they watched as dots moved around the screen like fleas on a dog. "I based my prog on old Google maps," Jeremiah grinned. "Yeah it's slow but it works," Jeremiah said. "It's ghetto man."

SEVEN

J EREMIAH dug another screen out of the chaff of his room and hooked it up to an auxiliary port on his system. "You'll see better with this one." As they looked they watched the resolution improve. It was slow but after a few minutes valleys, mountains, roads, and buildings, came into focus. They saw people like moving dots. Maria felt it was real and unreal at the same time like watching a documentary she didn't understand. "I can zoom in as far as ground level and get to a meter resolution like I said but I don't need to yet." He zoomed in a little further. Jeremiah pointed at the screen. A building squatted in the middle of the scene. "We're there." Ishmael looked up at the ceiling and Jeremiah laughed. "You can't see the satellites ace, but they can sure see you!" He zoomed out again. "I'll zero in on the mountains where the camps are, see what we can see."

The screen shifted and showed camps several hundred yards apart filled with people. Social distancing didn't occur to them. Other camps had been abandoned. Unneeded their dead campfires lay like splotches of lichen. "This is as good as I can get but you get the idea."

"Doesn't look too hard to get past," Wilton said.

Maria punched his arm. "They have motion sensors to pick up anything they can't see. Trust me, I've seen them. If anyone comes looking they'll find us for sure. Harder for five to hide than one. And besides, it won't take them long to use those unused campsites again when they need to."

"Should we let them find us?" Jesus asked.

"No," Ishmael pointed out. "If we get caught there they'll send us back in trash bags, remember the semi they left." It wasn't a question.

"You going out there?" Jeremiah shook his head. "You are wack man, insane. Why the fuck you want to die? Those people out there are

43

fucking serious. They shoot first then ask questions." He adjusted the focus and swung on his chair to face them. "They have weapons and lots of them, see those crates?" He pointed at the screen. "They got rifles, ammo, everything. And what have you got?"

Jesus remembered the pistol in his pocket. He took it out and looked at it before tossing it aside. Suddenly it seemed not as reassuring as it did on the streets. The slingshot followed it. "Nothing worth taking," he said with finality.

Jeremiah shook his head and the light from the desk lamp turned his face into stop-motion. "Look, you think we have it bad? At least we're alive. Every city on the West coast was left to die. And they all did, one by one. San Fran, Seattle, Portland. Every fucking city, every town, every shitty little hamlet. All gone, man. They swept Tacoma off the fucking map in less than a week. Everyone gone, dead, and the town flattened. Hell every city on the East coast for all I know. They got what they need to do it to us, everything but the wheels but they can get them soon enough."

"They're rumors, nothing but hearsay Jeremiah," Ishmael said. "We've all heard them ourselves, even repeated them, right?"

"Ishmael's right. If it has happened we need some proof. How do you know these things?" Jesus asked. He felt a pang. His parents had understood what was coming but died before they could get out. His resolved wavered, creaked, held firm.

"This." Jeremiah rose and fossicked around in an overloaded desk. He wrenched drawers out and tossed scraps of paper and pens on the floor. Covered as it was with detritus they couldn't tell if he made it messier or not. "Found it!" he exclaimed after a few minutes, brandishing a CD. "This is when I looked at San Fran, watch." He slotted into the drive and waited for it to load. "This is from two years ago; I copied it direct from the satellite stream."

The image was static, or looked like it was. "Remember the images I just showed you? You saw people moving around, a bit scratchy but moving. Here," he waved the image. "Nothing, no one is moving because there's no one there. No people at any rate. You can see the time clock at the bottom left." They looked and the clock was ticking. "It was real time too," Jeremiah confirmed. "I'll prove it." He zoomed in on an image, it was dark and it looked big. As he zoomed in it showed a bear. It was walking. "Lots of animals but no people. I've watched this for hours and not seen one person, never."

"We'll take your word for it Jeremiah," Jesus said.

"And it's the same for every other city on the west coast. I've run the same checks. Ident progs you name it. Nothing." Jeremiah almost looked he was going to cry.

"So this could be the last inhabited city on the west coast." Maria sat stunned at the images in front of them.

"I wouldn't doubt it," said Jeremiah. "And that's not the worst." He went back to the desk and dug around in another drawer. "Here." He slid another CD into another drive. Two images came up side by side. "Check out the difference. This is San Fran from four months ago." They watched as the screen filled with a different city. Green areas and buildings lined the sea front like an old computer game gone insane.

"Different, isn't it?" Jeremiah stated as the obvious lay in front of them.

"What the hell happened?" Jesus asked.

"The rulers of us happened." Jeremiah said. "They cleaned the place up and made San Fran into their own private holiday park because they could. I guess they still have the money and money always makes its own rules, does what it does. It's the same with the other cities like Tacoma, Seattle. Prime beachfront property sitting and waiting. Then when the people have gone the money moves in and there's no one around to stop you. You want to see the other places?" Jeremiah went to flip the image.

Jesus found it hard to look at knowing in his gut and who what was waiting to plough his city into the dirt. He shook his head, images of old memories being ploughed under ran through his mind. He quelched them, not wanting them to make his dreams worse than they were. "No, we don't need to. We've seen enough to see what is waiting for us out there and the lengths they will go to. I and my friends want to know why."

"They do it because they can my friend, because no one is able to stop them." Wilton watched the screens. He looked saddened beyond imagination. "It has always been so, always there have been those who have been beyond the consequences of their actions."

"The rulers, Jeremiah, you said the rulers of us. No one rules me." Maria folded her arms across her chest.

"Yeah they do, you just don't know it. It's the old con, keep the people occupied, keep them distracted so they don't realize what's going on under their noses. The old shell game." Jeremiah focused in on the map outside LA. There stood a concrete construction like a giant slab. It was huge, hundreds of yards across. "You know what this is?" None of them knew. "Look outside the window," Jeremiah said. They looked at the omnipresent spire, stretching past the few clouds. "You can look at it every day but on the feeds from the satellites I get into it's like it's not there," Jeremiah said. "I can't figure it out. They never show a picture of it. All you can ever see is the slab. It makes no sense." Jeremiah threw his hands in the air. "It's beyond me, man. I can see what's happening down here except for this. Whoever is at the other end of the spire are sitting there, watching us like rats in a maze. And when they get tired of watching, game over."

They looked at the slab lying on the ground like a vast shield. "It's a game to them isn't it?" Ishmael wondered aloud.

"And played out of our reach with rules we don't know or understand," Jesus replied.

"And they can shut down what we see anytime they want to. Your guess is as good as mine when they might do it or why. But when they do they will roll right over us." Jeremiah sat down and turned off his screen.

"Then there is only one thing to do," Jesus said. "We go and find them. And we don't stop until we do."

"Then what?" asked Maria.

"Tell them to leave us be. Or make them. If we die trying, it will be an honorable death." A dark cloud passed behind Jesus' eyes. It was like watching a storm approach, a storm to change their lives forever. Maria knew she wanted to be a part of it whether she survived or not. She knew Wilton thought the same so there were three. Ishmael was the unknown. He was older, more wedded to the city. Of Jeremiah she had no idea, he talked the game well enough but could he play?

"Sounds like a suicide mission." Wilton spoke up. They had forgotten he was there. "I'm not complaining, *por supuesto*, I am with you all the way as far as asking them to leave us be, but making them? Jeremiah can print us up some one way tickets if you like, straight to hell and beyond and save our energies. You talking *mierda* my friend. All bluster because when it goes to hell we'll be back like beaten dogs, cowering until the end comes. If we don't get killed trying first." Then he puffed his cheeks out. "But what would an old man like me know? *Ay* it does sound better than sitting around, and what the hell it might be fun until we die. Going out in a blaze of glory can make a good epitaph for us."

"The other thing I would like to know is who lives up there." Jesus continued to look at the spire. His eyes seemed to flare. "I want them to see us, pay attention to us, not think of us as less than ants, good only for stepping on without being noticed."

"But with only four of you how are you going to manage it?," asked Jeremiah. "I hate to bring this up, but if they pay any attention at all it will only be to smear you out like treading on a bug. They won't even blink. Anyone who can roll over all those cities, what do think they'll do to you?" He pulled out another disc and slotted it in. "Look at this."

The screen built up into the country beyond the hills. Jeremiah zoomed in. They looked at metal objects, concrete boxes, and buildings yards long. "What is this shit?" Jesus looked at the screen.

"I don't know but it's out beyond the hills. And there's a lot more, what you see isn't the worst of it. When I last looked a couple days ago there were more of them. Something is in the wind people and the smell of it isn't roses. Sorry but I can't see how you can do anything to make a difference."

Jesus sat on the chair with the least clutter. "I can see how they can roll over us anytime they want to. Only question is why are they waiting and what for? It might give us some time."

"Time for what?" asked Maria.

"To try and get more people to join us." Jesus stood and brushed off his ragged clothes. "And now is the best time to start, wouldn't you say, before we face the *enemigos* out there?"

None of them argued but all knew the same thing, numbers might help. It still would be like pissing into the wind but some of the piss might might get through. But how long would they have to try? They had no idea, no way of knowing. They sat like gargoyles covered in dust and grime, feeling the weight of what stood in front of them. It had been words up to now said with no expectation. Now it was as if they were in a rip with no choice but to let it take them where it wanted. Not one of them knew what would come to pass. The truth came to them like a slow cloud. They had been at a crossroads and now they had taken a step on a path which forbade any turning back. The gate behind them was closed. They remained immobile in thought as the sun melted into the horizon.

Then Jesus shook them out of the reverie they had fallen into. "Come on, we are all *despernada*, tired. Can we sleep the night here Jeremiah? We will need time to plan our next move. Or we can sleep at your place instead, Maria?"

"We need the best place to plan and we need intel to do it," Maria demurred. "And my place isn't it." She looked around at Jeremiah's set-up. "Such as it is, here is better."

"I'll clear some space." Jeremiah looked around. "If I can."

"I'll help," Ishmael said. They set to moving some of the junk Jeremiah had collected over to one wall so there was some floor space. They spread out some blankets and sat on them as the shadows grew. It didn't help the mood, it was somber and grave. The room had become a cell. Jeremiah rummaged around and produced a bottle.

"I don't know about you all but I could use a drink," he said. He dug around and found some cups and filled them. "A toast," he said. "To whatever comes next."

They touched their glasses together and drank. The liquid burned in their throats. It was a fire as smooth as honey.

"What is this? Did the disciples drink this after Jesus called them?" Ishmael asked, coughing from the spirit.

"Everything's a religious thing with you isn't it?" Wilton asked. "You ever get tired of seeing the world like in such a way, *predicador*?"

"Nope, it helps with the perspective. Goes with being a preacher or pretending to be. I admit I didn't start out this way but it came to me while I was living here and watching the city die. People need something in times like these and I tried to give it to them. But there are times I question myself. A lot of times." Ishmael drank the liquid and sighed into the distance.

"The baby?" Maria asked.

Ishmael nodded and sighed in assent.

"Seeing a baby die would rattle anybody, Ishmael, *agitato*. You shouldn't get down on yourself," Maria joined in.

"I'm trying not to but how else can I react? But anyway the past is the past and it will stay there and I will make peace with God the best I can and keep doing what I do. I don't always get it but God is standing with us like he stands with the poor, the lost, the sick, and the oppressed. God knows we are all that here and He will be with us no matter what happens."

"As long as he helps us to win I won't mind," Maria said.

Ishmael looked at her with grave eyes. "God don't work that way Maria," he said. "He let his son die on the cross and the Jews die in millions during the Holocaust. You think it will be different for us? All we can do is lean on Him and take strength. If we die on this journey so be it. It won't be his doing either way."

"You do have to wonder if God's around," Jesus said.

Ishmael laughed. "Coming from a man with His son's name. Yeah, I do. A lot. Don't stop me believing though."

"Not me," Wilton said.

"You think it matters? You think God will stop being around because you don't believe? Free will man, free will. He ain't gonna worry if you use it. He'd be a poor deity if he gave it to us and didn't let us use it. And we used it when we decided to follow Jesus to what might the end of us." He finished the drink and put the glass on a clear space. "Anyway I am tired. It's been a long day. You keep drinking, I'm getting some sleep." Ishmael stretched out on the blanket and the night closed around them. One by one the others laid out in whatever space they found. Maria stayed up watching the stars appear and the fires start on the nearby hills. She wondered when she would be out there again and wondered what would happen when she was. Then she found a place to lie down, and still wondering, slept as best she could. They all did.

EIGHT

O VERNIGHT the stars disappeared behind thick clouds. In the morning the air was heavy. It pressed down on them, making it hard to move as if quicksand mired their feet. Low dark clouds hung over the city. Under them the people went from place to place like zombies, conserving what energy they had. A light shower was starting to make the streets shine. In Jeremiah's apartment the five woke from fitful and dream-filled sleeps. They shouldered the air aside and got up. Jesus looked out the window. The hills hid behind rain that grayed the land, sapping the color. He couldn't see the spire or the shambles of the I-210. He turned away. It was a morning where the world looked futile and pointless. Jesus wondered if they would actually do what they had agreed to. The world was full of unrealized dreams and people who had let them slide past. Who would blame them if they did.

Jeremiah put coffee on. The smell seeped through the apartment and spiked Jesus' nostrils. He had almost forgotten what coffee smelt like these days. Then he wondered who could have coffee on a day like this in a place like this. He decided not to think about it or ask. It would serve no purpose and delay the inevitable. The others roused themselves in fits and starts. Complaining of sore heads they came up one by one to have the coffee Jeremiah poured into grimy mugs. Black, no sugar, it was the only way anyone could have it these days. Jesus accepted one Maria put in his hands. Tasting it, he wondered how it could taste as good as it did and if futility or action added flavor. "I will be going today." Jesus sipped the scalding liquid. "None of you have to come with me *entender?* But I will appreciate all who do."

One by one they replied they would. Even Jeremiah. "Hey man," he said with a wide smile "I've been behind a screen for way too long, know what I'm saying? Time to embrace life isn't it?" They did and welcomed him.

"So now there's five," said Wilton. "If we end up being thirteen it will be too weird, *extraño*."

They all knew what he meant. Ishmael's words from the night before were still bright in their minds. "Where will we go first?" asked Maria.

Jesus sipped again. The coffee was a bit cooler now. "To the sea. More chance of seeing people down there with Ishmael baptizing like he does, right old friend? Afterward, who knows, we will wait and see, *espera y ver*."

Ishmael agreed. "They do like to come and get washed. It's the only chance to get clean any of us have."

"Then it's agreed. And we pick up anyone on the way who'll come with us, *bien y bueno*." Jesus blew on the coffee.

"Don't tell them they might be on a suicide mission," Wilton pointed out. "You'll get more followers."

"No Wilton," Jesus said. "The truth is important. They must know the risk or there is no point to following."

"How about surviving? A lot of people put a high value on living." Wilton grunted as Maria punched him on the arm. He rubbed for a few moments. "That hurt," he complained.

"Be grateful I didn't punch your *cojones*," she replied. "You'd have something to complain about then." Maria paused. "If you have any. Living is more than surviving Wilton, if we go we live, if not we only survive for as long as they let us. I would rather live, wouldn't you?"

Wilton took note. She had strength in her he hadn't known before. He nodded assent to her question.

Jesus held Jeremiah's shoulder. "You sure you want to come?"

"Yeah man, I've had enough of my life sitting around here. Time to do something."

Jesus stood in the middle of the group. Outside the rain had started to fall again. If it was an omen it wasn't a good one. Ishmael crossed himself, so did the others, even Wilton. He saw them looking at him, a smile stroked Ishmael's lips. "It doesn't hurt to have an insurance policy."

Jesus spoke and they all listened. "I don't know what will happen. Whether we get somewhere or not I wanted to tell you all one thing. If you decide to stay here no one will think the worst of you. You can also leave anytime you want, there is no desertion. You must follow your own hearts and minds, always. I don't doubt it will be dangerous, some of us might not make it, there are no promises we will survive. But at least we will die knowing we tried. Which might have to be enough, *créame?*" He met all their eyes. None of them flinched from his gaze. Even Wilton held firm, even surprising himself.

By the time they reached the street the rain had changed from a shower to sheeting down. Rivers ran across the street and down the gutters, dodging past the rubble. The water banked up until it burst its captivity to rage along the boulevard. In the torrent, old and discarded toys spun and tossed. Dead rats and raccoons circled and lodged in the drains. The water built up around them and added to the froth spuming over the blacktop and concrete. The storm drains were full of lumber and bricks and the water flowed along and over them. "Not a good time to be making tracks." Jeremiah watched as a dead dog floated past like an obscene boat, its stiff legs like masts.

"No time like now," Jesus said and he walked out into the flood like a dirt-smirched Noah. The others followed him, sodden in seconds. They walked off down Wilshire, following the flood to the sea. They looked like a rag tag group of people with nowhere to go. If you asked any of them at that moment, there would be few dissenters.

In Vegas the skies were clear for now. When the rainstorm swamping LA reached there it would be a shadow of itself, its force spent on the mountains and the desert. Rantall Heyusser sat at his desk waiting for General Moore to arrive. He knew Moore was a good man despite his aspirations. Having a goal to reach was admirable; it kept a man on his toes and ready to impress. Moore needed watching and Heyusser was too savvy to let Moore get ahead of himself. Moore's ambition kept Heyusser on his toes too. The folder Heyusser tapped with his fingers was key. Certain things had recently come to light making Heyusser's position that much more safe. Moore wasn't so well-placed. He would be in a bad spot if they got out into the public.

Heyusser glanced down at the folder in front of him. 'Very interesting indeed,' he thought. Moore didn't know it but he had better tread very carefully for the rest of his career, no matter how short how long it might be. There were others jostling for his job, any one of them would be very grateful for a sudden promotion and would soon press their case to Heyusser. He grinned like a predator. He knew where the information had come from of course, he had good sources but he wasn't going to let the General know. Or would he? A bit of gratitude might be worth having. He was judging the pros and cons when General Moore knocked and entered.

"You wanted to see me Sir." Straight to the point. Have to give him his due Heyusser thought.

"What is the progress General?"

"We are moving men up to the line surrounding the city as well as materiel and supplies." General Moore remained standing as if he didn't want to remain there any longer than he wanted to. "It is taking a while of course."

"Why?" asked Heyusser.

"Too much movement too soon might alert the residents to what we have planned and spark a mass escape. We've been successful so far at preventing witnesses telling others what we're doing and neither of us wants to fail now. Our leaders wouldn't be very appreciative if we fucked everything up when we're so close to our goal."

Heyusser nodded. "You're right General. We don't want anyone starting some kind of insurrection. They tend to make things messy and I don't like it when they do. Neither do our overlords." He tapped the folder again. "Keep moving the men and supplies up little by littleand keep me informed. We have a week so time isn't an issue. Do you have the plan ready?"

Moore pulled a large envelope from his briefcase and slid it across his desk. Heyusser wondered if it was surgically attached, he never seemed to be without it. Heyusser opened the envelope, taking out a folder. "Thank you General, anything else to report?"

"Yes Sir, we had planned some drone flights but the weather over the city is bad. We'll have to delay until the weather clears up but I don't expect any major delays."

"I noticed. How severe is it?"

"Thunderstorms and tornadoes are forecast." General Moore stayed upright. It was as if someone had stapled a steel pole along his spine preventing any movement.

"When will you be able to get some in the air?"

"Tomorrow possibly, it depends on how low the cloud cover is and how long it lasts. We don't want to send drones down at low altitude; the risk is too great as you know." It was as if he was daring Heyusser to disagree.

Heyusser noted to himself how General Moore was a genius at the understatement. He recognized the dare and refused it. "Indeed not General," he said. "Keep me informed."

"Yes sir." General Moore snapped off a salute and vanished. A gentle snick of the door latch being the only sign of his departure.

Heyusser thought it went his way. The General had seen him tapping on the folder. He would have wondered what was in it and whether it concerned him. Which made Heyusser's decision not to say anything a good one. Now Moore had a bit of unease to work on the mind. Not enough to affect his ability of course. Only enough to keep him focussed on what he had to do and delay his personal ambitions for the immediate future. He leaned back in his chair and smoked another cigar. It felt better than sex. He pondered for a moment then picked up the phone.

The storm continued over LA. It rolled through to the beat of thunder. Lightning strikes brought down trees. Facades clinging onto buildings in the vain hope of staying there gave up and crashed to the ground. Jesus and the others huddled under part of the Columbus Transcont waiting it out. They were two hundred yards from where the woman gave Ishmael the doomed baby. He wept, the tears drowned by the rain. It was too wet for a fire so they sat and sprawled on the ground under what cover they could find. Dirt and dust stuck to them making abstract patterns in the creases of their clothes. Jeremiah fished a bottle out of his pocket, opened it, and passed it around. They each took a sip. "Is this the same as we had at your place?" Jesus asked between coughs.

"No," Jeremiah said with a straight face. "This is the good stuff."

As the spluttering stopped Jesus looked out at the clouds. "Could be a tornado soon." The clouds looked massive, a wall bigger than a dam rolled toward them. A green haze cloaked the shattered buildings and broken sidewalks. The clouds were moving, rotating as they moved east, the updraft from the city adding to their energy. A clattering roar penetrated the sound of the rain as it hit. They covered their ears with their hands and it wasn't enough. All but deafened they huddled further into the gap the collapsed road had left and hoped it would be enough.

The clattering turned into hailstones big as ping pong balls and the din was tremendous. It blasted the air into fragments and scoured their ears. Maria huddled closer to Jesus, scared like a child, they all were. They had been here long enough to know what was coming. There was a drop in the air pressure, the clattering din faded east and they heard the sound of hell. A low roar echoed between the buildings, getting louder. "Damn I hate it when you're right Jesus," Ishmael said. "I think I should've stayed in bed this morning." They knew a twister was on the way and it was as if he was silent, only mouthing the words. Jesus tried to get closer to the exit and craned his neck to see how far it was. He tried to get out to see but the others hauled him back. "Don't be crazy man!" Wilton shouted. "I know we all die sometime but you have a few things to do first."

Jesus tried to relax but he was like a cat on a hot roof. He couldn't stay still and he tapped his feet in a syncopated beat. He wasn't the only one. They sat there under the storm knowing their lives were on a knife edge. The roar grew louder. People say a tornado is like a train, a fleet of 747s on takeoff. They were wrong. It was worse. Louder. Magnitudes louder. They cowered under the assault. They cringed and waited for their eardrums to burst and bleed. The overhanging Transcont shuddered. Pieces of concrete fell with a splashy wham on the ground outside. The debris stuck in the ground, the mud miring it to itself. They wondered if the whole thing would come down on top of them. There was nothing they could do if it did and there was no chance of surviving if they moved.

A nearby rumble underscored the sound, a tremolo to the base of the tornado. It faded fast. In the path of the twister people gathered in knots and clumps in what shelter they could find. Anyone caught outside died. Flying debris crushed them or ripped their heads from their shoulders. The city hunkered down and waited it out while the storm battered its bones and tore through its roads. It ripped out trees and threw down buildings. It lasted over an hour and headed out over the San Bernardino mountains to blow itself out in the desert. By the time it reached Vegas all it did was rain, it had no energy left.

After the storm the surge left most of downtown underwater. The water ate into the bones and sinews of the city then retreated. It took concrete, metal, and bodies with it. There would be enough for the scavengers and when they left the people would come out, look at what remained then go about their lives. So it always was when the living envied the dead.

NINE

FTER the storm passed the five came out from the shelter. It had kept them safe, the structure sound enough where they were. The twister had veered left before it hit the Transcont and vanished over Pasadena. The humidity returned with a bang, reminding them even when things were good they were still bad. Soon they were sweating like running taps and felt miserable. They took off what they could to try and stay cool and dry off. It was a losing effort and they walked on towards the sea at Gardena hoping for relief. They passed by an old record store, the sign over the door could still be read—Doo-Wop Vinyl and Cds—but it was as empty as everything else. A young boy sat in the door, watching them pass. He had a dirty white shirt on, jeans, and worn out sneakers. A cap sat on dirt-streaked hair. His face was empty, his eyes devoid of feeling. His trauma ran deep.

Ishmael walked over to him, rested his hand on his shoulder. He spoke soft, his lips close to the boy's ears. The rest couldn't hear him. The boy listened. After a few minutes the boy came with Ishmael and joined the group. He didn't speak to them. Jesus dropped back to talk to Ishmael as they walked. "He's a little young to join in our crusade isn't he?"

Ishmael tutted at Jesus. "Not for long old friend. He's alone. His mother died in the tornado. He saw her crushed to death. Without some-one he will die. Who'll take him if we don't?"

"You know him don't you *eh pana?*" Jesus left unsaid the certitude he would die soon if they didn't do anything.

"Yeah, he's a tough little hombre. He'll be okay one day." Ishmael looked at the boy in a way Jesus had never seen but could understand. Ishmael was seeing the baby in the boy's eyes. The memory of that day made his eyes sting with tears. He shook them away. "We just need to give him time to get to know us, to trust us until we can find someone who will take him in." Ishmael looked at the boy. He was skinny, his cheek bones prominent. A swollen stomach spoke of malnutrition. "He hasn't eaten for a few days, if not longer. We'd best get him something soon." The boy stayed quiet. They walked on.

Ishmael shook himself then he started to speak. Soft at first but his voice grew louder as the need to speak out grew stronger and stronger and it drew people to the sound. "The storm has gone. It has taken many things from us but another approaches, it is here, now, it walks among us and will bring us to Glory. The Lord has listened to us! He hears us in our need and our loneliness! He has sent us the means of deliverance and all he asks is we follow the one He sent as He sent others before. Amen brothers and sisters. He has not forgotten us. He will bring down the high and the mighty that scoff and think we are nothing and see us vanish from the earth. But we will not go easy my friends. We are lowly but He will raise us up and He has sent the means to rise. We will lift ourselves people, we will lift ourselves!"

"Impressive Ishmael," Maria said when he came and stood with them after speaking. "Total crap but impressive."

Ishmael went to ruffle her hair and she let him. "Even crap can be convincing if you sound like you mean it." He grinned like a beacon. "Preachers have known it for centuries." Behind them a small crowd had gathered. Ten to fifteen people, men and women, followed on the walk to Gardena. Ishmael leaned close to Jesus. "Now you need to do your part old friend. Talk to people as we pass as Christ did so long ago."

"What would I say? I can tell you and the others, I know you." He ran a hand over his dreads. "But strangers? It's harder than I thought it would be."

Ishmael urged him on and soon Jesus went over to three men sitting in the remains of wall. His misgivings went with him. A runnel of water flowed into an open storm drain by their feet. He said little. "Come with me, if you want this to end as much as I do." It seemed enough to him and little else came to his mind. He would have to practice.

The crowd looked at each other and then at Jesus. They wore rags for clothes and had the look of the dead. Their eyes were flat. One man rose and came over to them. The others laughed. "You be kidding if you think he can stop all this crap man. You come back when you get tired of them lying to you and leading you around by your nose. *Idiota!* Pah!" The man spat on the ground and the water took the spit away with it.

"You don't believe that do you?" Jeremiah asked the man when he joined them, settling into step.

"What good is sitting on my *trasero*, my backside, and dying here? I'd rather die out there facing things like a man, *macho*." He shrugged his shoulders. Water dripped from his lank hair. "Here is full of shit. You're full of shit. What's the difference between what shit we choose to die in?"

"And you will," Wilton pointed out.

"We all die sometime. Better to die a man than a sheep." The man squared his shoulders. "I am a man after all."

"What's your name?" Ishmael asked.

"Arturo Hernandez," the man replied.

"You're in luck *hombre*," said Jeremiah. "You're actually walking with Jesus. Few can say they've been so fortunate."

A smile touched Arturo's eyes and they twinkled with humor. "I don't know about fortunate but it sounds about right." The six walked on looking back on the beginnings of the crowd starting to follow them.

"Looks like you're getting a following my friend." Ishmael pointed out as the street passed under their feet.

"As long as it stays small I don't mind," Jesus replied.

"It might not," said Ishmael.

"I know. I hope I don't have to do the loaves and fishes."

Ishmael grinned. The water lapped at the doors and the buildings of Gardena. Trash swam in the gutters and along the streets. The storm surge had left buildings broken and battered. Dead fish eddied around the scoured stores. On the roof of an apartment a block ahead of them a woman stood, waving a rag. On her hip was a small child. "We need to help her," Jesus said.

"You're the boss," Wilton said. They entered the building. It was white where there was still plaster. Holes big enough to climb through spattered the walls where bricks had fallen free. The stairs clung, rusting, to the frame of the building. There were no windows. The elements had long taken what boredom had left behind. The six clambered through the remnants the storm had left and soon cleared a path up the stairs. They groaned and creaked but held as the woman and the child came down. Someone produced a blanket and put it around them, the woman smiled a thank you.

She was gaunt, had once been beautiful. Lines dragged her eyes down. Her eyes were blue under hooded lids and straight brown hair framed her face. She wore a white dress and she had been beautiful once.

Jesus held out his hand and she took it, picking her way through to the door and outside. "Thank you," she said. "I had a family here when the storm came. The water took them. Will I see them again?"

Jesus shook his head. "Not in this world."

Grief appeared and stunned them all in a city where it had no place. "I didn't think I would but I hoped they might have survived." They knew how she felt. All had lost something. She bent her head and the child, a girl, tugged her dress. The woman rubbed the child's hair. "My husband died last year. Fever. It takes so many now. How can this happen?"

"I don't know, none of us do but it does." Jesus knelt in front of the woman. "I want to make sure it stops happening. Come with us, let's end this life and start a better one."

"I would, but the child, I don't want to leave her. I found her in the building after the storm. I'm all she has."

"She isn't yours?" Wilton asked.

She shook her head. "I don't even know her name."

"Is there anyone who can help?" Ishmael asked the people.

A woman came out from the back of the small throng. "I will take her, keep her safe. I lost my own daughter last year. We need each other."

"Ask and you will receive," Ishmael helped her pick the child up.

The woman watched the child nestle into the older woman's shoulder. Relief flowed from her. "I guess I don't have anything holding me. I'm with you if you want me."

"We want you as much as you want us," Jesus said. "Even if we don't know it."

"The more the merrier as they say," Jeremiah grinned. "If you don't mind the likelihood of death you're welcome."

"We're dead already," she said. "I'm Adeline, pleased to meet you." She looked around the group. "When do we get started on making things right?"

"Now I guess," Wilton said. "Am I right?"

Jesus squatted on the drenched ground. "Not quite my friend, we've already started, but today we've done enough. We started with four and now we're six. The night will be on us soon and it will not be a safe place on the street for anyone. Tonight we rest and tomorrow we go into the mountains and move against those who want us dead."

"Up in the mountains, I never thought I'd ever get there," Arturo said. "I have my own reasons for going, other than why you want us to go. Most of us do I think. My brother went hunting one day, I cannot be sure of when anymore, and he never came back. I'm sure he was killed up there by them and I would like answers. I will get them."

Jesus looked over in the direction of the mountains hemming them in, their backs to the sea. He felt like the fox that watched, helpless, as the hunter approached. "We all have different reasons Arturo, coming is the main thing. I hope you get the answers you want." He looked back to the people. "We may have to fight to survive. I hope you are willing for the battle if it comes to pass." Arturo said he was.

The crowd heard Jesus' last words as if amplified. They mumbled and muttered. Some of them started to leave, turning and watching as if Jesus was a madman and would come running after them. But he stayed where he was and with the rest he watched them go. At the end a few others remained, Maria counted ten. Ishmael said he knew of a place nearby they could shelter in for the night. They agreed and they left, Ishmael leading the way. Two blocks later they came to a decrepit supermarket on the edge of a long deserted strip mall. Part of the roof had caved in, the front windows shattered. But it was upright.

Ishmael led them into the rear where two rooms stood vacant, separated by a wall with a busted door. "These should be good enough for tonight," he said. He vanished back into the store, returning a few minutes later with blankets and pillows. They weren't clean, nothing was anymore, but they were dry and looked warm. "Make yourselves comfortable. I'll get some supplies for tonight." It was dim, the windows too high and too small to let in much light. The paint was peeling in strips from the plaster. In the gathering dark they heard Ishmael walking around the store. They spread what blankets they could find on the floors of the two rooms, shaking off the worst of the shit and dirt. "At least the roof is still up," Maria said.

Adeline moved around the room, pushing the walls. In places they buckled under the pressure of her fingers. Some had moved. "I'd ask for a refund from the desk clerk," she said with a smile. "Good thing we're only here for a night."

Jesus looked the group gathered around him and followed them into the building. "Let's get some rest, we'll need it."

"Something to eat will be good, and to drink. Make it beer." Jeremiah stretched. "Or whiskey, anything age makes better is fine with me."

Maria sat next to Jesus. "Can I sleep here?"

Jesus smiled at her, liking her combination of toughness and fragility. No, not fragility, tenderness was closer to it. "Fine with me. At least you don't snore."

"You do," Maria said.

"Do you hope for anything?" Jesus asked as they sat in the gloom. The others had sat down around the room and arranged themselves so they could sleep.

"Nothing." Maria turned her face to hide it. She was hiding something but he knew she would tell him when she was ready.

"Everyone has hope for something, Maria. It makes us keep going. Without it we stop and die inside. It is the fear of death which hurts us most because no matter where we go we can never be rid of death." Jesus rested his hand on hers.

"It's nothing," Maria said.

"No, it's something or you wouldn't be hiding it, it's no use keeping it inside without telling anyone. It will destroy you in the end you know." Jesus' voice was soft but unyielding. Inside it was steel forbidding any argument against it.

Maria knew she would tell him soon. "I don't want to talk about it. Not yet anyway."

Jesus felt relief, the door to her secret had been opened a crack, and it would be enough. Soon it would be wide enough to let it out. "Your choice Maria. I will be here to listen."

"And you Jesus, what do you hope for?" she asked him.

"An end to this." Jesus indicated the room. "For the people here, sitting like caged animals with nowhere to go, nothing to do except survive. Do any of them have any hope?" He looked down at the ragged sheet. "Is this is a way for a human to live, Maria? Scratching a living from dirt and shit in a city that no longer exists, only the old idea of it? All so the rich *bastardos* with their *anteportadas* will holiday on top of our bones and feast over our graves." He snorted. "I hope it will soon be over and for all to be free like people should be."

"As long as we don't die trying, what will we achieve then, Jesus?" Jeremiah asked from where he was lying near them.

"I don't know Jeremiah. Maybe we will inspire others when we die. Christ did, so did Gandhi, Martin Luther King. Death seems to have a way of inspiring action out of grief."

"Be martyrs? I don't know Jesus, you have to die to be one and I'm not sure I want to die yet." Jeremiah lay down and rested his arms over his eyes.

"It might not come to pass my friend." Jesus averred. "It's only a possibility."

Jeremiah considered the possibility as he remained silent. As he thought the shadows lengthened and the night closed in. Outside the wind shook the branches of the trees and they scraped the walls like fingers. Ishmael clattered in with dried food and some bottled water saying it wasn't much but it was the best he could do. They ate alone with their thoughts as the night settled over them.

TEN

NEXT morning the sky was bright blue and the wind blew from the east, pulling the desert heat with it. The memory of the storm was now fading. Inside the store the group roused itself with the rise in temperature. Ishmael fired up a butane stove and made coffee. Packs of jerky lay on a folding table next to it. "Not the most healthy breakfast," he said. "But it will have to do. Soon we'll be eating dogs to survive." he looked around. "If you haven't already".

"Worse, ourselves if we live long enough," Arturo pointed out.

"Let's hope it doesn't come to that," said a man from across the room. He pulled a tattered gray trench coat over his shoulders. It had holes in the elbows and cigarette burns dotted the fabric. His eyes shone in a face framed by a grizzled beard as matted with dirt as his hair. His voice rasped as he spoke. "I want to see this over before I die." He coughed, a ragged, choking sound then lit a cigarette.

Jesus went and took his hand. "Only if you can manage it."

"Oh I can manage it alright," the man said. "I've been waiting for something like this my whole life. I was born here, my parents died here, and I will too but not if I can help it. I don't know how long I have but I guess one advantage of not having doctors around to tell you is the bliss of ignorance. I've never been one for wanting to know." The man got to his feet. "I'm Nathaniel," he said. "Good to meet you people."

Jesus shook his hands. They were coarse, rough, but gentle, the hands of a man who had seen and done a lot. Jesus felt he had strength in him they would need. Ishmael was the last to greet him and he went to Jesus afterward. "We need to talk my friend. Let's go where the others can't hear us."

Jesus followed him into the store where the shelves stood bare of anything useful. "What is it, Ishmael, something about Nathaniel?"

Ishmael shook his head. "No. He's not what I want to talk to you about. "You won't like what I have to say but I need to say it." Ishmael looked like a kid about to give up his greatest secret. "I can't come with you Jesus, much as I'd like to." Ishmael looked saddened and determined as well. He had decided on his course and Jesus knew he would be unable to alter it

"What is stopping you?" Jesus wanted to know.

"Someone needs to stay here. Keep the spirits of the people up and I was thinking as you go east I'll head to Mt Baldy. I'm certain the spire is part of this and if we want to defend ourselves we need to do something about it. If they send in troops to clean us out we cannot stand by and let them. They need to know we're serious." Ishmael paced the barren aisle in front of Jesus. "And it will help me to rally some of those left here, rumors of you being out there won't be enough and you know it. People don't like to hear stories alone, they need action. I can give it to them."

Jesus watched his friend. "Doesn't sound like something a preacher would do, condone violence," he pointed out.

"You might think so but it's not unknown," Ishmael countered. "And besides it might be the diversion you need. I can keep them looking in one place while the real action is somewhere else."

"Yeah, you're right, Ishmael," Jesus said. "But I don't have to like it."

"You don't have to, Jesus but you do need to accept it. I have followers, you've seen them, but you need to be somewhere else, not here. There is a different road laid out for you old friend." Ishmael looked at Jesus out of eyes older than time. "And you know it will lead you to your destiny as mine leads me to my own."

Jesus nodded assent. His limbs felt leaden, tiredness seeped into his muscles. He would miss Ishmael more than he knew. He knew as well with a dread surety he wouldn't see him again. "I wish you could still come with me."

"God has other plans my friend." Ishmael looked out of the long broken window and sighed. "We could both be going to our deaths you know."

"I know. It won't stop us though will it?"

"Not a chance." Ishmael laughed. "How does it feel to be at the center of things?"

"I'm not sure I like it much," Jesus grinned at the man he had called friend for some years.

"There is one thing my friend." Ishmael walked over to the window and looked outside. "Things will never be the same, no matter the outcome."

"Why do you think so Ishmael?"

"It's what history tells us. It might be many years and many tears but things will change and we will see the start of something new" Ishmael sighed. "But we will never see the end. Israel is for others to see."

Jesus rose and joined his friend. "I will miss you, Ishmael."

"Likewise," said Ishmael. "Let's go, I need to say goodbye to more than you." They went back into the room where the others waited.

"Get together anything you can carry, blankets, and clothes if you have them, no more. There will be no one to help you carry it," Jesus ordered the group. "We will meet back here in a few hours. Then we will go."

The group disbanded. The demand was enough for them to shake off the dull complacency which had marked their lives for so long. It was like watching people come alive for the first time in their lives. The need to survive subsumed by the desire to act. They vanished like ghosts and Jesus sat with Ishmael to await their return, their heads close together. Ishmael's lips were moving. Maria had gone to the front door with the others but turned around. She came back and sat with them. "I can get my shit on the way," she said, brooking no argument. Jesus was glad she didn't leave with the others. Something told him he would need her close to him in the coming days.

"Thank you."

"You think they'll all come back?" Maria asked him as they waited.

Jesus waved his hands. "Some I hope, others will not but it is their choice. No one can tell them what to do. Not even me."

"I hope they all do and bring others with them." Maria said.

Jesus said nothing since there was nothing he could say. They waited in the shade as the sun climbed up and over the hills. The silence was deep, punctuated by birds and the bark of a dog. The hours passed and it was noon when the people started to return. A few more had added to the numbers but it was hardly an army that started to walk to the mountains. They looked higher than ever. It was as if nobody had seen them before. They were there like they always had been but now they were a barrier penning them in to await their fate and do the same to those who waited behind them. Ishmael stayed and watched them leave, his mind already elsewhere. The group turned right at the next street and vanished from his view.

"Does he need to stay behind?" Maria asked.

"No he doesn't," Jesus replied. "But he wants to. He has his destiny to follow as we are following ours."

"Did you try to stop him?" she asked as they walked in lockstep.

"No point. He'd only disappear if I tried. Make him stay and one day we will wake and he won't be there." Jesus kept his eyes on the gray-blue hills. "I've always wanted to see what lies on the other side." He had changed the subject and Maria didn't mind. There was nothing more to say.

The road was tougher to negotiate than most. The surface had buckled over the years and nobody had been there to repair it. There had been once, decades ago but they had left as well when the sea started to encroach too far. In time the city might become a modern Atlantis, a myth to scare people. The concrete and tarmac road looked like pieces of a puzzle board left on the floor as if a giant had thrown them there.

At least on this road there were only a few crumbled high-rises so walking wasn't impossible, only hard. In the distance over the crumbling roofs they could see the remnants of City Hall. The next quake would finish it off. Hollyhock House still stood in East Hollywood but it was only a shell now. In the past thousands of people would go there but only bats and scavengers used it now.

Jesus remembered looking at the ruins of the LA Coliseum. Where the Olympics had entertained millions trees made a forest. He thought about how it had all come to this. A city still fighting to survive and a ragged band of people who believed in him when he couldn't. He remembered when he had walked through the Zoo with his parents when he was not quite ten. It was a year after they arrived, hoping for peace, some stability they hadn't known up to then. The animals were long dead, skeletons where once there were living creatures.

He knew he would be leading the group out past the hills, past where the fires burned at night. Past where the desert started and didn't stop until it reached the plains of Iowa and Nebraska. Past the hills to challenge the people who would wipe out what was left of the city and remake it for themselves.

It hadn't been easy when his parents came here to find some sanctuary in a country where it was hard to find. Trying to stay alive was their only concern in a city where death came easy and often. Children, the old, the lame, and the sick all died and fed the creatures venturing down from the hills each night. Some of them stayed, finding the pickings were easy. He remembered the sounds of shots each night, fired by two-legged scavengers. He learned how to stay alive. Then when he was sixteen the fever came and burned through the people like fire. It took the hunters and the hunted. There was no defense, only avoidance and luck.

His parents were among those it took. People died all over, in the streets and in their houses. You couldn't escape the fever; only pray it didn't come to claim you for its own. Sometimes he'd wanted to feel it himself. He no longer saw the dead. He saw those who clung to life like limpets. They might die ugly, drowning in their own vomit and mucus but they sure as hell refused to die easy. He didn't know why they did. There was fuck all to live for but they hung on, surviving because there was nothing else to do. His Dad had a saying, *get 'er done Jesus, get 'er done*. That was all they could do now, get 'er done.

Jeremiah nudged his arm, interrupting his thoughts. "You look far away there man, you okay?"

"Yeah," Jesus said. "I was remembering shit, you know how it is."

"Yeah I do, I've been doing the same thing a lot lately. Enough to wonder why the hell I'm here, instead of being back at my place. Kicking back and minding my own business have their advantages." He kicked a rock and it clattered into the skeleton of an SUV. "And then I get to trying to figure it out, a little anyway."

"What have you figured out?" Jesus was glad of the company, the thoughts were too dark right now.

"Not much. It's more how I came to be here. It was much easier before you came along you know?"

"How was it easier? Easy doesn't come to mind when I look around. And it wasn't going to get easier. Ignorance isn't always bliss you know."

"Yeah I guess. Didn't help me much when I was growing up down south." Jeremiah looked as if the past was closer than he wanted.

"Where did you grow up?" Jesus asked.

"Down the coast near Carlsbad. I was born there."

"The caverns?"

"No dumbass, they were in New Mexico, or whatever the hell it's called now." Jeremiah guffawed, making some of the people look around. "The resort town north of where San Diego used to be. We do have some caves at La Jolla but not the ones you be thinking of, brother. When the sea started rising it flooded most of the place. A few of us got out before it got too bad and ended up in a compound outside of Escondido. It made a decent little community for the most part. My parents died there. I was seven. Not much later I took off, since there was nothing to keep me there and I ended up here in LA. I guess I figured I'd die here but now I'm not so sure."

Jesus knew there was a lot more unsaid than said. He saw the same signs he'd seen in himself. "We all have to die somewhere and sometime Jeremiah." Jesus pointed out a spire in the distance. "I went to there as a kid when we got here. I can't remember the name of it now."

"St Anne's," Jeremiah said.

"Yeah. I heard a lot about dying in there and being at peace when you do. For the first time in my life I finally understand it." Jesus smiled under the grime. "Why aren't you sure about where you die? And is it as important as how?"

"I guess not, the where isn't important," Jeremiah conceded. "But how? I mean I got no preference for getting shot over anything else. I'd like there to be some dignity when I die and it's quick. Is it too much to ask for?"

"No it's not," Jesus replied. "I meant it's how you live is what matters *amigo*. Whether you die doing something you want to do rather than waiting for it. Life is what it's all about, even at the end of it."

"Sounds morbid." Jeremiah looked at the hills as they drew closer.

"It does," Jesus conceded. "But it shouldn't. But you didn't answer why you aren't sure about where you die."

"I had hoped I'd die in a bed surrounded by family and friends. Now it isn't looking so great, I got no family and as for friends? Shit man I can count them on one hand."

"Aren't we your family now?" Jesus asked him.

"Hadn't thought about it," Jeremiah responded. "I guess you are."

Jesus nodded. "It's worth thinking about at least. But there's no hurry. If you don't think so now you will in time and then it won't feel so bad. It might be the case for us all, don't you think? One family together facing whatever comes next. I'm like you did you know, no family and I was born away from here too. Came here with my family when I was a kid. From Oregon of all places."

"Nice country up there, always wanted to see it," said Jeremiah. "Down in the compound people used to talk about it like it was some kind of paradise." Jesus knew it was far from it but he said nothing. "I kind of doubt I will but it's okay, few of us will do much traveling now." Jeremiah looked pained. "You know I haven't done much with my life. Feels like I've missed out on something, like I don't matter, I'm a little man in a big world that doesn't give a fuck."

Jesus exhaled. "Few of us feel much different. Look at Wilton, he owned a bar nobody went to but he did something. It mattered because we needed it whether we knew it or not."

"So what did he do?"

"He gave people a place to go and forget the world. You know sometimes forgetting can be a good thing, even if we can only forget for a little while." Jesus smiled again. "*Joder*, Listen to me, I sound like an old song going around and around."

"Don't worry about it," said Jeremiah. "There are worse things to sound like."

Jesus nodded. The group walked on.

ELEVEN

JEREMIAH wondered what it meant to die. Jesus' words rang in his mind as he walked along behind him with the others. More had joined the group, tagging along as Jesus spoke to them on the side of the road, others had gone. He figured it was the sudden realization this might be the end and he couldn't blame them. He knew how they felt, knew it himself, but the commitment to something bigger kept him walking. As he did, keds slapping his feet, he returned to the compound at Escondido and walking the coast to LA. Someone had built it when the sea started to encroach and make the shop fronts the new beachhead. He remembered the faces of the people living there squashed together like sardines. The lack of privacy. Seeing couples and strangers fucking their brains out as if there was no tomorrow. The realization they had it right.

He saw the old people and the children who sickened and died, dumped outside the compound for the bears and the wolves. The long trenches people squatted over to shit and piss. The work detail that cleaned them out and threw the waste over the compound walls. The shit in their eyes and hair. You could never remove the smell. He was on shit detail more times than seemed fair to him after his parents died from flu in less than a week. They weren't the only ones. The living envied the dead there as well.

He was one of those who threw their bodies out in an attempt to stop disease. He remembered going out of the gate of the compound, dragging the corpses on a wagon. They wheeled them out at midday and threw them in a pit a quarter mile away. The bears and wolves and anything else after an easy meal would go there. The almost dead, those who sickened and even just the very old walked off to meet their end.

Their usefulness was over. If they didn't the leader had them killed. There was no difference. Nobody spoke about it.

He had another job hunting vermin. There were no dogs to do it. He trapped and drowned them in buckets of water, watched them die. When he killed them he saw himself being more and more like them, a waste of resources until he died. Then he'd be tossed out like trash. He hated it. Hated how all he did was throw out dead people, dead rats and shit like they were all the same thing.

He chafed under the rule of the compound. The ruler, so called by himself, was a squat man almost as wide as he was tall. A beard covered a receding chin and he had a rotundity stopping him from seeing several feet in front of him. He had scars on his face but Jeremiah had never seen him fight. The nagging thought they were self-inflicted still stayed with him. He looked at the walls everyday and thought of getting over them. They were ten feet tall, escape proof, topped with razor-wire. Broken glass grew like plants in the cement below them. The gate was an option but guards stood on either side of it; not to stop people getting in but from getting out.

In the center of the compound stood a two-storey building housing the ruler and his personal guards. Jeremiah remembered seeing girls taken into the building most nights. At night he could still hear their cries. Some were only ten. The promise of safety had become the reality of brutality. Obeying was the key to living and disobeying saw banishment or worse. There was a wall near the building. In front of it, stained with blood were four posts. It was the execution site where dissenters met their end. Shot without compunction, their bodies taken away like sacks of meat. He'd done that job too. Just more vermin to throw out.

After his parents died he tried to find a way out. It took a year. He attached himself to a disposal detail. They didn't mind he wasn't supposed to be there, didn't try to send him back. The leader turned a blind eye to his being there and kept it closed when he disappeared. Nobody tried to find him. Why would they? He was a kid, he'd be dead in a few days and there were always others to replace him when the trucks came back.

But he survived. He knew how and headed north along the coast for some of the time and the mountains at other times to reach LA. He'd heard it was still there, Eden in a garden of death. LA was a siren call leading him on. He followed. It had to be better than where he'd been. He walked past the manure dumps that made him think he'd never smell again. They fed power to the fiefdoms along the coast to Oregon and further. He walked past a desal plant feeding water where needed. The pipes led inland. The plant didn't feed San Diego, it was gone by then along with the Oakland-San Fran sprawl. Only LA was left, a beacon drawing him up the coast. He hadn't told any of this to Jesus, he didn't need to know. Didn't need to know what he'd seen or what the world outside was like.

Here was bad but out there was worse. It was a world where the strong survived and the weak had to be lucky. He had been. He passed the derelict Camp Pendleton, a dump now, trashed and emptied of what it once held. He kept walking past San Clemente until he reached the southern reaches of the L.A. basin. It was little different from every other place he'd seen except most of it was standing. Gunfire followed him and he learned to dodge where it came from. Most times it had been staccato or the single shot from a hunter. Sometimes he heard them in the hills where survivors fought over food and water.

He scavenged dead things as he walked. He cooked what didn't smell too bad over small fires hidden from the sight of others. Sometimes he had retched for hours and when he could walk again he did. He fastened a homemade shank to the belt he'd taken from a dead man near San Juan Capistrano. He never used it. His shoes had torn themselves from his feet and he'd replaced them with pieces of tire, tied on with hemp. His skin blistered. He didn't know it would, he thought only white people got sunburn. In a store he had found dried apples, mangoes, and apricots in packets and ate until his stomach was in agony. He had trouble shitting for two days. He drank some bottled water he emptied packet mix into not knowing when to stop. It still tasted like plastic.

He passed by Laguna Niguel and Dana Point. His feet trod over the deserted streets of Costa Mesa, Fountain Valley, Seal Beach, and Long Beach. The rusted hulk of the Queen Mary lay in state. He saw animals roaming the streets and learned which ones to avoid. He kept going past Cerritos. La Mirada. Whittier. He turned away from the sea until he fetched up in San Dimas at the motel where Maria lived. There he stayed, scrounging what he could to survive. By then he was eight but felt much older. He found solace in computers and learned he was a natural at finding out how they worked. He got into what systems were still running and found out about the world. He settled in and there he remained until Jesus, Ishmael, Maria, and Wilton had taken him further. He wondered if he would ever return and wondered too about why not doing so didn't bother him. It was as if he had been there only until needed somewhere else.

He turned around to see Maria walking a few steps behind him. He'd known her ever since he'd arrived in the apartment below her. She was older by a few years, early teens then and she'd taken him under her wing. He realized she had never told him a lot about herself, it was always something she'd tell him later and never did. He didn't even know her. He waved and she waved back.

Maria saw Jeremiah looking at her. She knew him better than most, which wasn't a lot. It didn't do to get to know people. The loss of her parents had taught her a hard lesson. You didn't want people to know you either. You got feelings if you weren't careful and feelings always hurt. You needed to survive, to protect your feelings, there was no other way. She was native LA, born here. Like Jeremiah and Jesus her parents had died years ago. She was one of the lucky few born in LA who lived past childhood. Her parents had made sure she would before they headed out to search for the Shangri-La they told her was out there. They promised they would return but they never did. She was certain they wouldn't. She always had been. They were dead. It was a truth she accepted as she did the sun rising and setting each day and the truth became a shell, impenetrable.

She hadn't mourned them, life didn't let her. It moved on and she bore their deaths like a cancer sitting inside her gut like a stone. She carried her grief easy now. At first it had been so hard she wondered if she would ever move on from it. She learned to use it to survive in the middle of the rubble and death. She had taken to leaving the city at night to climb into the mountains. From there she looked down on the place that devoured her soul and drove her parents to their deaths. She knew it would do the same to her one day. It was doing it now, getting ready to hawk them up like spit on the hills. And she was going along with it.

In the mountains it was peaceful despite the camp fires and the men who sat around them. The camps deterred a lot of people from going into the hills but not her. She got past them when she learned how and found they were a line. Not much lay behind them except hunters after deer, bear and people if they could find them. Several times she was lucky she wasn't seen. It was the camps she shunned as they carried death with them, it hung on the air and she could taste it. There were hundreds of them. She looked as she walked, could almost pick them out even from where she was as she paced out the yards.

She knew the mountains as well as she knew the city, maybe better. She knew the way to Mt Wilson as well as she could pick the easiest path to Alhambra and Montebello. She could find water there easier than she could in the city. The rivers and streams ran faster and cleaner. In the city most of it was filthy and polluted and needed filtering and boiling before you could risk using it. She trod the mountains twice a week. It was an addiction she didn't want to fight.

She knew why. Her parents. They had gone into them and she wanted to find out what happened. She needed to know and feared if she found out she wouldn't be able to continue. She found herself caught on the horns of competing impulses. Following Jesus to a place she feared and couldn't live without. She was going to find out what happened to them, she needed to know how they had died. Out there, past the mountains, was someone who knew. She wanted to find him and get the truth so she could bury her past.

Now she watched the back of Jesus striding ahead, leading them into a future none could see. She hoped they weren't all about to die. She didn't like the idea. She wanted to survive. Martyrdom was over-rated.

Ishmael watched them leave. He didn't feel good about it but a different way beckoned. He might even believe it did one day. He wanted to gather who he could and who would listen and who had the skills he wanted and the nerve to use them. He knew they were out there somewhere. He went back into the store and looked around the room where they had spent the night. He closed his eyes and breathed in the memory. It would keep him going. He knew in his gut he would never see any of them again and found himself not grieving. His friends had left for the hills to break through the cordon if they could. Ishmael knew the likelihood of success wasn't high. They needed a backup plan and he was the one to supply it. Only he didn't have one. But he would think of something, or he couldn't do what he needed.

He looked out the window to where 110 still stood, straddling LA from north to south and then he saw the place he needed. The Cathedral. It still stood, more or less, and it would be perfect. Nothing else seemed to fit the bill and he smiled. The Cathedral stood downtown and people from miles around heard the bells when they rang out. The Campanile still stood but he wasn't sure about the bells. There were eighteen when first built. How many were still in place never mind working was anyone's guess. There was only one way to find out. Ishmael realized then why was there, had been all his life, why his friends had left leaving him behind at his asking. He knew God's will when he felt it act on him. His mind went back over the years to the time his parents left him by himself, an adult ready for what life had in store.

His parents had almost been apologetic. They'd loaded up their SUV with everything they could carry and left. Ishmael didn't know why then and still didn't but he'd come to terms with it. Such was the way of things. People came and people went and there was nothing anyone could do about it except pick up and move on. Grieving was not a thing for him so he ignored the feeling in his gut. The city was emptying and they wanted to get going while they could. Cars stacked themselves on the roads out. They became car parks spewing their load into the Mojave Desert like slow moving lava. Some made it further before the roads closed.

Ishmael hadn't known it then. All he knew was people left and those who stayed were stuck. He'd wanted to stay and he still wanted to, it was part of why he didn't go with Jesus. His parents had packed up and gone, the car gouting smoke behind them like a dying fire. In the days and weeks afterward he had wandered the city until he found himself in Compton and Gardena. He began to talk as he walked those streets. First he talked to nobody because there was nobody to talk to. He looked like a ragged-ass bible-basher and people shunned his presence. He talked and walked the streets not worried if anyone was listening. In a city where the end was in their faces every day the people knew about the end times. Only they weren't coming because they were always here.

He wanted to survive not because death held any terror for him; he'd made his peace with death long ago. He wanted to delay the inevitable. After it came he hoped he would live on in the words and actions of others. That was pretty much all anyone could ask for, even him. The afterlife lived in those left behind. He strode the city like an apostle, a prophet, someone to rail against the fates in a destroyed city. He would start again with his disciples, a horde of Elisha's to his Elijah. He needed to call them from a mountain top, or the nearest thing he could come up with, the Campanile downtown. It was the mountain he needed to climb, his Horeb. Everyone knew it like in the old times when the people knew the mountains were holy places but not here. They weren't holy but places of death, where the modern legions waited to plunge down on them like a tidal wave. In a city picked clean like a carcass the Cathedral still stood as if protected. In a sense it was, people left it alone, not afraid, but as if they had decided as one to leave one part of the city alone.

It could be respect, the respect people who had little else felt for symbols where there were so few. Ishmael wondered if the Cathedral was worthy of it. It was as if those left to die saw something they needed to hold onto. It was as if something deep in the spirit of the place had seeped into the psyche of the city. Ishmael could use it to bring them together and to get them to take action. To help Jesus to change things. To keep eyes elsewhere.

Ishmael knew whether Jesus succeeded or not, those who looked at LA and wanted it for themselves would take it. He needed something pre-emptive. If nothing else it would delay them from doing anything. And it could make them realize the true price for believing they were untouchable. He suddenly felt the need to bring down the mighty and lay them low. They would pay a dear price for their vanity. He started to walk the miles to his destination. It lay ahead, the last remaining high place. "I try all things, I achieve what I can." The quote came to his lips, unbidden and valid.

TWELVE

I SHMAEL reached the church in the afternoon and stood in front of the immense building. It was showing the passing of years. The huge bronze doors had started to sag and tilt. It was bare of half the windows and the cross was minus one arm and was listing to one side. The clean walls of the past were dirty with the years. Weeds had lodged in cracks, and some of the facade was missing. The Campanile still looked solid; he headed towards it and pushed open the doors.

He climbed the stairs, stepping past some of the bells, the cables holding them had rusted and frayed until they couldn't hold the weight. It was a hard climb. Most of the steps had rotted and they bent under his weight causing him to pause until he was sure they'd hold. He had a long way to climb. He needed several rest stops to catch his breath and wonder why he was doing this. After a long time he reached the top, hefting a piece of metal he'd pulled from the wall on the way up. Computer programs rang the bells in the past when they were working, but they had long stopped. The bells that remained were homes to birds and bats.

He murmured "Help me Jesus," raised the piece of metal, a two foot long bar and swung it hard against the top bell. It rang clean and true despite the billows of dust and accumulated bird and bat shit. The birds on the beams overhead scattered outside in a whir of wings and a spray of feathers. Bats huddled in the corners of the dome to escape the noise. "Thank you," he whispered.

He looked at the bell. Despite the rain blowing in, the shit and dust had hardened into a patina. It didn't matter. The bell shrugged off the deposit as if it was glad someone had paid it attention and wanted to repay them. Ishmael swung the bar again and then for a third time, then stopped and looked out on the city below. The peal of the bell rang out, making his ears sing. The city spread out below like an old quilt, dusty, ripped, and worn out with gaping holes where the years had taken their toll on the fabric. It was as if he was seeing it as it was under the memories. He rang the bell another three times then went down the creaking stairs to wait.

Jesus and the others heard the bell as it tolled in mourning in the distance. Maria wanted to know what it was. "Ishmael," he answered. "Doing what he needs to do."

They stopped and listened. Then the last of the peals died away, echoing into nothing. They were replaced by a silence where they doubted they had heard anything. They went on again along streets that looked the same in all directions. Around them the leftovers of the freeways were strewn around like broken spaghetti.

Jesus tried to imagine what it had been like back when tourists thronged Muscle Beach and Sunset Boulevard. The wail of sirens in the night. The hookers and pimps who congregated where the tourists hung out. The scent of celebrity that lured the curious for the Oscars. He'd heard all these things but never seen them. No one had. It was all so long ago now. Time had taken its toll since then. Soon the numbers would be zero.

The group of tattered remnants straggled along. On the way some tagged on and stayed. Others left who wanted to stay until they died. They preferred how things were because they knew no better. The group spread out along the road heading out of the city. They threw rocks at empty houses and buildings, bickered like family, and yelled to see if they could get an echo. They were boy scouts on the way to a jamboree with no idea of what was facing them in the mountains.

Ahead of them a man came out of a shattered pile of rubble. He raised his hands in the air and they could hear his voice from where they stopped to see who it was. "It is coming!" the voice said. "End times are on us all!"

"Oh crap," Jeremiah said. "It's him."

"Who?" asked a man called Nathaniel, standing at Jeremiah's shoulder. He'd attached to himself to Jeremiah two blocks back feeling like a puppy who had wanted to follow a stranger home. He hadn't said a word until then. They watched as a scarecrow came towards them.

"You a newjack or something? All know who he is, or of him." Jeremiah rolled his eyes half in jest and watched as the man came closer.

Dressed in rags, his hair was wild. His beard flowed over his chest and they could see the dirt on his skin and the fire in his eyes. "I've heard peeps talk about him. They called him The Madman, The Screamer. People said they come across him sudden, like he appeared out of nowhere to yell at them and then run away. I never knew he even existed, thought he was a fairy tale, a story."

"And yet here he is," said Jesus. The advancing man shouted imprecations. As he did he threw his arms around as if keeping them still would make them useless. "He exists."

The ragged man stopped in front of the group. Jeremiah thought the ragged man deserved his reputation. They had gathered behind Jesus like a coterie hoping if they didn't move the man wouldn't see them. "You know it's coming!" The group flinched, Jesus watched him. "I've seen it in my dreams! The end of things, of time. It's coming for us! Run before it takes you; there is little time! They are coming, coming soon, flee!" The man danced on his feet as if capering like a manic Pan. Wilton thought all he needed was a flute.

Several people stepped back, unable to make sense of the madman dancing in front of them. If Jesus saw them he paid no attention. "And where are we to go my friend? The hills stop us on one side and the sea on the other."

"Out of here!" The ragged man cried out and flailed his arms like maces. Jeremiah and Nathaniel ducked. Maria fished in her shirt and brought out a small object half-hidden in her fingers. Jesus waved her down and shook his head slowly. The man didn't notice. "The forces out there are huge, they are vast. And they are coming!" The man's eyes darted from side to side.

Jesus held his gaze, staring into the man's eyes like a man contemplating the abyss. The man's eyes were wild, they bugged out of his face like a rabid dog's. "You are he!" he cried out and fell back. "The one who will bring it! Great are you, great is the one who does the Lord's work!" He fell onto his knees. "Oh Lord let me see the end." He shuddered and shook and lay on his back, thrashing his arms and legs. Some in the group pulled rocks out of the way so he wouldn't hurt himself as he spasmed and threw himself around. The rest stood and watched, unable to react.

"The man's having a fit." Wilton watched as the wild man's back arched and he gibbered and thrummed his feet on the ground.

"Yes he is," Jesus said. "And mad too no doubt yet who would blame him for his madness." He stood calm, seeing what the man would do next. "Even the mad tell some truth if we are able to listen."

The man sprang to his feet with a shriek and ran off down the road towards the sea. He shouted all the way but even his voice faded in the distance and died away to nothing. The silence returned to the street as the group went on. The mountains were closer now. They would get there tomorrow Maria thought. She turned back from time to time but the wild, ragged man never returned. Later she would wonder what happened to him.

"You believed him?" asked Arturo.

"About me? No I didn't," Jesus said. "But that is not the point. The point is he did. He told us what he believed and he must believe or why tell us?"

"I don't get it, believe or not what's the freaking difference." Arturo tried to understand but it eluded his grasp. "What's going to happen will happen."

Jesus chuckled. "If you don't believe what you believe, you won't be able to act on it, and belief can change what will or will not happen. Beliefs can make us do good and bad things and only our conscience can tell the difference." Jesus said. "So my parents told me a long time ago. Belief defines us. It makes us choose one way over the other, makes us act a certain way and how we act shows others who we are. It cannot be any other way."

Jesus picked up a rock and threw it at a building. It span off the wall with a crack and added a little more to the rubble they walked in. "I have to believe in what I'm doing because if I don't I will not be who I am."

Arturo muddled with the idea for a while. "Conscience and belief, right. I get it." He deliberated for a few minutes. "No I don't. I'll have to think on it."

Jesus grinned, "You think as long as you have to my friend. Then when you realize you truly believe in what you do, your actions will show you who you are." Jesus tossed another rock. "How other people see you is another question. And not so easy to answer."

"And what will I do then?" Arturo wanted to know.

"You'll only know after you decide. The consequences will be yours alone to bear and remember, nobody else can make that decision." Jesus clapped his hand on Arturo's shoulder. "Don't worry Arturo, everything will work out the way it's meant to. *Dios Quiere.*"

Arturo wasn't too sure. He looked at the road they were walking on and kept walking.

Behind him walked Maria and Wilton. They marched in time, left, right, left. Every so often Wilton would kick a rock or stone in front of him. "Will you stop?" she asked him. Wilton could tell it was ticking her off. In a mood as childish as he could manage he kicked another, hitting dead center of a lamp post standing at an angle.

"Doing what?" He sounded almost aggravating.

"Kicking stones, what's the point?"

Wilton couldn't resist. He kicked another one. It ricocheted off a low wall to their right. "The point? Nothing, just like there's no point to this escapade or much else in this town. Perhaps there's no point to anything."

"What do you mean no point?" Wilton wasn't being good company. It seemed to her he hadn't been the nicest of people since they had set out. She hoped he would improve in the days ahead but held little hope. "There's a point to everything, Wilton. Even shit poor bars like yours and whatever we call living. There has to be."

"Ask the deer a tiger kills. No point other than simple survival for one and death for the other. Nothing else," observed Wilton. "It's the same here. Jesus thinks he's going to change the world by walking up to the mountains and asking them to leave us alone. It's another case of life and death and he wants to delay death to cling to life. But we all know death will come in its own time. It's the foolishness and stupidity of hope, wrapped up together. Each one adds to the other. I don't know whether to pity him or be angry at him. And look at the people around us," Wilton waved an arm around them.

"What about them?" Maria asked.

"What about them? It's everything about them! What will they do when we get there and nothing happens? Go back to what they're used to or sacrifice themselves for this fucked up little crusade? You know as well as I do it won't be the second choice."

Maria didn't know the answer. "They want to hope with him. Foolish or stupid, it doesn't matter. They want to try to do something even if it leads to nothing. At least they have some hope in the meantime. Even you're here so what does it say about you? Are you a man clinging to hope or life like the rest of them?" Maria drove the point home.

Wilton felt it hit. "Accepted, but at least I can see it's pointless. It makes me less likely than them to blame him when the truth comes out. I fear they will feel duped by a crusade that is bound to fail. Does it make me a bigger fool than the rest of you? Yes because I know better. Yet here I am wondering what will happen next and fearing it will be nothing at the same time."

Wilton aimed a kick at another rock and missed. "I'm here because I'm curious about him, about me, and our motives. And more to the point, those you see around him, wanting to do it with him. Have they considered what it is he will do? Do they even know? Do any of us know? Do any of us care or are we happier not knowing because we can't face the alternative?" He fixed Maria with a stare. "Can you?"

She had to admit to herself she didn't. "I don't. But at least I'm happy to be here, I want to be here." Her voice was fierce and her eyes flashed. "Do you?"

Wilton shrugged. "It gives me something to do and I'm a sucker for lost causes," he laughed. "Besides I could stand the exercise." He laughed and patted his still-bulging stomach. "I was standing behind that bar for too long."

Jeremiah had waited for them and heard Wilton's remark as fell into step with them. "You miss it?"

"It surprises and pains me but yes, I do," Wilton said. "The customers weren't anything special I admit but it was home and people did enjoy going there." Wilton looked wistful. "I worry about what will happen to it. Somehow the thought of it crushed into rubble offends me."

Jeremiah knew the importance of a place of your own. "If you stayed behind when those peeps out there start to move they'd ground you under them and spit you out the back."

"You're certain of that?" Maria asked.

"Yes. The signs were there on my computer for any newjack to see. Building up they forces is what they be doing." Jeremiah looked the ever-closer mountains. "Those peeps have a beef, and they be hardcore easy. I wish I knew the dilly on those boys."

The sun slid down the sky as they walked and as the shadows grew long, Jesus picked a spot for the night. A dilapidated complex, once a motel, on the right. He led them inside. The walls were sound enough and the roof looked solid. They made spaces for themselves and got ready for the evening ahead.

In the early evening while the light was still good two drones launched from Creech Airbase. Moore was pleased. Concrete progress at last. He would soon be able to tell Heyusser it was all clear to go with the plan. He had been developing it for months. Added forces little by little, moving them around to keep them occupied and ready to do what was needed at a moment's notice. So when Heyusser had asked for a plan it was ready. Moore hadn't been upfront in his meetings with Heyusser, he liked to make Heyusser think he had to order him to do things. It was good strategy to keep the opposition off balance; even better strategy when they didn't know it. And he was confident Heyusser had no idea.

The residents had been making themselves a nuisance but it wasn't as bad as he'd told Heyusser. Very few came out far these days and they dealt with those who did. There had been a few survivalists in the beginning but he'd seen to their eradication. No one could defend against a drone strike from miles out and no one could hide from their cameras. The resource wars had been useful training grounds and the lessons were still fresh. The world had descended into the chaos men like General Moore loved and craved. It gave them a reason to live.

He phoned the command center at Creech. "Patch through the feed to my screen, I want to see it firsthand."

"Yes sir. Feed commences in thirty minutes." The reply was snappy; quick. Moore sat down to wait. He smiled again. And again it didn't touch his eyes.

THIRTEEN

I N the late afternoon the drones began their runs. They worked across the grids taking video and thermal images of the city. The drones flew unseen, silent as owls. Nothing escaped their robotic gaze. Cameras and sensors quantum streamed the feed to the base. Moore waited and watched the images roll across his screen. Then he sat forward, the cameras had picked up something. A group of people were walking along one of the streets towards the edge of the basin. He counted at least twenty. They still had some distance to travel and would need to stop soon for the night. Sometime the next morning, he estimated they would cross into the mountains. He paused the feed, zoomed in and picked out faces, mostly men, some women. They reminded him of migrating elk and the hunter in him felt his pulse increase.

He smiled. Some of the camps would get their fun sooner than they thought. He picked up the phone. "Alert our people between Mount Baldy and Falling Springs. Tell them they'll be having visitors tomorrow morning so stay alert. Get on it." The phone squawked an affirmative. Moore leaned back in his chair. He poured bourbon into a glass and raised it to the screen. "Have a good sleep whoever you are. It will be the last one you'll have." He shut off the feed. He never saw the people massing near the Cathedral or he might not have felt so sanguine.

Ishmael had seen the drones from his eyrie. He was one of the few to notice them. The others who did looked away and ignored them. They were a fact of life like the rising sun and the tides. He'd paid them no attention before but he saw them as harbingers of what was coming. He'd been watching for people coming to see why the bells rang out when he saw them. They were invisible until the sunlight flashed them into existence. He watched a while longer but it was gone. They were high and small enough for survivors to miss them. It was by chance that anyone saw them at all. He'd heard stories of drones and knew in his gut it must be one, watching the city and the people.

With what he knew it wasn't surprising but expected. It could see the Campanile and the people as they came to be here. That didn't worry him, it had always been there and with luck, familiarity would breed ignorance of what he was doing. But not Jesus and his group. It would see them and so would the people who watched over them like vultures. He thought of the people in the mountains and beyond. A shiver ran down his spine and curled itself around his gut. The glint in the sky did not bode well for the future but what it foretold only time would reveal the answer.

He wondered if Jesus and his group knew it was there. Even if they did there wasn't much they could do about it except keep walking and trust in fate or God. It didn't matter which. Ishmael turned his eyes to the city. There was a scattering of people on walking toward the Cathedral, drawn by the chimes of the bells. It was working. He took up the metal bar and gave more strikes to the bell. The people looked up and kept coming. By twos here, threes there, a single person on this street, another on the next.

The bells rang out like a call to arms; a summoning for the defense of the city. He watched as the people came and kept coming, gathering into a larger mass in front of the Campanile. To Ishmael it looked as if they were washing up on the shore of somewhere secure and safe. Ishmael was glad they were here and he readied himself to speak.

During the night in the shelter of the old motel the group slept the sleep of the sound of mind. Raccoons came and went and bears sniffed the entry but the scent of people kept them out. They weren't brave enough to attack so many. There was safety in numbers even here. After the night animals moved on in search of easier food, other shadows moved in the dark and watched them while they slept. They strode on two legs and an intensity of purpose filled them. They walked around the sleeping group, unseen and unheard, moving light on their feet. They moved like ghosts, and wore long coats. Their faces tattooed and framed by colored dreads. They carried knives and clubs. Some carried pistols but kept them holstered. They didn't want to use them but they would if they had to.

They bowed to the one who came in minutes later and sat apart from them on a table. He wore better clothes and had a calm manner they trusted. He was the leader. He calmed their nerves by his presence. The arrival of so many people at once puzzled him. He wanted to know what they were doing here. He watched them until he rose and left leaving the rest to keep watch. He hadn't spoken a word.

Jesus woke before the others; something pricked his awareness in the gloom. Before he opened his eyes he listened. There was a scuttling sound, a scrape of a shoe on the floor, and he knew they weren't alone. He opened his eyes and saw the men who sat around the room watching them in the gathering light of the morning. Outside, the sun was not long up, just showing itself to the city. He sat up and one of the men whispered to another who stood, looked at Jesus and left the room. Jesus watched him leave and tried to get up. "You not rise, no sah, Jah want to talk to you and Jah want to know if everything be cook and curry with yah." The man was bathed in shadows and he spoke soft, without menace.

Jesus decided to stay where he was. He felt no fear. The air was calm but filled with expectancy. The others began to move and wake. "None of you be moving yet. Be staying like dat, be cool, all good here." The man spoke in a quiet voice they all heard in the silent room. Jesus nodded to them and they relaxed a little. Maria kept her hand hidden. He knew she had the same weapon she held earlier when they came across the ragged man and he didn't want her to use it. "Sistren not happy. We bow her tunti yah?"

She looked at Jesus. He shook his head, like her had no idea what the man meant. "It's okay, be cool. Let's see what they want," he advised her. She did. The rest woke and waited, unsure what would happen next and fearful of the worst.

"Jah coming soon. All cool, nobody want be sheg-up."

"Nobody want to be sheg-up," Jesus said. The man smiled and pulled a large joint from his pocket. "Good spliff. You want?"

Jesus shook his head. "Later." He relaxed and lay back waiting for Jah to arrive, whoever Jah was. He felt the need to know who Jah was and what he wanted, as much as Jah wanted to know about them. As the light improved, Jesus saw the weapons they carried. It was a good idea not to have moved. Jesus didn't want death on his hands. It might come to it at some point but he knew it wasn't to be here.

He guessed it was fifteen minutes, twenty at most when the man turned, stood, and ran to the door. He bowed. Through the door came a man, his skin black as night. He wore a top hat and dreads ran down to his waist. He wore a leather coat, worn at the elbows and a leather vest, fastened with a heavy gold chain. A matching chain circled the hat. He wore dark glasses and carried a cane with a gold handle. He wore the gold like a badge of office. Jesus knew this was Jah.

Jah pointed to Jesus, looked along his arm, asked a question without words. With a nod of assent given he walked over to Jesus and squatted in front of him. "And here I be just jammin' las' night, enjoying me ganja." He breathed leftover smoke. "Then kiss me neck if I not hear of people coming through here all hitey-titey like they be owning I place. What am I to make of this I ask myself? So I got to come to judging them inna da morrow. So you be telling I what you be up to?" He pointed the cane at Jesus. "But I be gracious and say you not look mafia to I. Come," he stood and beckoned Jesus to follow him. "Not the others, you. I sense you be leading them here with you, I talk to them later?" Jah smiled. "But I not be needing to now. Come." He left the room, Jesus rose to his feet, followed him, motioning the others to relax. The others wondered what was going to happen next. Jesus wondered too.

The man sat down and looked around at who Jesus had left behind. "You be cool now. Your man come back soon, we be jammin' later. Your man be massive I tell." He sat with his back to the wall and his smile was broad. His shirt had as many holes as fabric and a waistcoat of indeterminate color covered some of it. He had jeans cut off at the knees and a fedora perched on his dreads. A matted and oily beard ended at his chest. His nose spread along his upper lip and his eyes twinkled. He wore a billy on his hip and rings circled his fingers. "You all be staying right here now. No go moving or wanting to leave, dat be badda some hah? And we not wanting any badda." The threat was unspoken but they listened. A few of the men around them shifted to reveal what they were carrying. No one moved.

Jah led Jesus into a room further into the building down a corridor filled with musty smells. Paint was peeling off the walls in swathes revealing holes no one would repair. Posters of skulls, marijuana leaves, and Bob Marley decorated the room. Candles gave off the aroma of mangoes. There was a sofa along one wall and a large hookah stood in front of it. A woman in a green and yellow dress and a red bandu sat on a chair next to the door. Her eyes looked at nothing. The walls were solid and the windows were open, letting air in. "You man be partaking with I, then we talk this iwah."

Jah lit the hookah and dragged on the smoke from the ganja. "Now, with you ah deal with. Mi alright, but you? What you game be?"

Jesus had a toke, not having one would have seemed impolite, an insult. He didn't feel he had a choice. The ganja was powerful, his eyes watered and he coughed hard. Jah laughed at him. "You sure not be fish bowling man! Best thing I seen in years, ha!"

Jesus stopped coughing and handed the pipe over, his eyes red from the smoke. "No offense amigo but I will pass on having another. Too strong for me."

"And I no be giving you the good ganja man," Jah's face showed his teeth under semi-closed eyes It disappeared. He was serious now. The mood turned like a flicked switch. "I run de road here, I know who pass and who don't. Some I let, some I don't. Why I let you huh? What you got for me to let you all pass me kingdom?"

"We don't have anything, Jah. We're going to the hills, to talk to them up there. That's all. If you let us."

The smile returned, "Them people? I no think you be doing talking with them up there. They be well cold up there man. Dog-hearted they are, you not be flassing them folk. Tell you straight I do. They no tap a di tap people, we no reespeck them, they no reespeck us. Not be large those people, but we deal with them. I know dis, you go, you die. Unnerstan?"

"I do." Jesus said. "But it's where we're going, we have to. Me more than them but they're following, hoping for something better."

"And I let you pass huh?" Jah pulled long on the hookah. "Let you die like dat? For i-sire you be such a half eediat running up dere like a hot-steppa, you sight?"

"I hope you will, half eediat or not. It might be the only chance we all have to survive. If I succeed."

"Only Jah know that. Man you not know what is up there, we do. They are nassy, bright people. You go talk you not come back. But I help you. I like you, you a lion soul, righteous. I see something crucial, in you eyes. I no see dat all days here. Not even in my own people. They be followers, no leaders in them. If I know these people who be following you, they be crosses for me. But not you. You be needing them as they be needing you. You be Jah for them I be thinking." Jah looked at Jesus through the smoke. "You be irie dread head man." Jah grinned for a moment then his face turned grave. "You have seen them up there? They be true bald-head."

Jesus looked puzzled. "You speak different amigo. It's hard to follow you."

"Bald-head. Work in deep for Babylon. Wicked people up there and further, not good to see them. Why you want talk to them immaterial. Likely kill you as soon as see you. They be controlling things here, all over." Jah spread his arms.

Jesus wanted to have another toke, felt the urge to leave things behind, forgotten. But he was a link in a chain holding them together. He pushed the sudden desire away. The return to reality was a wrench. "That much we know but we've only seen the campfires, and some feed from satellites we can link into." Jesus shrugged. "Not much more. We can see the camps, what they have up there along the coast but it we only had old tech, low-res."

Jah waved the woman over and whispered in her ear. Her face was vague through the smoke. She listened, focused now, looked at Jesus. Then she walked to the door. Jah picked up the pipe and inhaled. Jesus wondered how he could smoke do much and not show any effects. "You go wit her, you need see things we see. Then we talk again."

Jesus followed the woman down one hall then another. Broken bottles and trash littered the way. Jesus saw Jah was less a King than he thought looking at the detritus. Or he was too fried to notice or care. But he knew he filled a hole in the lives of his followers. Then he realized Jah was like everyone else, holding on to a dream, wanting to survive. All of them wanted to. He and Jah helped their own followers. Jah was right, they were more alike than he thought. They came to a door and the silent woman stood aside to let him in, beckoning. Inside computer monitors sat on desks, wiring lay around the floor looped in coils. A man with a beard and a tam and a yellow t-shirt with a faded R on it sat in front of one of the screens. The smell of ganja hung heavy, miasmic. The woman walked over to the man, whispered in his ear and he swung his seat around. "You da man who came in here to rest last night huh? Hope you slept well."

"Wasn't the worst night we've had," Jesus said. He looked around the room.

"Jah must be wanting you to see what we see huh?" Jesus nodded. "Then feast your eyes man, we have the means to access the systems the people up in the hills use. Well situated we is."

"Black market?" Jesus asked.

"Yeah man, cost a lot to get it know what I'm saying? No digital here I be telling you. We see all the fuckery they be doing. Oh yah, there be more than us dat Babylon be hackling about."

Jesus knew what he meant. "You sound different to Jah."

The man laughed easy. Jesus warmed to him. "Most of us do, dat Jah, he like to talk like he think he ought to. The rest of we like de people unnerstan we. People call me Alfonse," he said putting his hand out.

Jesus took it. "Jesus."

"Jesus of death yah? Angel of death in the city of angels. I see some of dat in you man. Death is riding on you, like a jockey." The man punched some keys in front of him. "You feel him on you don't you?"

Jesus didn't answer, he didn't need to. "I didn't think anyone here could access their systems." He stared at the images rising up in front of him.

"Yah, this place is pretty bash, awesome. The people up dere," Alfonse tilted his head to the outside. "They want things and we supply things and we don't it for free, no chance, be nah good huh?" He tapped a few more keys. "They think we be bredrin, friends, but we not, never will be. Because of shit like this." He pointed and sat back.

Jesus looked. He was looking down from somewhere high up. There were buildings, and rubble everywhere he looked. Then he noticed the image was moving. "What am I looking at?"

"You be looking at here man," Alfonse said. "How Babylon itself sees us."

"I'll be fucked," Jesus said.

"Not something you see every day, yah?" He looked at Jesus as if he had never seen him before. "You not be seeing this before, I know." Alfonse sat like a peacock. He managed to strut and sit still at the same time. Jesus didn't know he managed it.

"Where is this?" Jesus watched as Alfonse zoomed the image in closer. "Is that the Transcont?" he asked pointed at the wide freeway that went left to right on the screen.

"Yeh sah," Alfonse said. "I know, I like to use proper rasta. Not all the time. Only to keep me grounded, yah?"

"Whatever you say," Jesus said. On the screen he could see a group of people walking down a broad street. The Transcont lay well behind them. The scene shifted. It was from behind them and ahead of the group stood the mountains. Recognition came to him in a Damascus moment. "Is that us? I mean my group?"

"Is you my friend."

"How was it taken? When?" Jesus was almost shocked, then he recognized who he was going to be dealing with. They could see long distances, were watching them all the time. Whenever they wanted they could observe everything they were doing, where, when. It horrified him for a moment then stiffened his resolve.

"They use drones to overfly LA You see them, yah? The feeds are quantum encrypted. But we know the codes, and we get them." Alfonse zoomed the image again. "Good thing they don't know or they be proper vexed with us. Raatid they be going, well true." Alfonse grinned. "This taken yesterday afternoon. It time stamped see? Woman told me Jah wanted you to see this." Jesus looked at the numbers on the top of the screen. They flickered in fast forward. "This be bad shit, man. And there more, you bet. Want to see?"

Jesus said he did. Alfonse showed him. It was thirty minutes later when Jah sent for Jesus again.

FOURTEEN

"WHY call yourself Jah?" Jesus asked when he was brought back to the leader's quarters. "It's your name for God, right?"

Jah chuckled. "Yeah man it is, but then I am as good as for they. I tell them what to do, and I reward and punish like any god would. So if cannot be calling myself Jah who can? There be nobody else here who can, even you." Jah crushed some ganja between his fingers and filled the hookah bowl.

"Gods perform miracles, as well, what have you done lately." Jesus said.

"We are alive man, and with I and I help my people will keep living. Is that not miracle enough in this place? Anyone say living is not a miracle is a foolish man."

Jesus had no answer. He could offer no miracle to his followers, only death. Nothing but punishment for those he led, despite his hopes. It had seemed so easy in Wilton's bar. Something only to talk about and pass the time but now it was as if he had his own crown of thorns. He knew living here was a miracle. The only question was how long it was going to last. When those who wanted the city for themselves would decide when the time had come to take it away. And would he be in time to stop them? With Jah he sensed he was wasting time but he needed to stay longer to learn more.

Jah looked again through hooded eyes at Jesus. "I be thinking you do offer something, not a miracle, no man, but hope." He nodded to himself and took in a deep toke. "Yeah that be it. Is a good thing."

"If it isn't futile hope."

"Hope be never futile man, never wurtless."

"Why did you show me all you see?" Jesus changed the conversation.

Jah chuckled again. Puffed out a cloud of smoke. "You not a chance in hell man. Not against those Babylon downpressors out there. Those not be wanting to talk to nobody, least of all a bunch of people they would like to disappear. You vanish, they happy, no one be vexxing them and they rule more than Jah do. They be their own gods, I ovastan, you have to overstan too. But I be good to you, I give you something to see. Like the drone who can track you so you ovastan bit more. Be harder to track you in the mountains but not too much with their tech. Hey but I be talking to someone who eaz haad, you know, you thick-skulled, not listen to I when it come to this, am I correct man?"

Jesus sniffed the air. He could feel himself getting light-headed even though he wasn't smoking. Much more and he was afraid he would pass out but he went with it taking small shallow breaths so it wouldn't affect him. "Pretty much, yeah."

Jah laughed loud. "You are Don man, true Don. You listen I. I say I help you and I will. Jah be good to people, it help me reputation. I give you a guide to help you, know where to go. We deal with them up in there, get weapons you can use. Otherwise you get into bad voodoo, bad things happen. I know this, they be waiting for you, they be tracking you all the while you be walking you know?"

Jesus knew they would be. "One thing I have to ask to you Jah."

"You ask I be answering."

"How do you get into their systems? Alfonse never told me."

Jah grinned through the smoke circling the air between them. "Ah man, you ask questions but how you know what you hear is truth? Better not to ask sometimes. Not lied to that way." Jah hoisted himself from the chair. "Now it be time for you to be leaving, Jesus man. We will take you people to where you need to be, the rest be up to you. Goodbye Jesus man. Jah be with you on your journey from now. And you be grateful I like you, yah? Or you not be ten toe turbo from here I promise you." Jah sat back down and watched as Jesus left to rejoin the others then he had another toke. Things were good in the world he ran. He called the woman over and the afternoon went on.

Jesus thought about what he had seen as he went back to where the others waited. he looked around as he entered, seeing the faces and eyes turned toward him. Maria stood, expectant, as if a doctor was bringing bad news and the wanting to know and not warred inside her. Jesus went around the room, murmuring to them in turn. He was getting them up, spreading the word of what they faced. Some looked confused, others concerned as if reality was finally biting. She knew some would stay behind and she hated herself for wanting to do the same.

Others looked determined as if they had stared down the fear inside them. Jesus roused them off their chairs, gathered them in groups. Wilton noticed how even those with a common purpose still gathered in smaller groups. They found a comforting solidarity there. He wondered what they would do when they faced the choice they couldn't see coming.

The man who had been there when Jah arrived was still there, sitting on a stool that wobbled as he talked. He glanced up as Jesus came in and watched him as he went from follower to follower. He laughed, his eyes beaming and he threw his arms wide as if greeting a friend long forgotten. "You be learning from Jah, man? Heh yeah, you know more now, why you be here. But that be for you to know, not for me." He nodded fast like his head would topple from his shoulders. "Yeah you soon face what you not be liking to face I bet. No shame dere. All do face it when they time comes. At they ends they face it."

The people in the small groups looked at each other. Then looked at the other groups wondering about what was to come and what everyone else was thinking. Was it the same as they felt? Did they all feel the fear wind around their guts to settle there? Did they all have a nagging doubt in their minds about the future and whether they'd live to see it. Wilton wondered himself as he watched them. He stood with Maria, Jeremiah and Arturo, they had gravitated together in the center of the room. It seemed to him that he, Jeremiah, Maria, and Arturo had grown to be their own little group. The first comers. A clique unto themselves in the hierarchy he knew had formed.

The others weren't like them, they had come to share the cause. He was there at the beginning with them, among the first called. He didn't like the feeling of superiority welling up in his gut. He told himself it was normal human behavior. It wasn't working well. He diverted himself by counting who was here. A few more had straggled in since dawn, they numbered near on thirty.

The rasta called out to Jesus. "A few more chase their destiny with you man. I hope it better than they think it will be." He giggled. Another man, so close in appearance they might have been brothers, came in like a ghost. He whispered in the man's ears. The man nodded and the other walked off leaving the man to look more serious than he had before. "Now you be following I. Jah tell me I be showing you the safest way to Babylon." He sprung off the chair and landed on his feet facing Jesus. Maria went to stand by him. The man looked at her as if seeing her for the first time. "I be not reespeking you early." He almost looked at her with reverence. "Not do that again I won't. You be taking care this woman." He pointed a finger at Jesus. Gold rings shone in the light from the windows. A diamond sparked fire. "She be special this one, special more than Jah knows, more than you know."

The man walked to the door. "I be calling I Gabriel. I blow horn, you follow. You come, follow I now. Jah commands it, we obey and not dis-reespek." The man left, dust eddied in his wake. They heard him continue to call as he left the building "you all be rope een!" urging them on like a ragged soothsayer. Jesus led the group after him, his stride had purpose in it. Maria noticed it. She wondered what it meant and what lay behind it, knowing it was something to do with Jah and what Jesus knew. She vowed to ask Jesus what had happened and knew she might not find out. She left behind him, not looking at the others as they wound out of the building and on down the torn up road.

The mountains were brown under the brutal sun. Even with the storms there wasn't enough water in the soil to stop the grass dying when the heat touched it. Trees with roots deep enough to tap the water table still had some green but even they were losing the battle. The city was behind and below them as they marched on. A loose straggle stretching to the last building they passed; a tumbledown barn. Gabriel had led them to the hills but more circuitous than Jesus had thought he needed to. "We go this way, bald-heads not watching this part, they look end of roads, we go tracks out of LA."

He talked the whole distance, words tumbling like fast water over rocks. Jesus wondered if he would ever stop. He never seemed to draw breath such was his capacity for talk. It never seemed to bother him there were few who replied. They crossed the old freeway dividing LA from the hills. Then Gabriel took them along a track half hidden in the scrub. Little more than a path carved out by animals, it was treacherous with loose slippery dirt. They picked their way along, testing for footholds when the track led up the slopes of the mountains. Gabriel exhorted them to continue. "Be hard here I know, only safe way. You follow, stay the path."

They fell more often than they wanted and soon were dusty and tired. Most of them bore cuts and bruises. They wondered when it was going to end. Jeremiah thought getting might be preferable if it meant not having to walk any further. Washouts hindered their progress. It was slow going, made worse by not knowing the direction they wanted or where the destination was. Gabriel kept talking. "All be good, know the safe way do I, you be follow I." Jesus felt they were going in loops, making progress then doubling back and going off on a tangent. It looked like Gabriel walked like he talked, his direction as random as his words.

"Where the hell are we going?" Arturo asked Jeremiah as they passed a familiar rock face and watched the backs of those ahead of them.

"No idea," Jeremiah said. "I'm following the man like I said I would."

"I'm going to find out. We've been going in circles I know it. We've seen this rock face before."

"It all looks the same to me." Jeremiah said.

Arturo made his way forward. It was like fighting through a slow mudslide. People crammed into a line behind Jesus and Gabriel. They kicked little rocks up and he tripped several times before he caught up. "Where are we going?"

"Where ever it is Gabriel is taking us."

Arturo found no comfort in the answer. "You're our leader, not him."

"Sometimes leaders have to know when to follow." Jesus walked on and looked ahead. His eyes raked the horizon. Around them the leaves on the trees were wilting. "They're dying," Jesus said in a calm voice. Arturo felt they were too.

Jesus watched Gabriel as he led them through a stand of spruce, some leaves still clinging to green. Some of the group snapped off a few twigs and a branch fell among them, dried out by the drought. Some dodged it. Some fell and picked themselves up. They looked like dirty rag-dolls the same color, all differences in skin and clothes hidden. They were all one now. Underfoot it was sandy and the fallen leaves snapped, popping like cap guns. "Where are you taking us?" he asked the dusty rasta who still jaunted ahead, skittering on the dirt and rocks.

"I taking you to Babylon as promised. Where the people be you want to see." Gabriel replied, pointing ahead. Trees and ridgelines hid their goal. "Only we can't go straight there, they be watching yesterday, watching today too. They be knowing of us. If they were I, I be waiting somewhere likely we be going. They be watching the spire, so we go different way."

Jesus had to admit he would. "People are getting a bit antsy about going around like this. Hard to blame them," he added, kicking a twig to one side.

"Yah I know, but need to take you like this, avoid the people waiting because they be waiting to hackle we. A true thing we need to go this way." Gabriel's face split into a grin. "We avoid them, Jesus, nah worry then."

Gabriel led them through the trees and into an open area of dry, dead grass. It crunched as they hurried on as best they could to avoid the omnipresent drones. Jesus worried about the sound carrying. It was like gunfire in his ears. Jesus wondered how Gabriel was so confident. In the mountains armed camps made sure nobody left L.A. "How do you get around up here?"

Gabriel grinned again. "We do much with the people here, we have ganja, they have tech. We do business and be knowing ways they don't. Be safer that way."

Jesus watched the group walking through the brittle grass. He saw their haggard, dirty, worn faces. They walked like the condemned. Their eyes looked down at their feet. Dust streaked their faces, sweat drew lines on their faces and their arms. They moved like one organism. They flowed over the ground putting one foot in front of the other. And another after that. Jesus wondered if he was doing the right thing. He couldn't answer. It was too hard.

The people walked as if going to their own funeral. He saw ragged and worn clothes, seams fraying along with tempers. He knew he was no different from the group attached to him like pack animals. He shuddered at knowing as little of their destiny as they did. He wondered what was going through their minds; what kept them going as the path seemed to lead nowhere. He sat on a fallen tree, off to one side. Maria came over and sat next to him as the group followed Gabriel. Like a herd of elk they ignored those that had stopped moving.

Jeremiah and Wilton saw them. They came over and squatted next to them. Concern veiled their eyes. "What's happening?" Jeremiah wanted to know.

Jesus shrugged. "Nothing amigo, a crisis of confidence. Keep with them, we'll catch up soon when we stop for the night."

"Are you sure?" Wilton asked. "It might be me but these people need something to keep them going and Gabriel doesn't seem the man to do it. Much as it pains me to say something positive but they need you. Me not so much." He smiled. It was more a grimace. "I don't expect much to come from this little trek following you like our own little Ahab, but they do."

"Ahab?" Maria stared at the fat man in the floral shirt. The white had turned a dusty brown and he had started to grow a beard, stubble furred his cheeks.

"Moby Dick, the search for the White Whale, Ended in death for everyone." Wilton scratched a line in the sand. "Except for Ishmael and the whale. The whale killed Ahab you know. Are you prepared for that Jesus, to die on the altar of your own making?"

Jesus didn't answer. Not at first. "I have no intention of dying, not that I'm sure it won't happen, *que así sea.*" He looked up. The group had stopped at the trees. Gabriel looked forlorn as if he'd lost his audience. They huddled together like zebra knowing safety lies in numbers. "Tell them to rest, we will sleep here tonight," Jesus told Wilton. "Give them some water too, it looks like they need some."

"They aren't the only ones." Wilton moved off.

Gabriel came over, questions in his eyes. "You be sittin' when we be moving man?" He scratched his dreads. "Resting not good in the open you know, we need to rest under the trees, harder for they to see, yah?"

Jesus looked up. The sky was blue, darkening in the east. A few scattered clouds hid nothing. The sun was low on the western horizon. Soon it would be gone and then the night animals would come out. He didn't like that. "Is there anywhere better than the trees to sleep under tonight?"

Gabriel said there was. "Over the ridge there be some caves. Use them when dealing with the badda men. Ten minutes we be there. Before the sun vanish we be snug." He pointed upslope to where Jesus saw the hill disappear as if severed.

Jesus rose and brushed sand and dead grass from his clothes. "Good enough, *bueno.*" Maria watched him close. Something in his eyes bothered her, niggled like a pebble in a shoe. Only she couldn't remove it as. She felt close to him, *intimo*, like no other. Not sexual. More than that. Deeper. "Back there," she said, quiet so no one else could hear. "What did Jah tell you?"

Jesus smiled at her. "Nothing much, it's more like what he showed me." He didn't say more. He felt it was a confidence he didn't want to betray. He gazed into the sky, eyes glinting and his dreads flopped lank against his cheeks. "There's a lot more to this than I thought, I'm not sure I'm up for it *corazon.* And I'm not sure I'm up for all these people following me like I'm the answer to the problems they think they have. They think I can snap my fingers and it's all fine and they can have their lives back and everything is back to normal. Except it won't be. Ever, *mierda.*" Jesus spat into the dirt.

Maria thought back to the man she had known without knowing for over a year. He was a man who had passed into and out of her life—once, twice, more? She couldn't recall—after her parents had disappeared in the mountains. She had lived and survived ever since, relying on her wits and street smarts. They had taught her well and she had learned more since. Her father had been a slight man, thin like a whip with a ready smile. Her mother had been taller, fuller without being fat and Maria had her eyes. They had made an unlikely couple. Her mother called her Maria, the mother of Jesus.

Maria remembered the shadows in her mother's eyes when swept up in the grief she never talked about. They took her up with them into the mountains as soon as she was able to keep up with them. They scuttled around the rocks and the washouts. Kept to the trees. Skirted the edges of the drying meadows. Tried to stay hidden. Her parents had told her to stay in cover. They never said why but the lessons stuck. She hated the open ground. Fear caused her to scan the sky. She craved the anonymity and invisibility denied them where they were.

She looked up and saw a condor circling in the last of the hot up-drafts looking for food. They were being looked for as well. They were prey for the camps if found. The only difference was they knew it. The condor was looking for something dead. It would know nothing. Life wasted nothing out here. If the camps found them they would die and the condors and other scavengers would make use of their remains. She wondered how long they would survive. Please God make it long enough she told herself, that's all I ask.

Jesus appeared resigned, accepting of what will be. She wasn't. Her parents had fought to keep them alive. She would fight the same as she had in the long years since they disappeared. They appeared in her dreams. She saw her mother's shadowed eyes and her father's face, hurt by the shadows and not able to stop them. She would stretch her arms out to them, still a child. She watched them turn away to vanish behind black curtains she couldn't get through.

In the months after they vanished the dreams had come every night, sometimes twice or more. Before the night in Wilton's bar they had diminished to once a month. Each time she woke with the same overwhelming sense of loss. The dreams were every night as if she was back in the days and weeks after they had vanished in the hills. They felt different now. There was no longing. They were a warning, an omen. Her parents stood over her silent, expectant, as if they wanted her to know something and couldn't tell her. They remained mute despite her questions. They could give no answers. She returned to the present. Jesus was looking at her. Wilton, Gabriel, and Jeremiah weren't there. She saw them standing under the edge of the tree line. Their heads were close together and their lips were moving.

Jesus was still beside her, looking at her face. "Are you okay Maria? You were miles away for awhile there."

She smiled. "It was nothing, only memories." The dreams of her parents lingered like the smell of death.

"We should join the others," Jesus said. "They might be missing us."

Maria thought they could wait a little longer but she held her tongue and went with him. Company would be good.

FIFTEEN

ISHMAEL had been busy. The people had gathered under the Campanile of The Cathedral. Dozens at first, then a hundred or more until they filled the ground. They were a trickle, then a flood that lasted the day. He spoke. They listened. Some left and came back with more. The process repeated. Ishmael kept talking. If he repeated himself it mattered little. The crowds heard the words and took them out and told them to others until they spread over the city. The words seeped into the tenements, rolled across the plazas and emptied into the river beds. The people slept and the words washed them and they woke to them and they listened.

Ishmael climbed down the Campanile in time with the setting sun and walked out into the crowd. People gathered in clusters and knots. Some grabbed his arm and thanked him. A woman, old, wrinkled, and smelling of shit and stale piss knelt in front of him. She kissed the ground. "We have heard you and we will do as you ask. Look around," she waved her arm. "What do you see?"

Ishmael looked. "People," he said. "But I'm looking for one man. If he's here."

"Followers," she said. "Followers, not people, not anymore and we will do anything you ask us, anything." A younger woman hurried over and picked her up. "Come on Maman, leave the man alone." The old woman went with her, looking back at him, her eyes glowing. The younger woman looked back as well. He couldn't read her face.

Ishmael waited until they vanished in the throng and walked further into the crowd. Finding safety in numbers most stayed gathered together, finding solace in each other. Ishmael had found the soul of the city. He walked on through the mass, absorbing it, and found a man. He wasn't the man he wanted but he knew where that man was in the city and told him. Ishmael kept walking and the crowd fell behind. None of them knew he had gone.

Two hours later Ishmael stood in front of a house near Compton. No riots could make the scene look as blasted and desolate as the one in front of him. The roof hung by a thread and the walls sagged and bowed. It looked like it would collapse if he breathed too hard. There was a door to knock on. It hung limp on one hinge. The windows were missing; remnants of them lay in shards on the ground. Weeds grew tall as the house, almost hiding it from view. A tree grew through the porch clinging to life best as it could. In the house was the man Ishmael wanted. He walked to the front door and called out. The man inside didn't like surprises. The shadows inside shifted and metal scraped against the floor.

"Andrew," Ishmael called into the gloom. "It's me."

"I need more." A voice called back, harsh, the rasp of a long term smoker.

"Ishmael, I need to talk to you."

"We all need things Ishmael, we rarely get them." The shadows thickened and took shape. Out of them came a short man, stocky, bald headed, wearing camo clothing and heavy boots. Ishmael wondered where he got them. Andrew always seemed to have them, it was one of his things. A beard, cut short, smeared his chin like paint. A large gun hung from his belt and bandoliers crossed his chest. Knife hilts jutted from his boots.

"You're looking good," Ishmael said to the man in front of him. He looked at the bandoliers and the gun. "Back from somewhere or about to leave?"

"Either or. How you look is a low bar these days," Andrew said. "Not hard to beat it. Take a seat. I haven't seen you for a while. What you been up to?"

"Been over a year. I'm surprised you still live here, that you're still living in fact." Ishmael pushed some debris off a nearby chair and sat. He looked around. "I've been here and there. Been told a few things, seen a few things more to open my eyes. And it's a wicked world in all meridians it seems to me, that's why I'm here. At least in part."

Andrew laughed. "I thought you'd have run out of Moby Dick quotes by now." He sat down in a spot clear enough to fit him. "It's not much but it's home." Ishmael said nothing. He'd seen much worse. Andrew had been born in here and survived a hard childhood he never talked about. Rumors surrounded him like a wreath and he did nothing to deny them.

"So tell me what brings you here after so long, I thought being a preacher would set you against me." He looked at Ishmael. "Has it?"

Ishmael shrugged. "Preaching doesn't mean I have to be a pacifist, it didn't for Christ after all." he leaned forward and felt his elbows dig into the flesh above his knees. He felt the pain. It was life. "I have a proposition for you."

"I'm listening."

Heyusser had suffered through a visit from General Moore. Moore had told him of the group moving through the city towards the mountains. He had told him the overflights the next day had revealed nothing more. The group disappeared like water into dry ground as if they had known they'd been seen or were being searched out. Heyusser was not impressed. He wanted to know where they were. They were a loose end and Heyusser hated loose ends. He hated having to make up lies about them when his masters asked questions. "You are doing your utmost to find them, General?" Heyusser asked.

"Of course sir. Drone overflights as well as search parties ready to move on any heat signature big enough to match. That should be enough until tomorrow when it will be daylight."

"When will you find them?"

"I expect a favorable result by tomorrow afternoon."

"Why not tonight?"

"It's a larger area than you might think. Sir." The sarcasm dripped like oil. Moore didn't even try to hide it. "I'm concentrating the search around the area leading to the spire. Most potential escapees go in that direction. That leaves several thousand square miles to cover. Assuming we know what direction we need to send the drones. Finding them will take time that's all." Heyusser deferred for now, giving Moore the rope he needed. Moore was getting a little tired of the man who had no idea of the difficulties even tech couldn't overcome.

And the game they played went on. After Moore left Heyusser waited to make sure Moore wouldn't come blundering in. When satisfied he pressed the button to send the signal to the overlords that he wanted to talk to them. He didn't like it. Speaking to them always made him feel like showering afterwards. He felt as if like there was something fetid attached to his skin. The answer came a minute later.

"Yes?" The face was stern, silver hair gathered at the temples hinting at age but the face was smooth and unlined. It was Woodhull Fleming. Heyusser felt himself shrink under the gaze until he was in a mental fetal position. The eyes were expressionless, basilisk-cold, and they saw everything. Heyusser knew in his gut those eyes had pared away layers in an instant. They saw deep into his soul, and dismissed him as an insect.

"We have a problem, sir." Heyusser hated how the words came, as if unwilling. He thought they sounded deferential without being servile. Hoped that was good enough. "A group might have left the city and reached the mountains. We don't have a location for them but we are working on it." He wanted to avoid questions but knew they would come anyway. Whether he knew the answers or could give a good reason he didn't was another question.

"Why not?" Fleming hadn't moved a muscle, the voice unchanged. Heyusser felt like a mouse seeing a rattler about to strike.

He took a breath to steady his nerves. He knew the face would have known this. "They must have known our drones had spotted them and changed direction. There's no other explanation how they avoided our ground parties."

"Could they see the drones?"

"They couldn't have, they're too high. It would be a fluke if they could. A glint of light is possible, but they wouldn't know what caused it." Heyusser had to be careful here. He knew if Fleming wanted, he could swat him as easy as he would swat a fly. And with as much finality. "It more likely was a lucky guess on their part, or being cautious. Either way we will see them in the morning when they start moving. It is only a matter of time."

"I don't believe in lucky guesses." Fleming leaned a little closer to the screen. "Someone told them. Someone who can access our systems. Find out who told them and take steps to make sure it isn't repeated. We don't like people wandering around, especially when the end is in sight. It upsets us."

"You are certain someone told them?" Heyusser asked the face.

"Yes I am and you should be too. They got information and they acted on it. Found out and close the loophole. It cannot happen again."

"Yes sir," Heyusser blanched under the snake-stare of the face. "Consider it done."

"I will not. Let me know when you have taken care of them." Fleming reached a hand to the off switch. "And find the missing group and take care of them." The screen went blank, the link severed.

Heyusser wiped his face. The contacts with Fleming always unnerved him even when he felt confident. He couldn't pull any strings today. He called his secretary. "Get me head of ops. If he's busy make sure he stops being busy." Heyusser sat back and waited.

A few hours later a man in a uniform with his status and rank on his sleeve hung up the radio phone and called his aide. "Set up a briefing with Patterson, we have a mission."

Later, in the early hours of the evening after the sun had set, twelve men left the mountains and headed into LA. They strode, full of purpose down the rubble-strewn boulevards. They were silent as shadows and their eyes were cold. They carried themselves as if on a mission and wore black uniforms, body armor, weapons, and canisters filled with gas and explosives and they made no sound. The streets were quiet, the people huddled down for the night. The men wore masks with night vision goggles to avoid using flashlights. They didn't want anyone to know they were there. No one did. Or lived to tell about it.

After two hours of marching they came to the building where Jesus and the others had sheltered and met Jah. Nobody knew they were coming and those still awake were too stoned to notice the arrival. The smell of ganja rode the air from a myriad of spliffs and hookahs. The men went from room to room, anyone in them would not wake to see the morning. They didn't speak a word as they brought death. One rasta went to the bathroom and ran into them, he dropped like a slashed balloon before he knew he was dead. Jah woke to find some of the men standing over him. It was the last thing he ever saw. The woman next to him never knew. She passed from sleep to death in an instant.

The men made no distinction between men and women, old or young. They had their orders and they were too professional to care. It took them less than thirty minutes. Then they left. When they were far enough the leader pressed a button. A low roar echoed through the streets and empty buildings. The building collapsed. Some people nearby woke up to the low rumble and the shake, wondering if there was an earthquake. They waited for the aftershocks that never came then went back to sleep. It was another building falling in a city where they fell all the time. The men walked back into the mountains, shaking the dust of the city from their boots. They had forgotten the people they had killed by the time they made the tree line. The leader congratulated them on a job well done. Within hours they were asleep.

Jesus and the group woke as the sun rose and dappled the ground outside the cave with shadows. They rose and stretched. Jesus felt the joints in his body snap and pop. Maria lay next to him and he knew she would no longer sleep anywhere else. It felt comfortable and uneasy at the same time. He sat up and watched her as she breathed. The thought rose in his mind, unstoppable and painful. He could be the cause of her death and the deaths of the others. He couldn't, didn't want that. His conscience crawled and cried at the prospect. They deserved better. He wanted to bring them life but might only bring them death. He came to the only conclusion he could. No other options were available to him. He had to leave.

But, thank God, not today. He had to talk to his friends. They could, might, understand. But not Maria, he didn't know if she would. He knew she would to try convince him she should go with him if he didn't stay. And he couldn't. Neither could she go with him, despite what she might believe. He had to face what was coming on his terms. He resolved to the course. He drank some water, his mind clear for the first time in days. The group woke as the sun brought Plato's shadows. Most of them would have killed for a coffee.

Wilton would have. His mouth was dry, it always was in the mornings but it seemed worse in the dust he'd walked through. Or all the tequila hangovers he'd suffered over the years. He wanted to change his shirt, have a shower, eat eggs and fantasize about sex with a woman that lasted from dawn to dusk. He fantasized a lot. It kept his nights happy and the days bearable. He knew it was never going to happen. He grimaced, stretched, and yawned. Next to him Jeremiah sat up and drank some water, he passed the cup to Wilton who drank with no pleasure. "I need a real drink," he said. "Something to make this taste better."

"Might take a while," said Jeremiah.

Wilton walked to the entrance of the cave and stared without seeing at the spruces. He sighed. "And I could be sitting in my little bar watching the sun rise through dirty windows." He grinned at Jeremiah. "Those still unbroken of course." He fastened his shirt as far as it would go. "One day I'll button this the whole way." It was the closest Wilton could come to being rueful.

"Keep walking with us and it might happen." Jeremiah drank more water.

"I doubt it amigo. Something tells me this jaunt among the woods will not last long enough to get back to speaking terms with my feet." Wilton sighed. "I have not seen them for so long I wouldn't know what to say to them if I did. But it doesn't matter I suppose, look at him; he has much on his mind I know. We expect much of him, and it worries him. This last day he was elsewhere in his mind. He looks different, as if he has decided something."

"A good thing, right?"

"Time will tell, a day, two." Wilton lay back against the cave wall. It was cool against his back. "I know a lot about people, you get to learn that when you talk to them every day, Jeremiah. Look around us, the people here are waiting, their eyes closed to what is around them. They see only another day to get through and hope they are alive at the end of it. They want something to happen but don't know what. They might not want Jesus to lead them, but they know they cannot go anywhere on their own. They are dead to the future. Look at them."

Jeremiah did. He saw people with blank faces and thousand yard stares. They shuffled out the cave. Gathered under the spruces. Ate dried fruit and some nuts they were handing around. They sipped water and he heard them murmuring to each other. "They seem pretty normal to me when you think of what's happened. At least they're talking and shit."

"Thus we see the problem Jeremiah, they are talking of small things, the weather, how well they slept. These are small conversations for normal times." Wilton rested his hands on his head. "But these are not normal times."

"I guess not," Jeremiah agreed.

"Not at all, the times have changed and so have we." Wilton paused. Stared into himself. "But we pretend they and we have not, and when something happens we do not react. We do not alter our thinking. Jesus has, I admit, but when someone changes their thinking, the rest of us let them think for us. We go along with them not knowing why. But the answer is simple Jeremiah, we cannot think of doing anything else. And so, we find ourselves here in a forest a day or so from all we know, such as it was, faced with the unknown. We find ourselves like the Israelites led by Moses toward the promised land. Or the crew led by Ahab in his doomed quest. Which I fear is closer to the truth. We will not reach the

Promised Land but drown in the ocean, dragged to our deaths by the whale Jesus pursues."

"You sure know how to bring a man down Wilton," Jeremiah observed.

"I'm being realistic Jeremiah. And more to the point, if Jesus does not do something soon I fear even the most positive among us will not stay long. When the end doesn't get any closer and they get more dispirited they will disappear like a river in the desert."

"But Jesus has given them some hope." Arturo walked up and squatted on his haunches in front of Wilton and Jeremiah.

"Hope only lasts so long," said Wilton. "It cannot survive without nourishment Arturo. it needs to feed on something. Unless there is something out here to nourish it, the support he has will vanish. It cannot be otherwise. I wish it was not so."

"He will help me find out what happened to my brother," said Arturo.

"He will do nothing of the sort." Wilton differed. "He will do what he must, not what we would want of him. You will need to come to terms with the loss of your brother on your own."

Arturo shook his head. "You are wrong Wilton, very wrong."

"Am I?" asked Wilton. "Look around you, there are more people than you here. They all want something from Jesus whether he likes it or not. Look at Maria, see how she looks at him. She feels for him, even loves him. That's something the rest of us can never feel *eh*? She wants something from him also, knowledge of what happened to her parents. He will disappoint her and whether she will survive or not it is up to her. And the others? They want something too and he cannot give it to them even if he tries so he will not please any. Like you Arturo, we will have to find our own answers."

Arturo huffed and walked away a few yards and sat. "I know. But what else, can we do?"

"Do not expect more from Jesus than he can give." Wilton had an almost satisfied expression on his face. "We should expect nothing and be grateful if we get it."

"I would rather risk disappointment." Arturo sounded like he wanted a debate.

"You might, but would all the others? Risky proposition my friend. People willing to risk disappointment always end up finding it." Wilton stood up and stretched. "And disappointed people don't react well. Think hard my friends. Now if you will excuse me I will make use of the forest."

He looked at the trees. "I hope I don't meet any indigenous fauna with my pants down."

"I wouldn't worry the bait's too small." Jeremiah cackled and turned his head away to hide his mirth.

Wilton humphed and walked off. The spruces were sparse and he had to walk further than he wanted to be out of sight.

SIXTEEN

THE buzz of the phone woke Heyusser from a dream involving lingerie-clad courtesans. They were being very willing. He thrust them from his mind, picked it up and held it to his ear. "Yes?"

"Done," said a voice.

"Thank you." Heyusser closed the connection and put the phone down. He didn't know the voice. It was electro-modded to prevent voice recognition. He rubbed his eyes. They felt like they had enough sand in them to fill the pool outside Caesar's Palace. He needed more sleep, a few hours so the courtesans would return. Afterward he would drown himself in coffee, black, the stronger the better. He lay back and closed his eyes.

Above him, beyond where no one would see were the gondolas where the overlords lived. Attached to the end of massive spires they speckled the planet like dandelion seeds. The spire rising from the mountains east of LA lofted four hundred miles on a pillar of carbon nano-fiber tube. On each side were thin rails for maglev transports. It was this Maria saw glinting in the sun from San Dimas. It was this the city ignored as part of the landscape, every time they looked at the mountains.

Woodhull Fleming watched from his Olympian vantage point as the sun rose behind the planet below. He felt a sense of missing something important. He sipped a cognac from the Borderies region of where France once had been. Some things couldn't be gone without.

He had overseen many changes over the years and he didn't look his age. None did. They could afford not to. There was one more change to come on the west coast of the country he had once called home. Sometimes he even missed it, or thought he did. He picked up the phone and pressed a button. "Cut off the water." He replaced the phone, drained the glass and poured another. Finally some progress might happen.

The desalination plant sat squatting over land turned to marsh by its own excreta. There had been others but the rise of the seas had closed most of them. Only three remained from San Diego to Seattle. Large pipes ran from the plant into and over the hills to the desert and Las Vegas. Smaller pipes ran south to LA. An hour after the message a worker pressed a button and the supply flowing through the pipes fell to a trickle. Less than twenty minutes later the water stopped forever.

In the hills Jesus and his followers sat among the spruces and waited. The sun spattered the ground between the trees and the cool was welcome. Below them the city still sprawled along the flatland it occupied. From here everything looked normal. It looked much as it did in the early 2100s. Distance gave the lie to reality. Streets and boulevards bisected the city. Water shone on them and they carved the city into segments like a vast chess board. Gabriel looked somber. Something had broken the jovial, chatty mood of the rasta who had brought them here. Jesus saw and wondered what was wrong.

Gabriel looked down at the rows of streets. "See down there man? I grew up there. I know most of LA, what's there and what used to be." An ineffable sadness radiated from him. Gabriel pointed out where Azusa University had once sat. The Marshall Canyon golf course. Where 210 sliced through Citrus and Claremont. The Santa Fe dam recreation area.

Jesus followed his gaze. "You grew up there?"

"Yah, all gone now, no family. Only Jah and my people. Only now my people, Jah, they be gone too." His eyes closed and his body shook. Unshed tears racked him and left him spent. "I know it true, I saw it in dream last night. Men come with guns. Shoot everyone, nobody alive, even Jah gone. All dead. I was bashy yesterday. Living was bashy. All nice things but gone, not bashy now."

Jesus sat next to the stricken man. "It was wrong, dreams often are."

"No not mine. Mama said I got the gift, see things be happening or will happen but not always. Man go mad if be other." Gabriel looked to the south-west. "Be our place there man, yah be bandulu, do bad things sometimes but we survive. We do what have to, like you." He pointed out a tall tower, still standing, stark against the flatness. "There be where Jah found me when I was eight year old. I remember the day. He was tall, looked the same as he did when you met him. Ah he was bright, it was like watching the sun rise in the morning when you look at him."

Jesus saw the wonder Gabriel must have felt. It flowed out of the man like a tide, washing over him. He knew Gabriel saw someone who seemed transcendent. To a small child alone in a city where such children died easy it must been like a rebirth. "It must have been a great moment, Gabriel."

"Yah it was, and it always be so with Jah. He would ask us to do things, sometimes he tell us and we do them, no question from we. Like me all were bruk when he found us. Jah gave us purpose, helped us live. We all like me at some point when Jah found we. All we owe we to him. No Jah we all die. I and I die too soon, I have no place now. Man not live with no place." He moaned, it keened on the wind and the group turned as one to see where the sound came from.

Jesus could do little. He rested his arm around Gabriel's shoulders as the man shuddered in his grief. "Who be so bad man? Who do this bodderation to us, who be so vexatious? We not be craven, we help you, help others too. It because of that they kill we."

Jesus had an idea who it was, who ordered it even if he couldn't know why. It seemed capricious to him, wilful. An act of insanity in an already insane world. It was unfathomable and he knew Gabriel was right. An evil thing had happened during the night. While he grieved with the ragged man, a cold fire sparked his soul and gave him reason to continue. Something greater had him. "It wasn't your fault Gabriel, it was the ones who want LA for themselves. They did it. If you were there you'd be dead too." He felt a pang of fear for Ishmael and the rest of the people who scratched out an existence in the city he had left behind. All who would die at the hands of the indifferent.

There was death coming and he could do nothing. It would all be up to Ishmael to do what he could to rescue the people. It would all be too little and the certainty of failure gnawed at him. Jesus knew many were going to die. It pained his soul to realize he might not be able to stop what was coming since if Gabriel was right it had already started. A storm bigger than anyone had known was building up ahead of them in the desert. When it reached critical mass it would roll over LA, leave it empty and the overlords would have dominion. He remembered Ishmael telling him their paths were different. With the memory came the knowledge they had their own purposes to achieve. The knowledge didn't help him feel better.

But the knowledge could help in other ways. He dug into himself and found much he didn't know. The cold fire in him burned higher and he knew he had to carry it through to the end even if it cost the most anyone could pay. And he knew if he paid, he would pay it again as often as he needed to, including paying the most anyone could pay. And he wasn't alone. He cast around, saw Maria, Arturo, Jeremiah, and Wilton who always complained. LA wasn't going to go under without a fight. Jesus stood and looked over the city with the limited lifespan. "Gather the people," he told Gabriel. "There is something I have to tell them."

The group gathered; there were enough to make several rings around him. He moved from the center to where the ground sloped down to the city below. Maria saw it as the backdrop Jesus needed. The scene looked almost prophetic. Something moved in her mind telling her all would be alright even if she wouldn't be around to see it. Below and behind him the grids of the city mapped out a past they had left behind. It was before noon when Jesus began to speak. By the time he finished the sun was kissing the ocean. Maria, Jeremiah, Wilton, all of them sat and squatted silent as he spoke. The group sat transfixed, unable to move. While he spoke Jesus sat on an outcrop of stone. He didn't move. He didn't drink. He only talked; questions came and went, unanswered. No one minded.

At the end the group dissipated, circled the clearing and sat on the grass and spruce needles. Some drifted into the trees. Voices and murmurings trailed away into the early evening. As Jesus spoke clouds ranged up over the eastern slopes as if gathering to listen and the air grew close. The clouds grew anvil heads for the gods to smite and they were black under the impact. A charge ran through the spruce and as one they all shivered. Rain was coming, lots of it. The clouds continued to mass up and rise over the mountains, challenged by the coastal winds.

It was as if the storm heard what Jesus said, turning his emotion into wind and returning it. It blew hard, shaking the trees, breaking branches, and blowing out the campfires of the men who sat watch. It turned his words into hail and rain and pounded the earth. The energy lashed the hills and the people and the city. All lay helpless. Jesus faced it without flinching. The land staggered and quailed. Jesus led the group into the cave.

They blocked the opening with leaves and branches to keep out the sound and the rage. They sat shivering and bruised. They held cloth and rags over their heads and ears, trying to keep the sound out. In fear they clung together, said nothing and shared the hell of the storm. The rain filled every channel and runnel and soaked the ground in seconds. The hail bruised the grass and the land. Animals clumped together and sought refuge until it was over. The men in the camps took it and hunkered down. In the cave Jesus walked among the frightened group. His touch soothed and he whispered words they heard over the vastness of the sound.

When it passed, they crawled out from their shelter and wondered how they had survived. The silence hurt their ears. They didn't talk in case they shouted and ruined the moment of calm. The rain had moved on but the rivers were still full. They overflowed their banks and spilled into the land.

Jesus stood on the side of the hills watching the water, silver and brass in the sun, flow across the city. He turned to the others as they walked over to him. "Storms last only moments, they have an ending to them." He smiled. "But we will bring a storm to last generations and leave the earth changed. Some of us will not live to see the beginning of it and none of us will see the end. You need to know this. If you want to leave you can, but I hope you don't."

Maria came over and held his arm. Wilton, Jeremiah, Gabriel, Nathaniel, Adeline, and Arturo followed her and watched, silent. They looked solemn and grave. The rest sat still on the ground. The water climbed up to them and they felt nothing.

"Gabriel," he said. "You have nothing left, these people still want life. We need to find it in our own way. You can help us find it our way or you can help those who don't want to come with me find it where they can get it. You can help them. I can't."

Gabriel knew what was going to happen. The group had gone as far as it could, its ending was now. He would go his way and Jesus and the people with him would go theirs. "Yah man, but be too bodderation for me most times." Gabriel said. "But they be bredrin of I now, I will help them, take them past the people here. I know the way, no bloodfire stop me now." He held up a ziplock baggie of green leaves. "Besides, I got the ganja we need." He looked around at the group. "I take them from Babylon to the Promised Land or I be not Gabriel.

Jesus laughed at the man he called friend. His dreads hung limp and his tattered coat looked worse than ever. He looked as if the storm had washed something vital out of him. He grinned back. "Disya not be something even Bobo Dread can help me with."

Jeremiah shook his hand. "You'll be dry in no time."

"Yah my body and clothes, but me dreads, they never be dry in my life. This be dread." Gabriel looked so forlorn Maria couldn't help laughing despite herself.

"You know what to do Gabriel." Jesus stood in front of the man who had lost much and then gained much.

Gabriel nodded. "Yah but I not be drop legging and blowing with a fancy or be back at ma gates ever. I be you fren Jesus, always will be but I fear we not reach it sometime soon."

"It took Moses forty years," Wilton said.

"Yah but we know what happen to him."

Nobody said what they all knew.

"But what about us?" Maria watched as Gabriel walked over to the rest of group. He gathered the remnants, the rest had scattered, vanishing into the forest.

"I be gathering the others now," Gabriel said over his shoulder. "Then I take them galang home." He waved. "I be gaan now. Goodbye fren Jesus, one day we be meeting again, Jah letting." He gathered the others with him and vanished like a wraith among the trees. The group followed him, silent amid the wet needles and mud.

Jesus looked at the few who stood with him. "Now the hard work begins." They watched the clouds split open over LA and wondered what was coming next. Jesus feared it more than he cared to know.

SEVENTEEN

THE morning following the storm crept in as if afraid of the heat that would follow. After Gabriel and the group left, Jesus and the others sat and rested until they fell into a sleep more like torpor. They didn't dream but their sleep had been uneasy. All had vague recollections of dark shapes that dogged their steps. They bore the smell of death and vanished when they looked at them.

Below them in the city, Ishmael turned on a tap to wash the grime of the last days from his face. The tap shuddered and spat a little water then a trickle tinged with rust appeared. It flowed in a fitful way then sputtered like a match and stopped. Ishmael wondered if he'd seen a mirage but realized he hadn't. There was no more water. He went into another room and tried one there without success. He bowed his head. He remembered reading somewhere that without water people lived three days. He doubted they would last that long even with the number of water tanks scattered through the city. If Andrew had noticed the water was out, he knew what it meant.

Ishmael knew he had to move sooner. In three days or less the outside would come in like a wave and would take the city down and the people with it. He couldn't get them all out now, he didn't have the time. He hoped his proposition to Andrew might still bear fruit and give the overlords a reason to think twice. If not it could at least be some revenge for destroying where they lived.

The people behind the mountains were moving. Ishmael knew shutting the water off was a means to weaken the city. To lower the will of the people, make them more vulnerable. Ishmael couldn't let it happen. He could see the Campanile from where he stood, standing like a beacon. He was glad something had drawn him to stay in the ruined Cathedral. He wanted to look out over the city from the top but he needed to do something else now, he left to talk to Andrew. The Campanile would wait for now.

There were some people scattered around the grounds as he left. They looked at him without asking where he was going. He didn't think he could tell them if they did. He nodded and they nodded back, acknowledgment was enough for now.

Another man rose in the mountains. The sun slashed ribbons on his face through the broken branches lining the sides of what he called home. He was the last one left in the area and he lived in a pit, twenty-five feet long and eight deep. A bed and a basin stood at one end and a rough-hewn table at the other. He had dragged fallen trees and turned them into walls braced with anything he could find. Dirt and rocks filled the gaps. Sheets of particle board topped with shingles and tar made the roof. He'd camouflaged his home from the air by small branches, leaves and mud. He needed to replace them often but the effort was worth it. The forces that moved around his base without knowing he was there had killed everyone else. Or, he sometimes thought with a grim smile, they thought he wasn't worth the effort to do something about.

He rose from the bed, dust trembling in the air around him. It was time to move. He dressed in fatigues, strapped his crossbow to his back, and wiped dirt on his face. Bears and wolves weren't the worst predators around here. You could figure out what they were going to do most of the time. The most dangerous had two legs and fucked up attitudes. He avoided them.

He looked at his supplies for the day. Jerky, dried fruit, and an old battered thermos filled with filtered water. Perfect. He had one more item to take care of. Walking to the door he picked up a small twig the size of a toothpick and wedged it between the door and the frame as he left. It would drop unseen if anyone tried to get inside, telling him they'd found him. It hadn't happened very often, only twice in the last twenty years. He'd learned to be careful and he wasn't going to change now.

He stopped outside, sniffing the air and listening to the sounds of the forest. The air smelt of pine, spruce, and mud from yesterday's storm. He heard a bear in the distance. Grizzlies had been moving south over the last few decades, coming back to where they had been years back. Their numbers were still small but he hoped it wasn't one. They were a threat if you were stupid enough to let them get close. The noise was from the north, so was the wind, so the bear didn't know he was there. He sniffed again, deeper. He listened harder. It was snuffling and shuffling from right to left. Black bear. Trying to keep quiet. Grizzlies never bothered about being quiet. They didn't need to. He kept the sound in his awareness, he would move if it got too close or was a female with cubs.

He started off in the opposite direction looking to bag a deer. A few quail would be good for variety's sake. He hadn't had much luck bagging them lately but he felt his chances were better today. State of mind sure, but the right attitude wouldn't hurt. He headed south and west until he felt and smelled the dead city and turned east feeling the pain rise in his gorge. LA bore too many memories and he didn't want to face them. Some things still hurt too much. Despite his resolve, faces swam into his mind. One was a young girl, his sister. She was six the last time he saw her alive. The quake that killed her sent his family tumbling out of their single-wide, carrying what they could. He still woke with the rumbling shocks fresh in his mind.

They had known she wasn't there the minute they were outside. When the rolling and shuddering stopped they had torn the house apart. They found her small body crushed like a doll under the debris. He hadn't stayed for the burial. He'd left the next day leaving everyone behind to deal with things in their own way, same as he did. They watched him go, stone-faced with grief, knowing their lives had ended. He was fifteen then and he ran far. He found solace in distance, unable to cope until by the time he could, it had been far too long and he never returned. The nearest he could go now was to stand on a ridge overlooking where the home had stood. There was nothing there, even the skeleton was gone.

By the time he was sixteen he found a place for himself among the hills and gullies of the ranges. He was twenty-one when he first went back. It was his birthday. He celebrated it by crying. LA lay in the clear light, the Pacific bright and blue, slashed by the white of breakers no longer surfed.

There had been a pull for his old life but it grew less and less and he stopped looking by the time he was thirty. He'd found some comfort in the survivalists in the area. He wondered why they'd been so pleased by the end of the world. He found out they enjoyed being right. With the men he found whiskey, guns, and beer, with the women, companionship, and the chance to talk. Then the forces came and killed the others one by one. They had swaggered and boasted how they'd stand when pushed. In the end it was empty talk, devoid of reality. Guns were no use against drones that hit unseen with enough firepower to erase city blocks.

Now he was the last as far as he knew from Mexico to Oregon. Shoving old memories aside he pushed on into the forest. He knew the most severe slopes and skirted around them, moving in a circular loop. His worn, dusty boots still gripped the ground as well as any animal.

On the air the smell of a campfire came to his nostrils. He shook his head, bewildered. The forces were either fucking stupid or didn't care about telegraphing their position. In response he turned right, giving them a wide berth. He thought for a moment about getting closer and seeing if he could pick off a few with his bow. He decided better of it, better to get them one at a time and leave them for the scavengers. An attack would bring them boiling into the area like fire ants and he didn't need the aggravation. Later he would send them a message but not now. He enjoyed pricking them a little, making them wary and scared of moving too far. It would never last long but he felt a touch of pleasure each time.

He didn't know it but he was going to get the chance sooner than he thought. In the distance was Jesus and his small group. They were making better time now they were more used to the hills, gullies, and forests. Jesus kept the sun in view and watched it track the sky. They too smelled the campfire and Maria took Jeremiah to check it out. "I've been up here a few times and survived," she'd said with a sureness she didn't feel. "I'm your best bet."

Jesus had agreed and let them go. They vanished into the trees. Jesus, Adeline, Wilton, Nathaniel, and Arturo sat down to wait. They flicked insects off their skin while the shadows lengthened. "I hate midges," Wilton complained, no one disagreed.

They passed around a canteen and sipped from it. "Anyone know where there's a stream to fill this?" Adeline asked. The only answers were head shakes. She sat back, rested her back on a tree and closed her eyes to dream of water.

Maria led Jeremiah through the trees, keeping the breeze in their faces. They trod soft to avoid snapping a fallen twig. They were lucky. A bear shuffled across in front, less than a hundred yards off, following its own path. They waited until it vanished in the trees. It was good. Any sound they made would be another animal the bear had disturbed. Then they moved on. Further on she held up at a trail of wolf prints but they were old. In ten minutes they found a clearing, clear of undergrowth. In the middle were a group of men. Next to them stacks of guns were in easy reach. A Humvee in camouflage paint stood off to one side. On it was a machine gun; belts of bullets festooned around it like warped Christmas wrapping.

The smoke they smelled rose from a fire in the middle of the clearing. Men sat around it waiting for the animal on the spit to finish cooking. She counted twelve. They looked serious, with blank eyes and unsmiling faces. They carried the ability to kill with them like cling-wrap. Like the others she'd seen in her treks, they were dangerous and best avoided. They were men who could kill like they killed for food, without thought. Something they would do when they needed.

She held them both back in the trees. Like most of the forest the floor was sandy. The storms had softened the leaves on the ground making it easier to be silent. She motioned for Jeremiah to stay where he was. She wanted to go closer and edge around the clearing to see if there was a chance to snatch some food or water. He didn't agree. He knew it would be dangerous and gestured for her to stay put. The men in the clearing had him spooked but he stayed where he was as she left him. He fretted as Maria drew closer to the unsmiling men. He realized these were the people they would need to get past to do what Jesus wanted. He knew how close to impossible it was going to be.

On the edge of the clearing Maria peered around the trunk of an aspen. It was dangerous where she was, too open. One look in the right direction by a soldier or a false step on her part and it would be her last. If they killed her, she would be lucky and not be able to give up information on the others. She hoped they would be trigger happy enough to save them looking for someone else.

She heard little she could understand. The soldiers were talking in low voices. The murmuring reached her ears like an out of tune TV. Two were prowling the far side of the clearing. Something nagged at her mind; scratched at her. Then she knew what it was telling her, there were others on this side, doing the same thing. It made sense; she'd seen it before and cursed herself for another mistake. This time it could be fatal. She needed to move and move fast. She turned away from the tree where she stood, away from where Jeremiah waited. If there was anyone close she couldn't let them know where he was. She needed them to believe she was alone. If they found Jeremiah there'd be no help for either of them. She took one step, then two. A voice came to her ears. "That's far enough." The voice sounded young.

She stopped and waited as footsteps grew closer. They came from behind and more than one pair of feet was making them. She sensed a man's presence and felt the barrel of a rifle press into her neck, hard and cold. "Who are you?" she asked.

The barrel pressed harder and she staggered. "You're not in a position to ask questions." The voice was quiet and menace edged around the words. It was the voice of a man who would shoot first and never ask why. "Move. Into the clearing. Slow." He pushed her shoulder with the barrel to get her moving. "Don't try and run, you'll be dead before you can take a step."

Maria allowed the guard to propel her into the clearing as if unwilling. She felt relief they hadn't seen Jeremiah and didn't seem to think someone else might be nearby. One prisoner seemed to be enough. She hoped he had seen her taken and left to tell the others. She wasn't going to be able to. She pounded herself mentally for being stupid. She hadn't watched for the sentries she had known would be there. The soldier pushed her further into the clearing and the group around the fire stood as one. "Looks like we got something for dessert after the main course. Well done, I could use her right now." one of them said, unwilling to take his eyes off her.

"Shut up Sanchez," the one who had found her said. "I found her, she's mine and you don't want to try to take her from me."

The man called Sanchez grinned. His teeth were yellow and the grin stopped at his lips. "Whatever you say man, whatever you say."

The flap of the tent opened and a man came out and came up to them. Authority was in his face. He was harder than the others. Maria knew he had to be. He stood a foot from Maria's face and his eyes searched her face. "Well, well, the forest throws up all kinds of wildlife doesn't it? Where did you find her?" he asked the man without his eyes leaving her face.

The soldier stood with his rifle pointed at her back. He was itching, she knew, to blow a hole in her they could drive the Humvee through. "Inside the tree line, she was watching us, seeing if she could scavenge some food."

"It's a possibility, one of several."

Maria stayed silent. It wasn't the time to talk. She needed to buy some time for Jeremiah and the others and silence was the best way. She watched the man's face. He was clean cut, his hairline ruler straight. He shaved and brushed his teeth. His uniform was cleaner and he had a pistol in his belt. He led them but he wore no insignia. He didn't need it.

He ordered the man behind her to bind her wrists. It was fast and efficient. She felt a cable tie tighten enough to keep her hands still but not so hard to stop circulation. Maria knew these men were good at this job and they'd had lots of practice. Two of them forced her over to the fire and made her sit. The leader sat in front of her. "I have some questions for you," he said in a quiet voice. Maria shuddered without thinking. She knew his type. The quietness hid a sociopath who followed orders without question and God help those who were unlucky enough to get in his way. "And you had better have good answers, lying to me is not a good idea." He grabbed her face. It was like she was in a vice. His fingers imprinted her cheeks and it made her jaws ache. "It will not go well for you if you do."

EIGHTEEN

MARIA needn't have worried. Jeremiah left as soon as he saw the man in charge start questioning her. The soldiers were too intent on their captive and he saw no others as he followed the path back to Jesus and the others. He didn't want to meet the men who had her and getting back to the group was the only thing he could do. Any distance between him and the soldiers was at least respite.

"What happened?" Jesus asked him when he lurched, breathless, to where he and Maria had left them.

"We found the camp, about two miles away." Jeremiah said. "The words tumbled from him, no order or sense to them. "Maria wanted to get closer, I didn't think she should but I couldn't stop her. She was close to the clearing where there were soldiers sitting around. She left me to go by herself. She got captured by a couple of soldiers. I didn't see them, I guess she didn't either." He motioned for water. Wilton handed him a canteen. "Anyhow this soldier, I guess he was a sentry or something, he caught her and took her into the clearing." He drank some more water. "Then this dude came out of a tent and started to talk to her. Then they tied her arms and made her sit down and the dude started in on questioning her. He looked bad."

Arturo urged him to continue. Jesus laid an arm on Arturo's shoulder. "Give him time, it won't help to rush him." Arturo relaxed under the words. "When you're ready, my friend." He nodded at Jeremiah.

"It looked like he was asking her shit, I couldn't hear and I didn't want to risk getting too close. I left and came back, not straight though in case someone was following me." He looked around to the group reduced by one. "Not that I would've known if they were. Those guys were danger-ous man, real pros. I'm glad they thought she was alone. If they'd got me as well they might have coming looking for you and we know what would happen then."

"We should go and get her, we can't leave her there." Arturo said.

"No way man," Jeremiah replied. "We can't match those guys, they have serious firepower and the attitude to go with it."

"Sorry Arturo but I agree with Jeremiah," Jesus said. "We don't have the ability to get Maria back, and we don't want them to know we're here. We have things to do so we have to leave her. With luck we can find her later, safe and then get her back." Jesus didn't like the option. "None of us like doing this but we have no choice. Maria will tell them about us sooner or later but she will not do it by choice.. She wouldn't want us to risk ourselves, she'd want us to go on and finish what we started."

Jesus looked at Jeremiah then the others. "When you have rested we will leave in case they start to search the area if she hasn't convinced them she was alone." Jesus could sense things were moving and he was getting closer to where he needed to be. He needed to keep going.

The men who had captured Maria were part of what he had come to fight. They had as little idea of what was going on as he did. They were acting on orders, pushed from behind as he was. Something different, but as real. No, something, not someone. Someone was pulling the strings and Jesus knew he needed to meet him. Jesus didn't know who he was but he was out there somewhere like a spider in a web, pulling the strings.

He had the sense they were all pawns in a larger game, one which he didn't know the rules. Something told him he would soon know when it was time to act and what he would need to do. Until then he was content to go where he was being led. The knowledge he was being led could be useful, there were no traps when you knew they were waiting for them. An old song, a verse long ago written came to him. *There is a place for everything and a season for every activity under the heavens.* "Let's go," he said, leading the group into the forest where destiny waited.

It was near noon. The sun was reaching its full height in the sky. The forest shadows were at their lowest, almost invisible among the trees. As the shadows went down the heat went up and it was stifling, drawing the moisture out of the earth. The man had walked far, avoiding the camps, favoring invisibility. Something told him the time was coming when he wouldn't be able to. It was going to be soon and all that he knew would be gone when it came.

Now he sat with his back to a cypress, chewing jerky as he watched a condor ride the updrafts, its feathers and wings spread. The man looked at the body of the deer he had killed. The condor would see it easy enough. He glanced up. The condor was scanning the forest floor, head turning left, right, assessing its chances of snaring some of the carcass. He smiled. "Patience buddy, you can wait a little longer."

He had cut off the portions he wanted already. Wrapped in plastic they were secure and weighty in his pack. He stood and waved to the condor. "Ciao buddy, your turn, better make it quick though." He walked off, heading downhill, the deer smell rising and drifting through the forest. Soon other scavengers would be there, following the scent through the trees. Wolves, mountain lions, and bears were not averse to a free meal. He wanted to be long way off when they started to gather. Being part of a banquet had its place as long as he wasn't on the menu.

An hour later he reached a gully slashing across the land. The sides were steep, hewn by water from last night's storm. Trees lay strewn around, brought down by the water that pulled the earth from under them. Holes patterned the sides and mud covered the bottom. He shook his head. Not worth trying. There would be a way across further down the slope. He followed the gully until it started to shallow and widen out to where he could get across. He listened. There was movement nearby. The sound of footsteps was a few hundred yards off, on the opposite side of the gully. They were noisier than they ought to be out here. He knew they were a group of people either with no idea of how to stay quiet or weren't concerned about it. Soldiers? No, too loud.

He listened long enough to find out what direction they were moving in then moved to find a place to watch for them. He wasn't concerned about who it was, they were making too much noise for that. He made himself inconspicuous, hiding wasn't necessary.. If he came out of nowhere they could do something stupid and someone could end up getting hurt. He wasn't worried about himself, but one of them. In a few minutes the people making the noise came out of the trees. Six of them, disheveled and grimy.

They had the look of being from the city, haunted and shadowed. The man in front, the leader he assumed, had long hair and it hung like it was in braids. No, dreads. He had forgotten what they looked like. The rest looked down, beat. They had lost something, no, someone close. People always looked different when they lost someone and the loss was still on their minds. He saw it in the way they walked, silence wrapped around them like a shroud. He knew in an instant the others had her.

They were going nowhere it seemed, as if they wanted someone to find them. And they had, only they didn't know it. They were lucky the others hadn't found them first. None of them carried weapons so he made sure his crossbow was slung and pointed down. He decided to raise his hands, to be certain there was no foolishness and to look as non-threatening as he could. He thought of the best way to introduce himself. "Hi there," was all he could come up with.

The group stopped short. He felt like he had stopped a group of kids about to raid an orchard, wondering what the hell they would say to get out of the shit. The leader of the group raised a hand in greeting. He did the same. They were less than twenty yards away.

"I am Jesus," said the leader. "I was told of you, the one who was left."

Jesse noted the accent. "I'm Jesse. Where are you from and who told you? I wasn't aware I was famous, and here fame has a hard price."

"LA, what's left of it." Jesus said. "Who told me isn't important but I was told as well you might help us."

"I have a little place nearby. I call it home. It's not much but it does the trick. Don't ask me my last name, I can't remember what it was. Out here I never seemed to find anyone who would need to know it so it kinda drifted away." He watched them. They stood like deer, not sure about fighting or fleeing. He needed to relax them or they would bolt or attack. He decided to sit, taking off his crossbow first. "I was walking and hunting and heard you all coming along. You make a bit of noise if you don't mind me saying. Not a good way to keep low if you ask me."

"We aren't usually this far out of the city, we aren't used to being quiet, more used to making noise to survive." Jesus sat down as well.

"Out here you don't only have dogs to watch out for." Jesse thought it was going well so far. Still had to take it easy, these people were green to the forest, they'd be easy prey. It looked they had found that out already. It would explain the silence emanating from them. "What brings you up here? I don't get to see people from the city here anymore, not for years. Don't ask me how many, time has a way of passing out here without you noticing."

"You're from there?" One of the group asked him. He was a large man with a patterned shirt trying hard not to fit .

"A long time back. Came up here to forget about things and never seemed to have enough of a reason to go back." He scratched his head.

"There was a reason once, personal, but over the years it kind of faded and this became home." He looked around. "Such as it is, but I like it here."

Jesus knew it. "We never had reason to leave either. Until now."

"Is it still as bad as I knew it?"

"Worse ," said the only woman in the group. She was tallish, five ten or so. Slender, curvy. Jesse could hardly take his eyes off her but he did with a wrench. "And it's going to get worse soon."

"Worse?"

"Long story, the main reason we came up here in the first place." It was Jeremiah.

Jesse saw a man who was black and he looked intelligent. That was good up here. He could survive with some luck. Had sense too. He had wanted to interrupt the woman, make sure she didn't let anything slip. It made sense, they didn't know him enough yet to say more. Smart move, Jesse thought.

"You better come with me." Jesse had made a decision. "Looks like you could do with some food and drink." He waved in the direction of north. "I have room, trust me and you can ask me what you think I can do to help and I can decide if I want to."

"You look the trustworthy type." Jesus stood and led the group across the gully. "We'll come with you, how far is it?" They stood face to face, they were the same height.

"A few hours, two or three at most. I have food in my pack if you need any. As long you don't mind venison tartare and granola you'll be fine. It's fresh, real fresh." Jesse started walking and they followed. "So what happened out there?"

Jesus wondered how he knew. "What do you mean?"

"You looked like people who've lost someone. Someone pretty close right? Not judging you folks of course. I know the feeling well, been carrying it myself for quite a while. You get to know the signs when you see them in yourself every day. Feel them too."

"A friend of ours, they captured her not long ago. We would like to get her back but we can't."

Jesse kept walking but slower. "You were close to her huh?" Jesus didn't reply and the silence went deep. No answers there. "Where was she taken?"

"Back there, in the forest. It was my fault." Jeremiah said. He sounded forlorn, begging forgiveness.

"Don't blame yourself," said Jesus. "We don't know where, we don't know this area well enough. And we wanted to get out of there in case someone came looking for us." He didn't need to say who the someone was, Jesse's posture told him he already knew.

Jesse stopped. He knew with clarity who would have taken her and he shuddered. He didn't want to be in her shoes. "Take me there."

Heyusser took the call in a mood nobody would call good under any circumstances. "Yes?"

The voice on the end was quiet and without inflection, it was like talking to a robot. "We have someone you might want to see Mr. Heyusser," it said. "She says she is with some people who want to stop us and will try to."

Heyusser contemplated the words. He didn't doubt she was telling the truth. He knew whose voice was on the phone and he could be very persuasive when he wanted to be. His mood lightened . "How many does she say there are?"

"About twenty, sir. She claims they're going north, past the spire."

"Doesn't sound a lot." Heyusser pointed out.

"No sir. But every insurgent acts for ten others. They could pose a significant threat unless dealt with."

Heyusser remembered the call telling him to cut off the water. Getting more numbers wasn't going to be an issue for much longer. They'd be dead or close to it soon enough. "Bring her here. And look for her companions. If you find them you know what to do."

"Yes sir." The voice clicked off.

The quiet man turned from the radio to Maria. She'd had better days, but few were worse. A cut showed on her cheek and bruises were coming up under her shirt. She could feel the muscles stiffening around her ribs and shoulders. She moved her shoulders, her arms still tied behind her back. She shifted as best she could and grunted with pain. At least nothing seemed broken but she would be stiff for a few days. The interrogation had been rough. She'd told them things to send them in the wrong direction and look for more people. Jesus and the others would be able to go undetected for now. At least she hoped they would but it was the best she could do. It hadn't been easy, having to give up the information without making it seem it had been too easy. She'd kept the lie simple, easier to remember. She held her face blank, hiding any sense of victory. These men would spot it in an instant.

The leader came up to her, speaking to a soldier, they were soldiers she knew that, not some civilians playing war games to salve an ego problem. "Get my car ready." She heard him, they wanted her to know what was happening. They were going to take her somewhere and she had no choice but to go along. Some time bought would at least give her time to think of a plan. And time for the others to find her. She remembered the ghosts of old TV shows. This wasn't Survivor, it was survival in its purest form. No cover, no special effects. It was raw, primal emotion, the lust to survive at any cost.

"You're coming with me. Someone wants to see you." The leader bent over her, she could smell his breath, felt the death in his soul, he wore it like a familiar friend. He knew death well, had seen it and delivered it in turn but this was on another level. She kept herself closed, not wanting to give anything away.

She felt a sharpness in her as he bent over her, wanting to see her shrink back. The sharpness in her soul refused. It steeled her, she knew she was going to live for at least a day longer so she had nothing to lose. She stared back, unbowed. "Good, I was getting tired of this party anyway."

The leader smiled. It was like looking at the mouth of a rattler from the eyes of a mouse. "A sense of humor, interesting but you won't keep it for long after you meet him. That's if you do." He held her jaw, his fingers bit into her bone. "Accidents happen out here and no one will ever know what happened to you if one, must we say, befalls you."

"Not to me." She refused to buckle. "If I don't get there then he'll be after your ass not mine and you won't be able to think up an excuse good enough to save it." She almost grinned in his face. "You might want to keep that in mind."

He almost slapped her face but held himself back. "You might be right but you wouldn't be alive to know, would you?" He walked off. "Bring her," he said to one of the men.

The soldier hauled Maria to her feet and drag-walked her to the Humvee. The doors were open and he shoved her into the back without ceremony. She arranged herself into a sitting position and braced herself for what was going to be a rough trip. The doors opened in the front and the leader and a soldier got in. The engine hummed into life and the vehicle lurched forward, settling into a steady roll. She was right. The vehicle jounced and jarred its way along the forest and she wondered if the ride would ever smooth out.

Ishmael had found his way back to Andrew's house. The door was closed and the windows curtained off. It had the effect of keeping the outside world at bay, hiding the inside from view. Ishmael nodded to himself, Andrew was getting more secretive since he'd talked to him last. He knocked on the door. There was no answer and there was no sound from the inside to tell him Andrew was home. Ishmael hoped he wouldn't be long and he would have what he needed when he came back. Time was short and Ishmael settled down on the front porch to wait.

It was getting on for night when Andrew's return roused Ishmael from a reverie. He wasn't alone, a woman was with him. Her hair was long and matted, her clothes were rough and she bore tattoos on her arms and legs. She didn't smile at Ishmael, only looked at him with an inbuilt suspicion in her eyes. She followed Andrew into the house, showing him he was third in line here. She had a claim on him Ishmael couldn't compete with. Ishmael smiled to himself and followed them into the house.

Inside nothing had changed. Andrew opened the pack he had carried inside and laid several blocks of a substance on the table. Ishmael didn't know what it was but from Andrew's handling it wasn't modeling clay. The woman stared at the substance almost with reverence. Ishmael wondered about her state of mind. Andrew didn't seem to mind her attention, seemed to revel in it. "This might be what we need Ishmael," he said.

"What is it?"

"Explosive. Pretty powerful but as it is now, stable. I could drop it off a skyscraper and it wouldn't go off." He tossed a lump over to Ishmael who flinched a little when he caught it. It was heavier than it looked.

"How much will we need?" he asked.

"There's enough here to do the job. I've looked at the spire and how it's built. All we need do is enough damage to weaken the structure. Its own weight will take care of the rest." Andrew looked pleased. "Then it's bye bye spire and bye bye overlords. I hope they know what's happening, they'll have plenty of time to think about it but they won't survive the trip. What will the others think when it goes?"

"I hope it's enough to make them think twice about what they're doing. You know we have no water now?"

Andrew said he did. "Looks like having a bath is a thing of the past now."

The woman was still staring at the explosive lying on the table. "We should do it tomorrow."

Andrew and Ishmael agreed. "You can sleep here tonight Ishmael," Andrew said. "It will save us time in the morning. By night we should be close to the spire."

"Thanks," Ishmael said. He looked at the woman whose eyes remained fixed and wondered if he was doing the right thing.

NINETEEN

"I⊤ was here," Jeremiah said to Jesus and Jesse as they sat back in the trees. Jesse had followed the general path Jeremiah had taken, avoiding his twists and turns. It hadn't taken Jesse long to get there. Jesus wondered as they followed him if he hadn't been there before. He wondered who Jesse was behind the face he presented. The night had fallen, covering the ground with a blanket hiding everything under it. The men in the clearing were sitting around the still burning fire. A heap of fallen branches lay to one side to keep it going. The smell of burnt food and stale coffee hung beneath the trees. The air had a chilled edge. The winds were blowing from the desert, bringing lower night temperatures. It was a blessing after the heat and humidity.

"So where is she now?" Jesus asked.

Jesse pursed his lips and shook his head. "She could be anywhere but my guess is they've taken her east. That means Vegas."

"Which means against her will, doesn't it?" Jeremiah looked through the trees to the men camped a few hundred feet away.

"Generally the case when you get captured." Jesse said. "You stay here I'm going to look around." His eyes were bright in the dark. "Spread out and wait. Don't move, don't make a sound. They'll be patrolling the area and you don't want them to know you're here. They've got one prisoner already and they won't need others."

Jesse vanished into the night leaving the words hanging in the air. He was gone for a long time. Hours passed and in the air the night birds hooted and called amid the rattling buzz of crickets. The soft sound of owls after prey merged with the squeals of the taken. Surrounded by the dark, Jesus and Jeremiah waited. The moon had moved degrees by the time Jesse returned. They heard his movement and froze, relaxing when the sound coalesced into solidity. He sat next to them, putting some rifles on the ground .

"Like I thought. They took her to Vegas for interrogation. The boss headed out with her before dusk with one other driving. From what I heard the rest weren't happy staying here. They were going to come looking for you tomorrow." He scratched his head. "I heard you'd be good for taking out their frustrations. Don't ask me why they took her, no one in the camp knew. They were pissed they didn't get to kill her. After having some fun first. Whatever the reason it won't be good for her."

"What's east of here, and why Vegas? I thought it was long gone now." Jeremiah asked.

"You don't know much do you." Jesse said. "I should give you a little history lesson." He drew lines in the sand and leaf litter. "Years ago when the climate started to change for the worse a lot of people said it wasn't happening. It was all some big fucking conspiracy so they sat on their asses. Then when the sea started to rise and the climate went bat-shit crazy, some people started to get organized. Some blamed the governments, like they could do anything. Survivalists took refuge, and governments all over the world fell like dominos. We had wars. Starvation was a fact of life. All that happy horseshit. Long before it all went down the big end of town had figured out what was going to happen. They'd known for years. Even helped keep things confused to buy time while they built their escape routes. Up there." He pointed to the sky.

"The spire Maria could see from her apartment." Jeremiah said. "And from mine. The one with the encrypted feed I can't get into, that's where they went."

"What else do you know about them Jesse?" Jesus asked.

"Not a lot," Jesse responded. "Whispers and rumors is about it. Way back when a few people did stories on the spires. Most were nut jobs and dumbass conspiracy theorists, easy to ignore and discredit. No one gave much attention to them. So while people laughed and pointed and ignored the reality, hundreds went up. I've seen a few in my time, up and down the coast. Always inland or on high ground safe from the sea. And around the spires are little fiefdoms run by little men who take their orders from those who live up there. Our overlords. Some of the fiefdoms are bigger than others but the overlords don't worry about all that shit. They still have all the power, more since they don't have anyone challenging them. And they run the whole fucking world like they always have and no one knows or cares as long as they can feel like they're free."

"How did the fiefdoms come to be?" Jesus asked.

"And why do they surround the spires?" Jeremiah wanted to know.

"When the governments around the world collapsed, they left one hell of a power vacuum. And people rushed to fill it," Jesse replied. "Tech bros first, they had more money. Built massive compounds first but took to building spires when they felt it still wasn't safe on the ground. People protested and some were angry and far from peaceful but it got sorted out by the overlords. They did their deals to sort out who owned what patch of land and set the boundaries in place. Made things peaceful for the most part and they had their private armies for when they weren't. They still do, those guys over there are part of one."

"You said they knew what was coming?" asked Jesus.

"Knew about it? Hell most of them were making money from it. They made money from trying to stop it and from keeping it going. They owned everything in every country and they had the money to escape. Up there are the richest of the rich. Every immoral, money-grasping son-of-a-whore is watching us like a kid watches ants. So they built their escape from the shit-storm they helped cause and got off-planet. Not all the way though, despite all their money they couldn't go far despite what they wanted. There wasn't the tech to do it, still isn't. But there was the tech to build their escape, and to keep them supplied."

Jesus was alert. "Supplied?"

"They can't feed or water themselves up there. They still need what the planet gives them. The fiefdoms around them are no more than big-ass, glorified supply dumps. Food, drink, people. They take what they want. The best goes skyward. We get the crap left behind."

"Looks to me like things haven't changed." Jeremiah noted. "Way of the world, man."

"Yeah, some things never change much. And the other thing they owned? All the coastlines of all the countries in the world that has them. When the people escaped the sea most of the coastlines were empty except for the major cities. Most of it was ripe for the picking and there's one thing the rich know what to do. Pick up a bargain and keep it for themselves even if they had to purge a few places to do it. But you know already don't you or you wouldn't be here." Jesse stood. "That's a little of what you're going up against. But enough of the lesson, we have to get your friend."

Jesus watched Jesse. Jesse had a look to him he hadn't seen before. It wasn't anger, it was cold resolve, the will to succeed despite the odds.

"You said Vegas, how do we get there? Getting across the desert will be impossible on foot."

"I have an idea about getting a car to get us there. Lucky I know where one is." He strode off and Jesus and Jeremiah scrambled to keep up.

After a few minutes Jesse hauled them up where the tree line ended. In the glow of butane lamps a line of vehicles stood. Three guards stood on one side smoking, as if guarding them was below their expectations in life.

"Wait here, I'll find one we can all use." Jesse told them before sidling off, returning in a few minutes with a panel truck. He pulled up, electric motor humming. "Get in," he ordered. The doors closed behind them. "Let's get the others." Jesse aimed the truck down the road, lights on low beam, picking the way ahead.

"They let you walk up and take this?" Jeremiah asked.

"I didn't give them a choice." Jesse's tone stopped further talk.

Jesse jinked between trees, looking for where they left the others. He pointed into the back of the truck. "We can get dressed too, uniforms are in the back. They might be useful to get us through. How does it sound to be guarding prisoners?" Jesse chuckled as he swung the wheel to guide the truck through the trees to where the others were waiting.

An hour later they were heading toward Vegas, wondering if Maria would be alive when they got there. The high mountains were now behind them and the road sloped down in front of the truck. The desert sprawled either side under a moon that made the land white and the trees skeletal. The occasional billboard whirred past and old gas stops blurred in the windows. Barstow loomed ahead.

Then came desert and the border. Primm made them look in stupefied awe. Casinos lined the interstate. Signs shouted their names and enticed vacationers and drunks and gamblers alike. The contrast was immense. Affluence belched out of every structure. Jesus wondered if LA had once been like that. Then came lights bright like mini suns shining over arrays of solar panels that ran for miles over the flat desert floor. "They don't lack electricity out here," Jeremiah said.

The road had little traffic. The occasional military convoy ran down the opposite lanes. They held their breath each time, looked back to see if they would turn around. "Is all that for LA?" came a voice. Jesus couldn't tell who it was over the roar of the tires.

"I guess it is," another voice said, it was Jeremiah. "It won't be long before they flatten it like a carpet."

"Poor Ishmael." Adeline spoke.

"Poor us," said Wilton. "I said before we were following Ahab to his doom and now I am certain. We are all his crew, heading for the show-down with the white whale."

"Ahab died," pointed out Jeremiah.

"They all died," Wilton demurred. "Only Ishmael survived to tell the tale. They died at the hands of the whale, led to their doom by a madman. I doubt Ishmael will be as fortunate as his namesake. We won't be." He rested his head against the juddering side of the truck.

"You are not the most comforting of people, Wilton," Arturo said, eyes closed. Next to him Nathaniel sat with a rifle between his knees. "Almost as much as Nathaniel here pretending to be a guard." Arturo looked at the rifle. "I hope you have the safety switched off *amigo*."

Nathaniel said he did. The truck drove on, following its lights in the dark.

Jesus sat in the front next to Jesse. The hum of the engine and the drone of the tires almost calming to his soul. His thoughts centered around Maria. What had happened disturbed him. He felt responsible for her welfare. He was responsible for all who had come under his orbit and followed along and all those he had met along the way. Even Jesse who seemed to be able to take care of himself.

Everyone expected him to do something. He knew they did. No one followed anyone without wanting something for themselves. Maria wanted to know what happened to her parents; Arturo, his brother. He had nothing to offer them. They had come with him despite that. Joined with him on his campaign he knew had no real goal. Onlythe hope of stopping something someone, from destroying what he held dear. Did they think the same? He hoped they did. He couldn't tell them he hadn't thought of the consequences. They were only coming to his mind now. And as they did he wasn't able to do anything other than watch the road unroll beneath the wheels.

In his mind Jesus saw Maria as she moved, walked, and talked. He saw the flash in her eyes when she looked at him when she thought he didn't see her. Saw the pain when she talked about her parents and being alone in the city. Saw the strength beneath the surface and wondered if he had the same. He closed his eyes to the road and looked for her smile. It came rarely but lit her face when it did like a ray of light pushing through storm clouds. He saw the push and pull of her muscles in her arms and legs as she moved. He felt the stark realization of the hurt he had done to her because by dragging her into this. It cut deep into his gut and curled itself around his spine. It was cold.

It was his fault it had happened to her. It would be if anything happened to any of them who still followed him. Their faces swam behind his closed eyes and each one accused him in silence. The knowledge was beyond his ability to deal with. It cut across his soul like a knife dipped in acid. Every thought arriving in his mind added salt to those wounds, increasing the pain by degrees. He wondered what he would do if it ever got to be too much. He kept his eyes closed as the miles rolled past and tried to rest.

Jesse watched him out of the corner of his eyes. Jesus was one hard man to figure out. But he'd get there.

Sometime in the early morning, Ishmael shuddered and woke in the front room of Andrew's house. Goose bumps had turned his back into a relief map. He pulled his torn sweater back on, walked to the window and looked out onto the street. He heard breathing and turned to see the woman crouching by the door, watching him like a cat. The city hid itself in the dark and he couldn't see the mountains from where he was. They brooded there, hiding a multitude of woes and foes closing in on the city. The irresistible force soon to move against the once immovable city. The force was a Damoclean sword of men and machines. Above all the overlords watched and waited.

He rose and walked outside, it was quiet there, cooler. Around the back of the house he saw the spire stretching high to its vanishing point. Ishmael saw it as the beacon lighting the way to the future and yet leaving them out. He wrapped himself up in his sweater and watched and waited for the sun to brighten the eastern horizon. He heard a noise and turned to see the woman walking barefoot on the tall grass overgrowing the backyard. She walked up to him. "I know what you want to do, Andrew told me."

"I have made no secret of it. I don't talk about it much that's all. Whether it's a wise course or not is another matter." Ishmael searched her face in the dark and saw nothing.

"There is wisdom and there is woe," she said. "I forget the rest."

"But there is woe that is madness." Ishmael finished the quote. "You know Moby Dick?"

"My daddy used to read it to me, some parts of it I remember better than others." She faced the direction Ishmael stood. "It seems a good book for the times."

He looked at the woman, seeing her for the first time. Seeing more than a dirt-streaked bundle of ragged clothes. He realized she was younger than she looked. "You don't strike me as a reader of the classics."

"You don't strike me as much of a preacher considering what you're planning to do."

The point struck home. Jesus had said much the same thing and the truth still scored at him. "Sometimes even preachers have to take action and do what they need to do." He grinned in the dark. "Now I sound like John Wayne."

"I prefer Herman Melville," the woman said.

"So do I." Ishmael stared into the night and felt fate turn its face towards him. "So do I."

The woman took his arm and led them inside. She lay next to him on the couch and with her presence a close comfort he fell asleep in moments. She stayed awake longer.

Two men watched from the gondola as the day marched west across the world. There were no stars to see up here, the glare of the sun blotted them out. The men stood behind a glassteel window one inch thick and impenetrable. The two men waited for the day when even the moon would be theirs. It would be a great day.

Fleming chafed at the lack of space where they lived. Most of them in the gondolas did despite their size. But they had paid their price and had learned to deal with such things. At least they were safe here, able to live and rule the world below like they had until nature made them move. Fleming was dying and wanted things completed before the end came. The man standing with him was taller and wider. It was like seeing a bear next to a deer. He was hairy, his hair dyed jet-black. Where his companion was thin he was weighty to the point of corpulence. He smoked a lot, and was far more sanguine about matters. He had long put away his concerns about space. He needed little and lived in smaller quarters than most of the other residents. "Anything bothering you, Woodhull?" he asked his companion at the window.

"Things aren't moving as fast as I would like," Fleming said. "L.A. should be vacant but the idiots keep hanging on."

"How long has it been?" asked the ursine man.

"Three years. I had to order the water turned off to force the issue and weaken the population. It took less than four months to clear out San Francisco, six for San Diego and Tacoma. LA is another matter." Fleming watched the Earth come to life. "My backers are getting a bit touchy." He looked at the march of dawn. "Why they hang on is beyond me."

"You sound a mite testy Woodhull," said the other. "People don't always act in a rational way, experience has told us as much. Why not give the order? You've done it before in other places."

"Sentimentality Stephen, simple sentiment. I grew up there, not far from the barrios. They infested the city, filling it with gangs and drugs. They were a blot then and I expect it's worse now, the good people moved years ago leaving it to the damned Spicks."

"Don't let Hernando hear you say that."

"It wouldn't bother me if he did and you know it." Fleming reached for the cognac and refilled their glasses. "Still, it never hurts to put more pressure on, which is why I arranged for the water turned off. That will force a few out before I do give the order, no matter how much it pains me to do it to the city I owe my existence to."

"And the rest?"

"Collateral damage, isn't that the term? The sad result of progress is it doesn't stop because a few people don't get out of the way or can't keep up. People are always on the wrong side of the battle Stephen." He watched the line marking day from night as it advanced, crossing Vegas and moving to the coast. "Isn't it funny how some things cannot be stopped? Take the day and night, each follows the other, never stopping and never catching up to the other. Ancient tribes used to see them as parted lovers, never reunited. Even the bible has them separated forever from the beginning."

"But we've moved much farther from then."

"To the point where nothing can stop us as the people in my city. will soon learn." The intercom, a discreet appliance on his desk, buzzed. "Yes?" Fleming answered and sat listening for a few moments. The reply was a muted voice, Stephen wasn't able to hear what was being said and wouldn't pay attention if he could.

Fleming stood up after a time to stare out of the window. "And there are people wandering around in the mountains with some foolish idea they want to stop us. And will actually try. Amazing isn't it what some people will try and stand up for." He laughed, it was a harsh sound, devoid of any humor. "We will deal with them of course."

"With prejudice?"

"Extreme." Fleming watched the day as it dawned below. "Isn't the sun a wonderful thing?"

TWENTY

ARIA felt stiff as a board. The bruises from the interrogation had bloomed like macabre flowers. She winced every time she smacked into the side of the truck at every bump. Sunrise glinted through the windows. The wheels thumped down into the many potholes and rocks spanged off the chassis. She missed the aches in her feet walking gave her. "What a way to travel," she said to herself. A battered and faded road sign said a town called Jean was a few miles up the road. The population read zero.

She had become more certain with each rumble and bounce they were heading to Vegas and her life would end there. In the front the two soldiers hardly spoke. Maria tried to make conversation but it was a failure and she gave up. She wasn't going to learn anything that would make the effort worthwhile. The road ahead didn't curve, it jinked left or right as if on a whim. Whoever built it seemed like they were in too much of a hurry to worry about corners. Something in her gut told her she was in for some bad trouble when she got there and she hoped it would be worth it. She watched the signposts bring their destination closer along a blasted landscape. She was grateful she hadn't seen too much outside and was able to dream as they drove on through the night.

Now the desert stood out as the sun hit, turning it gold like the dreams of the gamblers who won and lost each day. She watched as creosote, Joshua trees, and sagebrush appeared and vanished. She soon tired of it and tried to look up the road as far as she could. She saw hawks circling in updrafts of warm air as the sun started to heat up the land like a hotplate. A flash of white caught her eye as a jackrabbit dove for cover in the rocks by the road.

In a moment of grim humor she thought it was likely the jackrabbit would survive the day when she wouldn't. "Run rabbit, run rabbit, run, run, run." She sang the old song her mom sang to her when she was a child. "Don't give the farmer his fun, fun, fun! He'll get by without his rabbit pie. So run rabbit, run rabbit, run, run, run!" Funny thing she thought, her world was ending and the rabbit would keep on trucking. She giggled and the leader turned in his seat. "I'd save your breath if I was you, you might not have many left."

"Nice to hear from you, I thought you'd lost the ability to speak."

The leader snorted and turned back to the road. He had no interest in another damned taco jockey, what she said or did. She belonged to others now.

The drone took off from Creech at 08.00. Twenty minutes later it flew over an area where the mountains trailed into the Mojave Desert. It took motion and still images. On one the images a ragged group of people gathered round a sputtering campfire in the shadow of the hills.

Five minutes later Heyusser was looking at the group. He zoomed in on them as they sat, unaware they had company. He was looking at his prey and he smiled without mirth. They were the ones he had been wait-ing for. He had no doubt. For a moment he wanted to see them, speak to the leader and find out their reason for being there. He decided the hassle from the overlords wasn't worth it. It was better for them to disappear into the camps. When they were out of the way he would report he'd dealt with them. It was better than killing them. Heyusser didn't mind extreme prejudice. He used it to maintain fear and servility. But not this time.

They would die soon enough but he would make use of them until they did. He picked up the phone to General Moore. "You know where they are?" It would surprise him if Moore didn't; news always passed through him first. Moore replied in the affirmative. Of course he had. "I thought you might." He listened for a few minutes, smiling to himself. "Thank you General, get some men ready. I want them picked up, no extreme prejudice at this stage. Yes I know those were the orders but I have my reasons." He listened for a moment. "The camps, separate them as much as possible. Let them know what their future is not." He put the phone down, the matter closed.

In the camp where they sat, as the sun walked across the sky, Gabriel looked at the fire. It was starting to sputter, about to go out. It had been hard going since he had gathered the group and set out east. People had been bickering like children and he had been hard pressed to stop it. Some had left to find their own way. Less than two dozen remained; more from not knowing where to go than from any sense of loyalty. They felt cast adrift with a lunatic they couldn't understand. Listless and fearful they were jealous of those who had left and wishing they had as well.

Now they sat, wanting to go somewhere but had no idea of where. The idea of somewhere became the reality. Ahead lay the desert. Behind them the only place they had ever known and it pulled at them like a magnet. They feared the future that they couldn't know and longed for the past they hated. LA had been their home; where they were was nowhere. Here the future had no meaning. They had nothing to look forward to and nothing worth going back to. They were static figures in the landscape, stone circles of humanity.

Gabriel poked the fire, knowing the rest would leave unless something stopped them. He knew that he could not be that something. He felt as they did despite what he'd told Jesus about taking them home. It was only his promise keeping him going, pulling against that tug LA had on him. "Come on bredrin." He rose and stretched his back then walked around the group, prodding them into movement. "We move now, not stay here in de open. We seen by Babylon." He looked at the sky. It was cloudless, empty, a speck glinted silver as if in response and vanished. He knew what it meant. They weren't alone out here; eyes were on them and he felt small as if still a child. Babylon was watching them. Better it was them and not Jesus. The group dragged itself together, listless like beaten dogs staked out in the sun. They grumbled at the sight of the desert. Some shook empty canteens and wondered if they would ever see them filled again.

"We have to cross that?" One of them, a man with torn pants and a remnant of a shirt asked.

"Yah we do but there be an easier way, Jah told I years ago," Gabriel replied with an assurance he didn't feel. "We follow the mountains north to the river then follow it east. Can't go across the desert without water Jah knows, need full canteens so we follow the water."

"Well I'm not going with you and sure as hell I'm not following the word of a man who has a God delusion," the man said. "I'm going back to take my chances there; at least we'll have a chance. Anyone with me?" He looked around, almost beseeching others to join him. A few hands went up and back down. Other stayed up, quavering with uncertainty

"Why go back, man?" Gabriel asked. "You die back there, you know it."

"We're going to die here too, Gabriel" the man retorted. He waved his arm around them. It was dirty and scarred. "And where the fuck is here anyway? It's a piece of dirt we're sitting our asses on. And out there? North, south, east, it don't matter. It's the same wherever you look. I don't want to die someplace I don't know. Only place I know is LA." He huffed. "I'd rather die there, you understand? And I'm not the only one."

Gabriel sighed. This was one bodderation to him and he found it hard to find the words to dispute the point. A part of him agreed with them. He wasn't made to lead but follow. Jah was leader and not him. He sighed again. He put his hand in his pocket. The bag of ganja was still there, untouched. This seemed a good time to smoke some of it. He pulled it out. "Tell you what man, we smoke the herb. We talk. We be irie then. If you still want to go back to Babylon you do with blessing of Jah. If not we go north. Yah?"

The man looked at the bag. It was tempting; he hadn't had a good smoke for so long he couldn't remember. "Alright," he said. "Let's talk."

It was a smoke they wouldn't get to have. "Dust!" someone called out.

They all turned as one in the direction a woman was pointing. A dust trail was heading towards them and they heard the sound of engines. Gabriel knew with dread what was coming across the desert and he felt his stomach clench. "Dis be badda thing, real fuckery here." Four vehicles were coming across the desert floor. Dust plumed behind them, hanging like veils. Even from here Gabriel could sense the menace they had with them. He remembered the glint in the sky from earlier and knew there was nothing they could do. There was nowhere to go under the gaze of the drones. No matter where they went Babylon would find them. Destiny has its own way of doing things and bringing things to pass. It was stronger than anyone knew, stronger even than Jah who was bringing things to an end for him. He felt calmer than he had for days. No more leading.

"We need to run, find somewhere to hide!" The words ran through them like a chant. They were about to run. If they did they would die. Hunted down and shot like vermin. Gabriel waved his arms. The chant slowed and stopped.

"Be bashy bruddahs and sistahs, they be knowing we here. Let's see what they be doing with us." He threw the bag on the ground. "At least they might be having water, yah?"

The group watched and waited as the vehicles drew closer. As they did they became three trucks and a Humvee painted in desert camo. They trailed far enough behind each vehicle to stay clear of the dust. Guns sat on the roof of the Humvee. The trucks were windowless. Sunlight glinted off windscreens and aerials whipped in the wind. Gabriel knew they meant business and they were about to find out their fate. A strange calm came over him as he waited.

The vehicles pulled up fifty yards distant. Doors opened and men in fatigues with rifles spilled out and marched toward them. One ordered them to stay still. "Do not move!" he called out.

"We be staying right here man, we not be wanting badda, you be cool and we all be cool, yah?" Gabriel replied.

"On the ground!" The leader barked.

Gabriel did as ordered, the rest of the group followed suit. Except for the man who'd wanted to leave. "Fuck you!" He turned and started to walk, there was no command to stop. The commander nodded to the men with him. There was a rattle of gunfire and the man lurched under the impact of the bullets and fell as if hitting a wall. Gabriel felt piss run free. "Dread man, dread," he whispered to himself. "I sorry fren Jesus, I try but this be the ending for us."

"Anyone else want to be brave or stupid, there's no difference either way," the leader asked. There was no answer, even Gabriel kept his silence. The leader nodded to the soldiers who ordered them up and marched them to the trucks and pushed them inside. They weren't kind to the captives. Then the convoy turned and drove back where they came. Destiny had put her finger on them, Gabriel knew. Only Jah could help them now. He looked at the soldiers in there with them. They were hard-faced. It was like looking at statues except you can read meaning into statues. Something in them was of their maker. It was like they were dead inside, they had no emotion. They were robots, automatons, without minds of their own.

Gabriel leaned towards the nearest of them. "You got water fren? I be thirsty, we all be thirsty. You help a brudda?" The soldier didn't answer. Gabriel sighed. It looked like a long trip. Gabriel watched the sun travel over the sky as they drove. No one talked as the truck rattled and bounced across the desert until it reached the main road east. It had been I-40 in better times; now the desert floor was smoother. On the road the truck bounced and rocked. By the time they passed Barstow the prisoners looked like one collective bruise. The guards passed canteens around for them to sip but they did little to assuage their thirst. The water was tepid and bitter. There was no food. Gabriel ran his tongue over his chapped lips and his stomach growled. No one paid attention to it.

Gabriel asked where they were going. No answer. He didn't expect one. Guards never had the best interests of prisoners in mind. It struck him hard to realize they were prisoners. He closed his eyes, leaving it to Jah to let him know their fate when he pleased. It was mid-afternoon when he got his answer. The trucks pulled up with a lurch and the ever present dust billowed around them. Gabriel looked out and saw a sign. Fort Mojave. The sign was bright lurid red and the letters were yellow. Gabriel was reminded of a pus-filled sore. The door at the back opened up and guards waved them out. Even the soldiers got out and stood with the guards, rifles at the ready.

They lined up in twos as ragged as they felt. In front of them stood a long wire fence held up by steel posts. Colored tops made it known the fence was electrified. Gabriel didn't want to test it. Behind the fence stood rows of low Nissen huts. Prisoners lolled around in what shade they could find. More guards with dogs patrolled the fence, inside and out. Other guards, silent as stone, pushed Gabriel and several others towards the gate. It opened to let them in and closed behind them. Gabriel turned as the guards herded the rest back on the trucks. Then they drove away and Gabriel knew he would never see those gates open for them again. "Jah protect me," he whispered.

Andrew woke Ishmael and the girl shortly after sunrise. If he wondered why the woman was sleeping with Ishmael he made no mention of it. "Coffee," he said, holding out two mugs. "Don't worry the water's purified."

"How much do you have?"

"As much as we need."

"We go to the spire today?" It wasn't perfect but the coffee tasted as good as any Ishmael could remember.

"Yeah we do."

"It won't be easy," Ishmael said.

"I know, it's a lot farther to reach it than you think," Andrew pointed out. "Plus if they're already looking for Jesus and the others they will be on the alert even more than normal. Getting past them will be the hard part. Then we have to plant the explosive and get out. Nothing more than a stroll in the park."

"Trying to lighten the mood?" Ishmael smiled.

"Only for you," Andrew replied. "It won't work for me, trust me I've tried." He busied himself with preparing caps and putting them into his backpack.

"I hope it's safe." Ishmael wondered.

"Until I hit the button." Andrew said.

"Not very reassuring."

"It wasn't meant to be since we don't have much chance of coming back." Andrew looked serious.

"Martyrdom has its benefits, Andrew."

"Except you have to die to become one." Andrew zipped up his backpack and slung it over his shoulders. "Let's get moving."

Ishmael said a silent prayer and followed Andrew out the door. The woman followed, silent again. He wondered if she would survive and if she wanted to.

TWENTY-ONE

HEYUSSER stood at the window. Behind him his morning coffee steamed on the desk. The day had started out well. He smiled. The group was picked up and dispersed and the other escapee was on the way and would soon arrive. He was glad he hadn't had them killed but kept the option for later consideration. He almost asked for a woman, one of the perks of the job he reasoned but he put it off for the evening. He decided it was time to let the overlords know. They would be appreciative of his efforts. The screen clicked on and a face filled the space. It was Fleming's lackey. Heyusser wondered if he ever slept. "Yes?" asked the face.

"We have picked up the group."

"Terminated?" Always the same monotone too, not one shred of an inflection.

"Taken to work camps," Heyusser informed the face. "Killing them seemed hardly worth the effort. They'll die there and this way they might at least be useful until they do."

The face didn't shift its expression. "You disobeyed your orders." It said after a staring minute.

"I delayed them. My judgment, my call." Heyusser stared back. It was like looking at an image frozen in aspic.

"It was an order." The face repeated as if there was a tape stuck in its brain.

"Down here we have a thing called initiative." Heyusser watched for any little tic to twitch a muscle in the immobile visage watching him. There wasn't one. "You could check your dictionary."

"My master will not like the change in plan." The face showed no emotion.

"Plans can change, and it's not a major change. If he doesn't like it you can always get rid of me and have my replacement dispose of them."

The face still didn't change. "I will put it to him." The screen went blank.

"Asshole," Heyusser said to himself. He pressed another button. "Any news on the arrival of the woman?"

"Twenty minutes sir. It's been slow progress with the state of the road."

"Bring her to me when she gets here. After she's waited a while of course." Heyusser clicked off. State of the roads, at least he had more people to help fix them. He poured a drink and sipped it as he waited.

The desert began to give way to the outskirts of Vegas. Maria watched as the first house went past marking the return of civilization. She didn't fancy her chances of finding out what happened to her parents. It had been so long ago but you never knew your luck and here was her best chance of a lead. At least she was still alive. She was grateful even though her gut told her something bad had happened to Gabriel and the others. Experience told her it never lied. About Jesus her gut told her nothing. It was silent like the empty crumbling buildings scattered along the sides of the road.

Then people started to appear like still life images. As they passed she saw them frozen in place. A man walking a dog; a woman with her purse, small child in tow; a light pole with a dog pissing against it. She watched the fragments like she was sitting at the movies watching a newsreel. They drove past houses that looked like pictures in a scrapbook. Whitewashed walls, fences with flowers crawling over them, lawns like carpets.

She was in a Neverland where time had stopped. It was a fantasy, a place where LA never existed. It was as if something or someone had erased all knowledge or memory of the city. Maria wondered where Jesus was and what he was doing. Was he still going and behind her somewhere. She wondered if she was going to see him again. She realized she missed him. His gaze lying between angst and serenity. The way he looked off into the distance, his eyes clouding over when the vision of what was coming filled his mind. She missed his willingness to try to do something despite the likelihood of failure. She missed the way he could calm them when they fretted with a word or a gesture. She missed the way his hair moved when the wind blew and lying awake at night near him listening to him snoring . His absence left a hollow place she couldn't fill. She wondered if she would ever see him again and the hollow place echoed her thoughts.

Maria didn't know but Jesus and the others were only a few hours behind. It had been a slow trip. Each checkpoint made them a little bit later, taking Maria further away. Distance and time chafed him. He fretted as the miles rolled by, marked by downed billboards, rotted barns, and old truck stops. They rolled through Jean, waving at soldiers as they passed through. Vegas lay ahead in the glittering distance, unseen, using Maria to lure them along the road. Jesse's hands stayed on the wheel. He hadn't shifted them in hours and his eyes looked through a windshield blurred with dirt and dead bugs.

"I'm going to pull over at the next stop," Jesse said. "We need to recharge and rest up a while. We need to be fresh when we get there if we want to help. Tired people are no help to anyone." He didn't mention Maria, there was no need.

Jesus didn't want to stop. Any delay hurt him like a knife in his spine. Maria needed them to get there but he agreed. Jesse was right, he felt the tiredness seeping behind his eyes and he stretched. Jesse pulled off at a gas station ten miles past Jean and rolled up to the one charger still powered. It was slow going as the truck recharged. They got out to stretch their legs. Adeline went inside to find what she could, not expecting it to be much. Jeremiah went with her. They came out with jerky, buns, water, a pack of Twinkies, and a twelve pack of soda. "Not the healthiest but was all they had left ," she said as she put them in the back of the truck. "It should be okay. I guess soldiers took the rest."

Over an hour later they rolled out and continued northeast toward Vegas. Jesse wanted to stay longer but Jesus said no. "We don't have the luxury of time." His manner brooked no argument. They remained silent and the dust swirled up behind them as they pulled onto the interstate.

The closer they got, the more the silence mounted as if they didn't want to face the inevitable. It was the best way to keep it distant. They kept their thoughts to themselves. Even Wilton's normal manner shifted to taciturnity. They brooded, drank slow and ate even slower knowing they needed to eat but found it hard. Unheeding, the miles continued to roll under the wheels bringing Vegas closer.

"I'm glad of one thing," Jesse said as he stared through the hazy windshield. He'd kept looking ahead since they had started driving. Jesus wondered how he could concentrate for so long. "At least they have their shit together about the roads." Jesus couldn't tell if he was joking or not. Jesse relaxed his grip and shifted his hands on the wheel. "Want to try and find some music? There might be something out there we can listen to."

Jesus played with the radio. Country music blared out of the speakers for a second before he was able to squelch it. Jesse swerved and recovered while dirt smacked the chassis as the truck slid off the road and came back. "Shit that was loud." He shook his head. "And what else would it be but country, it's always country."

Jesus cycled up and down the band. Most were country and he hated it. A rock station came and went and then the sounds of jazz issued from the speakers. Jesus leaned back and closed his eyes.

"Jazz man huh?" Jesse asked.

"Yeah but I haven't heard any for so long I'd almost forgotten what it sounded like."

"I like jazz myself," Jesse said. "Something about it gets to me where it matters, right here." He poked his chest. "It's from the heart, you know? Emotion."

Jesus knew what he meant and he signaled agreement. The jazz flowed through the truck and soothed. They said no more until Jesse poked Jesus' arm, waking him from a sleep filled with uneasy dreams. "Ten miles to city limits."

Jesus turned his head and watched the first building roll past. Then the second until they ran into each other, undifferentiated. He thought of Maria.

Vegas looked like she had imagined it from the old stories she'd heard. The strip lined with casinos. Signs telling of old of acts and shows and fortunes made with a pull of a lever. The casino lights were out. There was a glare in the morning light that made them look like washed out photos. The color had drained from them, waiting to come back when the sun went down. People shuffled from one casino to another hoping to find luck waiting for them. Unlike the people in the suburbs they looked almost hopeless, their eyes cast down at their feet. She wondered what was going through their minds. Then realized even here the people had no way out. They were more like the people of LA than they realized.

The car pulled off the strip into an area the signs said was the Arts District. Only a few sculptures on street corners and faded signs saying art gallery and museum gave away the past. The driver pulled up at the front of a building resembling a turtle. The realization stirred that this was her final stop. The driver got out and stood by the back door, rifle held loose but ready. The leader got out and opened it. "Out," he said.

She stood in a courtyard with flags arrayed on poles. Guards in uniforms stood each side of the entrance, rifles at the ready. Other armed men in uniforms paced up and down. There was a lot of security here she thought. She wondered for a moment what kind of building would need guards and knew she would soon find out. The leader grabbed her arm. "Move." She did.

Inside the building was light and airy, unlike what she had expected. An atrium lay under a glass dome and people in uniform came and went. The green of the glass gave a hue like being in a forest. The leader marched her to a desk where a bored man sat, watching computer screens. He looked up as they approached, his face asking the question.

"Prisoner for upstairs." The leader pushed Maria forward. "Mr. Heyusser's orders. He wants to see her asap, I would suggest you make sure he does."

The man nodded. He had a badge on his shirt telling whoever cared he was Security. Maria almost laughed, people in uniforms all around and they needed a security guard. Like most he was overweight. "Sign here." He pushed forward a clipboard.

The leader signed it. "She's all yours," he said. "Don't lose her, it was a long drive to get here and I don't want to think it was a waste of my time."

"We could have picked her up from you on the way, if that was a concern." The guard almost sneered. He'd seen enough people like the leader, small men with big ambitions ready to come back down to earth.

"As if. You'd get lost finding your own bathroom never mind our vehicle on a straight road." The leader looked at her for the last time. "I'd wish you good luck, but luck won't help you anymore." Two guards came up and cuffed her arms. The leader smiled. "End of the road lady, you're in their hands now."

They escorted Maria to a pair of gray doors. Behind them they closed with finality, marking her transition from human to nonentity. On the other side it was like a prison. The walls were white, only notices stopped them from being blank spaces. The floors were gray linoleum. Painted lines directed their steps past doors with numbers set above heavy locks.

Set in each door was a small window, thick glass inset with wire mesh. This was a prison and one door was hers. The certainty smacked her spirit. They marched past them beneath ribbons of fluoro lights, one guard at each elbow. They didn't say a word.

There was little point in protesting and she could no more run than an ant could avoid honey. They would gun her down before she'd taken a step and if she wasn't where could she go? She couldn't open any doors, they had thumbprint locks. She could only wait and see what happened next. What room was hers. Who would talk to her if anyone and who was Heyusser.

It didn't take long to answer one of her questions. The guards opened a door along the second corridor they marched along. Inside was a bunk, a chair, chemical toilet, and nothing else. A bare bulb burned in the ceiling. Like everywhere else the walls were white and the door was gray. Nothing marred the surface, no spot, not a speck of dust, not even a cobweb in the corner dared to appear. This was her home now. The door closed behind her and a brief hum told her it was locked. Maria lay down on the bunk and closed her eyes. She needed rest and wanted to be ready when taken to Heyusser. She could see nothing through the window in the door and the walls shut out all sound. It was as if there was only herself in the world, isolated. She knew it was aimed at breaking her spirit but she wouldn't let it. She closed her eyes and retreated into the place in her mind as she did every time there was danger outside. In her safe place she waited.

Time passed, as in the Casinos there were no clocks to mark its passing. Without her noticing guards looked in, checked she was still alive and moved on. More time passed. Minutes that felt like hours passed before the door opened. A guard came in and stood to one side leaving the door clear. Another stood outside in the hall. The first guard gestured and Maria did as ordered and left the room. She could have taken them but it would have been pointless. She wanted to see the man who wanted to see her and they would take her to him. The guards were like the rooms and the halls. Gray pants, white shirts, close cropped hair, pistols on their hips. In her mind they merged into one organism. They took her to an elevator and led her inside. She felt it rise, a soft push on the soles of her feet, No lights told of its progress. It came to a halt and she passed into a room with plush black carpet. A desk sat in front of expansive bookcases. A man with gray hair and a detached expression sat behind it, flipping through some papers. He looked up and indicated the chair in front of him. "Please. Sit."

She did as Rantall Heyusser ordered and waited for what was to come.

Ishmael sat under the tree, shaded from the sun. He rubbed his shoulders where the straps of the pack had cut into his flesh. He felt older than he had for years, tired to the bone and he wanted to sleep the day away. The woman sat nearby, Ishmael still didn't know her name. Andrew sat with his back against a spruce, eating some jerky, a water bottle by his side.

They had made good progress at first until the presence of the troops made their going slower. Andrew had led them the easiest way possible but it wasn't going to last. Ease was second to avoiding contact. Ishmael looked at the woman and she moved closer to him, sitting next to him. He liked her presence and wanted more of it. "What's your name?" Ishmael asked.

"Nancy." She sounded edgy, like she didn't want to give too much away.

He wanted to respect her wish and wanted to push her further to find her motives. Something had to lie behind the quiet. "Why are you here?" Ishmael asked.

"Why are you here?" A question answering a question. He knew he might only know what she wanted to tell him.

He knew the answer without thinking into himself. "I want it ended. Nothing more."

"Destroying the spire will end it for you?" She looked into his face, seeing what Ishmael couldn't hide.

"It will either be the end for me or the end for them." Ishmael looked into the distance. "I hope it will be the end for them so the city will live."

"Then what's the point?" Nancy scratched the dirt with her boot.

"Doing something is the point. A friend of mine told me that a few days ago." He thought back a few days. "Now he's out there, somewhere, trying to do what he can, same as us." He closed his eyes as they blurred. "I was a preacher once. I gave people hope but it was false. I hid behind words and ignored reality. Now I know what we need to do, draw a line and make a stand so the hope means something."

"A line in the dirt?" Nancy looked at what she had scratched by her feet.

Ishmael sighed. "Yes. And the spire is where we draw it, if we get there."

They watched Andrew get to his feet and wave them on. "We will," Nancy said.

Ishmael wondered what would happen then.

TWENTY-TWO

MARIA waited while the man finished what he was doing. As in the room like a cell there was nothing she could do but wait. She couldn't control what he did but she could control herself. She put herself back under the crumbled overpass when the wolves were waiting for her. She calmed her mind and blanked her face. Let him make the first move. He thought he held the upper hand but she did as long as she wanted. As long as she didn't let it slip with a bad play. She sensed he liked to be the wolf looking for a weakness. She would show him nothing. She heard papers shuffling on the desk. They rustled as they fell into place. She felt his eyes on her and raised her eyes to look at him. She assessed the predator behind the desk and what she should do next.

"You came out of LA?" he asked. His hands rested on the desk and he gave no hint of malice. He was as unreadable as a stone.

Keep it simple she told herself, it was easier to misdirect and not forget anything. "Yes I did."

"As part of a group?"

She thought back to the interrogation in the forest. No point in lying, he was confirming what he already knew and she wanted him to believe her. "Yes I was."

He ignored the unsaid. "May I ask why?" He steepled his fingers, the tips resting under his bottom lip.

"You may." She sat relaxed and upright. Her hands rested in her lap like pet mice.

"And you have permission to answer, no force involved. I ask out of idle curiosity, no other reason." He smiled. He looked like a viper about to strike.

She didn't believe him but held it to herself. He sounded like the good cop about to turn into the bad cop. There was something dark in him despite the words. She knew in a second he was a man who wouldn't stop at torture. He would have no compunction about it. Those who give the orders are worse than those who carry them out. "I'm not sure why, some wild goose chase," she replied. "A dream, *sueno.*"

"Ah yes, dreams, the things we use to keep us going when we lose hope. Martin Luther King had one once, it helped him in his life and you hoped yours would help you too, am I right?"

She didn't mind saying yes. "Don't they help everyone?"

The man nodded. "Yes they do, even me. My name is Rantall Heyusser," he said. "What's yours?"

"Maria, Maria Carranza. What am I doing here?" Take the front foot she told herself. Don't let him dictate.

The man stopped smiling and the atmosphere changed in the room. A worm of fear squirmed around her spine. "You know why, it's as I told you," he said. "I want to know why you came out of LA and what were you doing in the forest when we caught you. People don't escape LA for no reason. You and your group are up to something and I want to know what it is." He tilted his head as if seeing her for the first time and was weighing up what he was seeing.

"*Escaparse*, escape." Maria said.

"Escape? Why, would you want to escape? What is there to escape from?" Heyusser shrugged, enjoying the cat and mouse thrust of question and answer.

"Nothing. There was nothing to keep us, nothing, *nada*, better ask why we stay." She mock spat on the floor. "No power, no food, fighting to stay alive every day, nothing to keep us except death. As for the others, who knows. But we all wanted better, who wouldn't?"

Heyusser bowed a moment. "I can't argue since it sounds plausible. Yet," he leaned forward. His voice went quiet, ominous. "I fear you aren't being honest with me. Who did you come out with?"

Maria remembered what they had seen in Jeremiah's apartment. "Nobody in particular, a few of us who wanted to take a chance."

"No Maria, someone was leading you. And there were too many of you to be simple refugees. Do not lie, I know more than you think. Who was leading you?"

She shrugged to hide the impact of his words. "Nobody, everybody. What does it matter anyway?"

"It matters to me." Heyusser was blunt. "I don't like loose ends and not knowing who led you is a loose end. You know we caught the others and in time I will find out what I want to know. It's up to you how hard it will be on whether or not you join them. You should think hard. They are in labor camps and trust me when I tell you they are not pleasant places to be."

"Labor camps?" Maria felt shock and surprise follow each other through her soul. Then she realized he only had some, not all. They had split up by the time they caught her and Jesus and the others weren't with her. She'd have known if they'd caught Jesus and the others. They would have been in the truck with her and the man in front of her would have been crowing about it. She felt for those in the camps but Jesus was still out there. She kept her face blank by force of will against the flood of relief. She couldn't let Heyusser know there were more out there than he realized.

"Of course, we need people for various projects and they will be very useful. Here in Vegas, and elsewhere."

Maria saw him look up. "I don't know, we sort of got together and decided to get out. It was a group decision. It's happened before after all."

"But why did you leave them? There is safety in numbers and being alone out there makes little sense to me." Heyusser was on the trail and he clung like a terrier to a rat, wanting to shake the truth from her.

"They didn't want to listen to me when I said there was a safer route east." She tried to sound smug; it would help him believe her. "I didn't agree with where they wanted go and went out by myself. I was doing well until your men found me."

"That may be," Heyusser said. "But it doesn't help me to know why you left in the first place. Or why you chose to do it now and why there were so many of you." He tapped the desk with a finger and the sound was like fingernails on a chalkboard. "There is a reason you decided to leave now, not earlier and not later and you will tell me. But you can have some time to think about your answer. Overnight should be enough." He pressed a button. The elevator doors opened and two guards came out. They could have been the same ones it was impossible to tell. Heyusser nodded at them. "Take her away."

In the elevator Maria thought she had managed to dodge a bullet. The next time she might not be so lucky. She went back over the story she told in her mind as the guards took her back to her cell. Heyusser would call for her again.

Jesus watched Jesse angle the truck through the streets of Vegas. They were aiming for the old Arts District south of the Strip. Jesse was keeping as low a profile as they could manage, using residential areas as much as possible. As far as they had found out by vague questioning and vaguer threats it was there they would find Maria. A few buildings were empty but far from the scale of LA. It looked prosperous, alive. People walked the streets with a purpose, an aim. They saw no shambling wrecks of human beings hoping to survive one more day. It made him think, made him look and recollect to where he had been only days before. From sitting in a wrecked bar with notions of change in his head he was in the city of the overlords. All he had to do was figure out what he was going to do next and when.

The streets they went through ran between single story bungalows fronted with lawns. Flower beds exuded undisturbed placidity. It was a far cry from the strewn streets of his home. Far enough to make him wonder how two places so different could be in the same country and so close together. Then he realized the truth. These were the people who didn't know what lay across the desert and over the mountains and didn't care. These were the people who would let his city vanish and become a resort for those who lived above them. And they wouldn't bat an eyelid when it happened as long as they weren't disturbed. Nothing mattered but their world.

Jesus thought of LA steamrolled into oblivion. He saw in his mind the images of other cities redeveloped over the bones of buildings and people. They would never feel the ghosts of the dead who made way for them. None of the overlords knew the scarecrows shambling along the streets looking for a meal. None of them had to watch for the wolves that would take the sick and the wounded. Jesus did. He wanted those who refused to die and struggled day after day to live to see the next sunrise.

There was a dignity to the broken bones of LA he didn't see in Vegas. It was like coming from someplace real, true, to a lie so all-consuming it had become reality. But it wasn't his reality, not Jeremiah's, Wilton's, Maria's, and the others. This was the reality he had come to change. Only he didn't know how.

He sat in the seat and watched in silence as the streets, houses, and apartments rolled by. Then small offices with neon signs in the windows that morphed into office blocks, malls, and cinema complexes. In the distance the temple casinos lined the strip. They still supplied the glitz and glamour. Kept the minds of the people away from the truth, kept them brainwashed. The overlords had dominion. He faced the question of how they would react to the challenge, he didn't know the answer and hoped the others wouldn't ask him.

Jesse piloted the truck to a stop in the forecourt of a Motel 6. He turned to Jesus. "Okay, now what?"

Jesus stared out of the windshield. "We get Maria." He knew how. It was the only way.

"How?"

"I don't know yet *compadre*." Jesus smiled at the world outside. If he told them they'd stop him going. "We may need to wing it."

"Sounds like a good plan, let's see what happens then huh?" Jesse turned and opened the hatch to the truck. The others were sitting, eyes closed. They stirred when the hatch opened. "Time to get Maria."

Wilton spoke. "Once more into the breach dear friends."

"You don't have to quote books that's Ishmael's job." Jeremiah punched him on the arm.

"Ah friend Jeremiah, books say what one wants to say most of the time, and a lot better. What's the plan?"

"Jesse and I will go to the building where she is to check it out and see if we can come up with something get her out. I do have something in mind. We'll leave you here. It's somewhere safe to hole up. We'll be back later to get a plan together." They started to protest but Jesus waved them off. "This isn't negotiable, I can't risk you like I risked the people with Gabriel."

Adeline leaned forwards, hands on her knees. "They've caught them anyway. None of them had any idea how to get over the desert and with the drones flying around, a big group is easy to spot."

"Or they're dead." Nathaniel pointed out.

"You could have saved them, kept us all together." Adeline glared at Jesus. "You sent them away knowing what could happen. They could die."

Jesus knew the truth. "It was their choice to go or not. It was a risk either way. Can you say they would have lived if they'd stayed with us? Can you say we didn't face the same risk of death or we don't face it even now?"

She couldn't.

Jesus continued. "I don't know if they are better off where they are or not." He turned to face the world around them. "But it's better for you all to stay while Jesse and I go see where they have Maria. We must go alone. You cannot come with us, not in there."

"They might prefer three birds in the hand than one. We could lose both of you." Wilton pointed out.

"I expect so, but there is no choice. And it might not happen. I expect we'll be back soon."

Wilton didn't speak; none of them did while they sat in the truck; the sun beating down outside as it rose. Wilton fidgeted in his seat. "It will soon be like an oven in here and I do a very bad imitation of a roast pig. Let us go inside where it's cooler, see if we can get a room to wait in."

Ten minutes later they were waiting in adjoining rooms, the door open between them. They sat in weary silence, grateful for the lack of noise after hours on the road. The silence held while they waited as Jesus and Jesse went to get Maria.

Inside the truck, it was also silent. Jesse said nothing as he drove; following the directions on the GPS. Jesus sat; thoughts running through his mind he couldn't stop and didn't resist. They ran like an unending tape. Maria's face swam in and out of focus, the line of her jaw, the curve of her back. The thought he might lose her wrenched at him. The knowledge he might be the cause, almost tore him in two. She wasn't responsible, he was and unless he got to her she would pay the price he knew was his alone. His freedom didn't matter if she had none.

The building that looked like a turtle loomed ahead. People walked in and out past deep levels of security. Guards stood in numbers calculated to deter. Around their shoulders automatic weapons hung loose. Jesus and Jesse saw more behind the full length glass windows. Jesse pulled up in a space marked for official vehicles and grinned at Jesus. "We aren't official but they don't know that."

Jesus nodded. He puffed out a breath. It felt like life left him. "It looks like force isn't an option."

"Good thing we don't have any then," Jesse responded.

"There's one thing in our favor though," Jesus spoke as he looked at the building.

"What?" Jesse asked.

"They might not expect the soft approach."

Jesse knew what Jesus was going to do. "You lied to them back there, didn't you?"

"I had to. They would have tried to stop me. I couldn't allow it."

"When did you decide?"

"When we got to the motel. I had to make them think I was going to do something different. You understand?"

"I do, a man's gotta do and all that shit, right?" Jesse wondered at the singularity of purpose Jesus had at that moment. He almost admired him and felt he was stupid at the same time. "Why?"

"They want me, not Maria. I'm offering myself as a trade." Jesus looked again at the brooding building.

"Risky," Jesse said.

"It gives me the chance to talk to them, save the people and city. Keep them from looking for you. And it's what I came for."

They sat in the truck for a minute longer. The sun beat down on the city like a hammer. Jesse broke the humid silence. "How are you feeling, Jesus?"

"It sounds stupid but I feel like I'm being dragged along some street in Jerusalem to meet Pilate."

"That makes me Judas then?"

"No, but it doesn't matter much either way does it?"

"I guess not." Jesse opened the driver's door. "We'd better get moving."

Jesus got out into the full sun. He stood for a moment in the glare. "Better make this look good," he said.

"Yeah I guess." Jesse pulled some cuffs out of the truck and turned Jesus around by the shoulder. He wasn't gentle. "Making it look good." He slipped on the cuffs and tightened them.

Jesus winced. "No need to try too hard."

"You can thank me later. Let's move." He shoved Jesus forward, almost toppling him over on his face. "Move it." He spoke louder to make his voice carry. Guards watched them get closer, parting like the waters to let them into the building.

Inside Jesse marched Jesus to the same desk Maria had stood in front of hours before. A different man sat there; his neck sloped into his shoulders balancing a small head. He wore sunglasses and hadn't shaved for three days. Jesus wondered if he was cultivating what passed as style in his life. "Yes?" the guard asked, as bluff as his looks suggested.

"Prisoner." Jesse shoved Jesus forward and his breath huffed out as his stomach smacked the counter.

The man pushed a clipboard at them. "Sign here."

Jesse signed.

"Where is he from? We had another in earlier today; the boss was anxious to see her."

Jesus kept his face blank. Maria was here. He was almost relieved. "He might want to see this guy too. We picked him up in the mountains outside LA. It took me a while to get him, led me on quite the chase." Jesse was chatty. Jesus realized he was quite the actor. "I thought rather than take him somewhere else he might have information the boss might like to hear."

The guard put the clipboard away behind the desk. "Paperwork, wasn't it supposed to vanish when computers first appeared?"

Jesse laughed aloud. The man pushed a button and two guards came out from the doors Maria went through. He looked at Jesus and grinned with no mirth. "After we've got the information from you we can send you to the camps, new labor will be handy. There's always a place for someone with youth on their side and a bit of stamina."

Jesse wondered if the man couldn't do with some exercise himself. "Okay if I wait here awhile? I'm kinda beat from the drive and I could use a coffee like I never thought."

"Sure thing buddy," the man said. "Over to the right we have a canteen. They have the best burritos this side of the border if you want something to eat."

Jesse thanked him and turned to Jesus. "I can't say it's been a pleasure buddy, I'll have these blisters from chasing you for days." He walked off, limping for effect.

The guards took Jesus by the shoulders and led him away behind the doors.

The spire stood glowing in the late afternoon sun. It was a beacon lighting the way for Ishmael, Andrew, and Nancy. It beckoned them, leading them towards it and the destiny it would bring them. Lights glowed over the hills that lay between them and their goal. The low hum of engines echoed in the hills. They spent the night feeling as if they were treading the valley of death.

TWENTY-THREE

J ESUS made no fuss as they took him. It would have been futile. It was part of the choice he'd made when he had led them out of LA. He knew it couldn't be otherwise. Here were the people he needed to see, here was Maria. The path he started on when he was walking to Wilton's bar had brought him here and it still hadn't stopped. It beckoned him through the doors. So he went with the guards along a bland corridor. Closed and blank doors watched them pass.

The guards escorted Jesus along the along the same corridors they had taken Maria. They came to the same elevator and waited. There was no speech. The doors opened and Jesus stepped inside, one guard in front, the other behind. Both were close enough to intervene if Jesus tried to escape. It was second nature, unquestioning, learned over years until done without thought. The idea of Jesus not wanting to escape didn't come to them. That a fly would enter the web by choice was unthinkable.

The guard in front pushed a button and the doors closed and the elevator rose then stopped. Jesus followed along a corridor until they reached a door like all the others. Jesus realized this was where he would remain until the next step, he wasn't going to see one of the overlords yet. They wanted him to wonder when he would. He didn't know what floor he was on but it wouldn't matter if he did. He closed his mind to thinking and stayed in the moment.

The moment was all that mattered. At each moment he had to be ready for the next. He stilled his imagination. He wanted nothing to distract him until the inevitable meeting. Like Maria he couldn't do anything about the wait. The guards pushed him into the cell; the door closed behind them. Like Maria's, it was sparse. The guards removed the cuffs and he sat on the chair, facing both of them.

He decided to speak and see whether it would affect how long it would take for him to see the overlords. He saw no harm in stirring the pot a little. "I am, or was, the leader of the group who left LA several days ago," he said. "Your leader would like to meet me." He saw them look at each other and felt a warm glow. He had made them question something. "You might want to tell him I'm here. We need to talk." He closed his eyes and lay down on the bed. The guards left. Jesus heard the door shut as the guards left. If he cared how long he would wait, he gave no sign.

In the sky the drones continued flying. They flew at will, the pilots weren't worried about stealth. The time for secrecy had gone. At night they flew lower, images enhanced by IR optics and thermal cameras. They missed nothing and the images streamed back to computer banks.

Experts pored over the data and images in a building shaped like a half-pipe turned upside down. They ran them through programs, determined what was happening and kept watching. Caffeine and energy pills kept them going. They watched moving images of people, stills of others frozen in mid-activity. They watched the crowds in front of The Cathedral and the Campanile. Some images showed people in mid-speech, their arms thrown out in supplication. They reported what they saw then left others to make the decisions.

They had done their job and done it well. What happened after they made their reports was of no concern to them. They lacked the imagination to consider anything that didn't appear on their screens. Dead, captured, interrogated, and imprisoned people were collateral damage The men and women sat, watched, recorded, and reported every day of every month. There were no windows to the outside, no clocks to measure the time. They sat at their desks until told it was time to leave or allowed to have a break. They didn't know what the outside world was anymore. Finding out there was one when they came out at shift's end often made them blink in surprise.

General Moore had the reports and photos on the desk in his office. Splashes of color from highlighter pens marked out targets of interest. He looked at the images, made notes on a pad, and assessed what to do next. He knew the command to send the troops into action to come down on LA like a wolf pack was imminent and he wanted to be ready when it did. Not for Heyusser but those over them, sitting high above the Earth, immune and inviolable.

Moore's office looked like a caricature. A flag he'd sworn allegiance to years ago when he first enlisted stood in one corner. A map adorned one wall. A model cannon sat on a corner of the report-strewn oak and leather desk. Medals lay on felt cushions in a glass fronted cabinet under micro spotlights. Some were his. Opposite the map were photos of men who fought in the recent resource wars. They looked proud accepting medals, and parading in ranks at military schools. One of them was Moore. The remaining wall was bare apart from a framed diploma and surrounded the door to the office. At his back, a row of picture windows looked out on the airbase.

Around LA the noose was getting tighter. The defunct city stood on its platform, not knowing when it would drop to its death. Moore walked into an adjoining room and the light flickered on. A table in the center sat under spotlights. On it was a relief map of the city and the surrounding mountains with push pins showing the arrayed forces. Moore liked technology as much as the next man but a relief map was tactile. It gave him insights a computer image never could. He walked around it, touched it, and smiled at what he saw. It was coming to the time to let loose the dogs of war and send them howling down the hills into the city. It made him feel very good.

In the motel rooms, the air was as silent as it was when Jesse and Jesus left. Then it was as if noise had run from the vacuum their absence created when Jesse returned. The questions had run fast. Jesse had answered them as best he could but he couldn't say a lot. He'd been gone for three hours by the time he returned. He'd waited in the cafe as long as he could before leaving without them. The others weren't mollified, they'd wanted Jesse to come back with both. Adeline most of all, she wanted to go and get them out. She demanded the keys but bowed to the inevitable and sat down. She wasn't happy about having both of them behind prison walls and felt more helpless than ever. Jesse understood. He felt the same way. Jeremiah sat next to her and put his arm around her shoulders. It didn't help.

Not knowing was the problem. It always is for people left wondering with no way to find out and unable to stop the imagination. None of them could come up with anything. Their suggestions ranged from vague to ridiculous. Wilton pondered it more than the rest. Jesse had distanced himself, keeping his mind clear. Arturo still wanted to know what had happened to his brother and knew he was no closer. It niggled at him; a flea bite in his mind he couldn't scratch.

Nathaniel wondered why he was here. He felt he was in limbo. He'd had his reasons for coming on what was to him, an adventure; a little more like being in a Scout troop. He had wondered most of his life what lay behind the mountains but had been too scared to find out. He'd avoided the question too long and found himself in the middle of the answer he'd never wanted to find. It lay all around, inescapable and inevitable. It was death. Around him he saw the dealers of it, the soldiers armed with assault rifles and more.

Something was behind the death that surrounded them. Something or someone needed to have it around to deal with those who tried to change the world. Someone needed death for a lot more than wiping an eyesore from the land. He wanted to know more, who were they and why did they need the coastal areas. And why now, after all this time were they making a move. He had to ask someone. Nathaniel walked over and tapped Jeremiah on the shoulder. It was a start.

Jesus was sitting in the cell, heedless of the passage of time. He looked for, and found, something deep in his mind; it kept him focused. He was at the mercy of others he didn't know and couldn't, at least yet, reason with. The time would come when he met the man he had come to see. He kept his mind calm so he could react better, and not be at the mercy of those outside the cell door when they came for him. He allowed no thought of Maria and the others to distract him. He kept his eyes closed, waiting.

Maria was waiting as well. She knew Heyusser wanted to speak to her again. It was up to him when he would. It didn't take long. The door opened. A guard came in and gestured to her to follow. "Do you people ever say anything?" she asked. There was no response, not even a nod of a head. It didn't surprise her, it would be far too much to expect. In the elevator she thought of the meeting she was going to.

In the room on the top floor Heyusser still sat behind the desk, looking like a gargoyle. Maria stepped out of the elevator when the door opened. It was like going into the lair of the spider. She wondered for a moment if Heyusser ever slept, he even wore what looked like the same suit. She didn't let the emotion she felt show, at least she hoped. "What do you want?" she asked Heyusser, taking what initiative she could.

Heyusser said nothing but poured some golden liquid from a bottle into a glass. He held it out to her and smiled like a wolf. "Have a drink."

She sat in front of the desk and lifted the glass and sniffed the contents. She looked at Heyusser, puzzled at what he was doing.

"Cognac, the finest money can buy." Heyusser leaned back, the chair he sat in creaked a little. "Power has its privileges you know, having money and the finer things in life are part of it."

Maria sipped the cognac it burned a warm, sweet trail down her throat. "Not bad, not my taste though. I prefer tequila. You aren't showing me this for nothing, are you?"

Heyusser smiled a thin smile. "Ah yes, tequila. The Hispanic side of you no doubt. Or is that a stereotype?" He put his glass down on the desk. "And no. I'm not. The reasons will become clear later."

Maria smiled back. "I'm not the only one around who likes tequila. Lots of *gueros* enjoy it too, if you haven't heard." She mimicked Heyusser's position. "Only there's not much of it around to enjoy where I came from," she said, remembering Wilton's grubby old bar. The memory brought sadness and anger with it. She downed the cognac to hide her face.

"True, sorry for being insensitive."

"I'm from LA," she said. "We deal with it. You should know." She put the glass on the table. A thin trickle of cognac ringed the inside of the glass before pooling around the base of the glass. Maria watched it.

Heyusser watched her. He wondered when it would be worth telling her the news. Not yet, he decided, he'd let the scene play itself out a little first.

"I do, still we can all learn something from each other and from new experiences, correct?" He gazed out of the windows for a minute and Maria waited for him to speak. "I want to know more about the group you came out of LA with, who they were and so on. To be honest I was a little worried about the one who said he was the leader when we picked him up. He didn't seem the type people would gravitate towards; lacked charisma. Help me and you can get all the top-shelf tequila you can drink among other things. I am after all in a position to help you a lot."

"You needed to see him in the group, it worked for us." What was he leading up to and why her? What was he going to offer in return for the information?

"But hardly a man you would follow, wouldn't you agree?" Heyusser poured some more cognac into the glasses. "A toast," he said. "To absent friends."

Maria realized with a sudden shock of clarity what he was up to. He had a bad poker face and couldn't conceal his glee at being so close to the answer he wanted. So be it, she thought, I'll give him the answer he wants, but not the one he needs. It would take him hours to find out otherwise. She watched him as he drank. She remembered her father would have the same look on his face and her mother could always tell. Then she took him down with a stare or a well-chosen phrase. Then they had vanished. Here she was still wondering what happened to them. She knew too finding out was a vanishing point in the distance. "What do I get if I tell you?"

"Straight to the point, I like that." Heyusser grinned like a cat. "As long as it's not overused. Small talk has value after all." He tapped the desk. "What would you like? I can help if it's at all possible. It's the least I can do for a guest."

"I'm not a guest I'm a prisoner so don't play games. I can read you better than you think."

"No games, I was only hoping we could get to know each other. I know you must be after something out here, why else try to get over the mountains? It wasn't to follow the man we captured and we both know it. Nobody would try." Heyusser shook his head and fake empathy oozed around him. He swung to look over his demesne. "And not people like you. Something else drove you and it was more than you have told me. So let me know what you want and we can make an arrangement suitable for both of us."

Maria wondered if she should tell him. She didn't want to give him any advantage she felt she had. It felt as if she was in a chess game, a novice against an expert. She decided to tell him enough. "I want to know what happened to my parents. Nothing more, nothing less." Which she knew wasn't true. "Give me what you know and I'll tell you what I can."

Heyusser raised his glass. "You have a deal." She was deep in the game, wondering who would first claim checkmate. She hoped it would be her.

TWENTY-FOUR

JESUS was sitting on the cot with his legs crossed in front of him. His breathing was slow and even. He was calm, withdrawn. The window in the door opened once, then once more a few minutes later. Eyes he didn't see looked in at him, saw no movement, vanished. The window slid shut. He paid no attention. There was a reason he was being kept waiting. He didn't know what it was and he kept his mind from thinking of it. He'd heard long ago the old police would keep a prisoner alone for hours to soften them up, get them to talk. Yes that was it.

Songs ran through his head and when he got all the way through one he enjoyed it. Then he sang it in his mind one more time. He found himself enjoying the solitude. The last few days had merged into a blur populated by faces and sounds he couldn't control. All wanting something different and pushing him against his will. He was at the center of a whirlpool, buffeted and shaken; unable to find the peace to think. Odd to think how the peace and quiet he needed came in a place he wouldn't have expected. He had the time and he used it. In the closed area around his soul, kept out by old songs, he didn't notice its passing.

In the motel room the others were chafing at their inactivity. Wilton was the most aggravated. He paced up and down, from room to room, and in circles. He drank coffee after coffee. The rest watched and tried to calm him without success. "I am very tired of waiting around, it is most wearing on my mind. I want to go outside, and I want to go now. Is there a problem?" He stood with a fighter's pose, an angry man with nothing to take it out on.

Nobody could think of reason to stay indoors. Jesse almost snickered. Wilton looked more foolish than brave but he couldn't argue against him. "We're all feeling bored, so since the truck is outside, who wants to have a look around?" Wilton dared someone to stop him. Everyone agreed. Minutes later they were sitting in the truck, watching the suburbs roll by.

It was the same as when they first arrived in the city. The buildings stood whole and clean, whitewashed brick and picket fences. In front of them people watered, weeded, and mowed their lawns as if there was nothing abnormal. The coterie of people in the truck sensed the banality of the normal around them. It was as if they were watching an old sci-fi movie where the people were no longer people. When someone looked, it was without interest, devoid of curiosity. The roads were smooth, unobstructed by the corpses of cars or people. No wolves or mountain lions patrolled the streets. Over the roofs of the houses, the spires and heights of the high rises overlooked them, reflected the sun. It was a difference as stark as between light and dark. Here tidiness ruled instead of the broken glass and concrete. Yet it seemed as if it was a forced order, a veneer over the chaos. Something dark lingered on the edges.

In the truck Wilton wondered if the people they passed noticed they were different. They felt as if they were refugees in a hostile land. Most of them shrunk down in their seats like rabbits trying to avoid a hawk. Only Wilton sat up straight, staring at the new world they were in. The road rolled under their wheels, only the odd jolt from a pothole moving them in their seats. Downtown drew closer as they circled around trying come to terms with where they were. They avoided thinking about Jesus and Maria. They could do nothing for them and the paralysis of uncertainty lay in wait if they did. To stay sane, they watched the suburbs and the city pass by and thought of other things.

After an unknown period of time Wilton spoke. "Have you noticed anything?" he wondered aloud.

The others turned their heads to look at him, even Jesse took his eyes off the road for a second. "Noticed what?"

Wilton kept speaking. "Soldiers, police, have you noticed how many uniforms there are? Even in the old times I remember nothing like this, not in pictures or print or old TV shows. Yes, they were there but here it's another league." He watched a patrol car pass going the opposite direction. Two burly men sat in the front wearing sunglasses. It gave off a menacing air, palpable even in the truck.

"Now that you mention it, there have been more patrol cars than there should be," Jesse noted. The patrol car accelerated away with a sudden blare.

"Lots of crime?" Nathaniel asked.

"Hardly seems to reek of it," Wilton remarked. "Everybody looks like poster children for prosperity. So why are there so many soldiers and police?"

They shrugged as one, even the truck seemed to shrug with them. "That's why it's so peaceful, nobody can commit a crime and get away with it," Jeremiah said.

"I doubt it," Wilton said with a touch of asperity in his voice. "No crime or little crime needs few police; there is no reason for them to exist. This is very different. Something is very wrong here. The people behave so well out of fear, not of committing a crime but of something else. That's why they dare not look at us or they show any curiosity. They don't want to draw attention to themselves. They are scared." He sat back and looked out of the window at the rows of cultivated trees and the scrubbed clean city.

Jesse watched as another car rolled past. Three men wearing suits and the same dark glasses sat inside. "Scared people are the easiest to control," he said. "Give them the illusion of security and they will give up everything else. They always have and governments know it. Even before the overlords took over and we lived in a democracy, that was the case. They play a long con to keep us in our place."

Down the street a Humvee sat at a crossroads. Machine guns and antennae made it look like a bizarre beetle. Nobody seemed to mind it blocking a lane. The cars ahead of them drove around it not looking as they did as if not wanting the soldiers inside to notice them. It was odd, when Jesse thought about it. Odd and scary. He didn't like it. They passed by; the air of menace almost visible. Jesse wondered if the people knew the cost they were paying.

"And another thing," Wilton said. "Everyone looks the same, have you noticed?"

They looked out of the truck at the people on the sidewalk.

"They look different to me," Jeremiah said.

"Not their clothes or their looks," Jesse clarified. "It's their manner, how they walk. Eyes ahead, a nod or a wave but nobody stops to talk. It's like they can't or won't interact with each other."

"I can understand why," Adeline said. "I wouldn't want to stop in case the cops asked me what I was doing."

"We should pull over in a parking lot by a store." Wilton said. "Let's observe until we draw attention to ourselves. And with all these authority types around it might not be long."

Jesse pulled over into a parking lot and they waited with the engine idling in neutral. People walked past, one by one, no more than two. All were neat, trim. Nobody stood out. After ten minutes they coalesced into a generic mass of humanity. Nothing to distinguish one from the other.

"I can't remember what any of them look like even when I've seen them," said Jeremiah.

"They all look like they shop for clothes at the same store," Adeline said watching a couple walking a dog.

"It's a fucking police state. No wonder everyone doesn't stop to talk, Do they have a law about illegal assemblies?" Arturo spoke the thoughts they all had, as more police and military vehicles rolled past. "They must have a good secret police set up here too. The last two walked by had their eyes on us. If we didn't have this truck, we'd be in cuffs by now, *bastardos*."

"Time to move people, let's see if we can get our friends out," Jesse said finally. "We'll keep going in a roundabout way, check escape routes onto the Interstates if we need them." Jesse pulled out and headed to the building where Maria and Jesus waited. He didn't tell them he thought it was a fool's errand.

General Moore was waiting by the phone for the order. LA was on the scaffold and the man with the mallet was ready to knock out the support. Then LA would die. The prospect was giddying. If he could salivate he would. The phone buzzed. Moore picked it up, he'd expected it to be Heyusser. Being correct disappointed him. Only the thought it wouldn't be him one day gave Moore some comfort. "Is everything ready?"

"Yes sir," Moore replied. "I'm waiting for the last recon groups to report to make sure of the plan and make changes if I need to." He picked up the file of photos taken thirty minutes ago on the last drone flights. He'd canceled them after they'd taken off. There was no point in sending any more. "I can forward the last images if you like."

Heyusser's voice demurred. "No need General. Let me know when you're ready. Our overlords would like to know the state of affairs before we give the go ahead but be certain it will be tonight."

Moore assented and hung up. He pored over the images, a large group still gathered around the Cathedral. Moore guessed the crowd at a couple thousand. Moore thought it must be most of the remaining population. It made things easier if it was. He disliked having to send men into houses, having one big gathering made an easier target. One drone strike and the city would be empty. He would still send in the troops of course, they needed to feel useful. He waited for the phone call, eyes closed.

After he made the call Heyusser walked over to the windows to look out over the vista beneath him. Down there little people lived little lives unaware of who allowed them to live. They felt secure, safe, and were happy enough to ignore what was going on. He grinned like a wolf baring its teeth. In his hand he held a brandy. It had done its job. The woman, Maria, had been able to loosen up. Not a lot, but the promise of more information was enough. She was back in her cell and he had thought little of her since. Finding her parents was the driving force for her to leave, following the man he wanted.

He drew breath enough to sigh, what a sad little reason to risk her life. As if they mattered in the bigger scheme of things, but then very few did. And one who did was out there somewhere. The man who had led her and others out. Heyusser wanted him. Wanted to find him in time to realize there was nothing he could do. The he was too late to stop the inevitable. Heyusser laughed. He realized why they had come out to risk their lives while talking to the woman. A large group needed a large purpose. They had learned about their fate and they wanted to do something about it. They needed someone to pull them together with the ability and charisma to get them to follow. He thirsted to show him his efforts were futile and watch him collapse like the rest. How pathetic, how useless their efforts. He almost felt sorry for them. He should video the whole thing, they could watch it on replay if they missed it. With peanuts.

On the top of the mountains around the city Ishmael saw the glinting of ocean in the distance. The sun had started to set, turning the sea into mercury. The city shone in the light as if daring the forces to try and ruin it. Ishmael felt sorry for the place he loved and lived in. It was lying like a sacrifice to the gods who would soon rip its heart out and toss it aside. Near him lay the spire. Impressive from a distance but up close it was huge, vast, tens of yards across above the trees hiding the bottom from view.

They had marched long and as the evening fell they saw how large the compound was. It was huge, bigger by far than he had realized. The bare expanse of concrete they would have to cross was more than daunting. A large gate was at one end and tire tracks led to and from the base where a large building stood. It surrounded the spire. Huge supports and cables stretched from each corner of the compound. It was its own immensity and it took Ishmael's breath when he looked at it and tried to take it in.

He wondered how they could bring down something so massive but when he looked at Andrew, he saw his friend smile. "To weaken it enough, remember?" Andrew hefted the backpack.

Ishmael looked over to the spire, stretching to zero point in the sky. The scale of it forced him to look away and blink to bring his vision back to normal. It would be dark soon and the spire would be lit from below by floodlights. He returned his gaze to the city. The sun was burnishing the afternoon. Metal glinted everywhere, even into the forests and the hills where the sun could reach it. Ishmael felt the pangs of fear scuttle down his spine like fleas. For the first time he knew what they were up against. It was easy to be brave when you couldn't see what you were facing, something else again when you could. He walked to where Andrew and Nancy were waiting. Andrew finished tying the straps on his pack and stood, hefting it onto his shoulders.

Ishmael felt a sudden, jolting tiredness and hoped it would be over soon. "So many people," he said to himself. "So many people wanting help. And I don't know whether I can or not. I don't even know what to do except what I'm doing." He prayed he would find the strength to do what he needed to do when he needed to do it. He picked up his pack, feeling the weight of the explosive and the movement of the detonating devices. Andrew had told him about weak points, stressors, and physics. All they needed was to weaken a support and the weight of the spire would do the rest. Failure was a certainty. All they needed to do was attach the explosive, set the timers and fuck off quick. Ishmael smiled at how Andrew had said it and he wondered if it would be so easy when the time came.

"Tonight we bring down the tower," Andrew said as he turned to lead them to cover where they would shelter until the time came.

Nancy smiled at Ishmael. "I'm glad I came, no matter what happens," she said in a quiet voice.

Ishmael only nodded. It was all he could do. If he spoke he was afraid his voice would give away his fear and stop him. He followed them out of the small clearing and into the forest. It would be over soon, one way or the other.

TWENTY-FIVE

ARIA had been in her cell for what felt like an eternity since Heyusser had returned her there. The lights stayed on. There were no windows to see the passage of time. There was nothing to do but wait and it was harder now she knew he was using the time to arrange things to his advantage. But she still got something, more than Heyusser had imagined. In a strange way she realized Heyusser had given her something to cling to. Her parents might still be alive. She clung to the hope despite the knowledge he might be lying.

She was sitting on the bed when the lock shifted and the door opened. The guard beckoned her out, silent as always. In the room where hopes rose until dashed down Heyusser stood by the window. It was getting dark; the lights of the city glowed bright. Maria walked in and the doors closed behind her.

Heyusser turned and smiled like a raptor would smile at a rodent. "Welcome," Heyusser said. He waved to a chair. "Take a seat. I have a surprise for you."

Maria looked askance at the man who knew so much and held so much back and who urged by a gesture. She sat in one of the chairs behind the desk and watched him as he turned back to the window making her wait. He seemed to be enjoying himself and it played on her mind. The other chair was sitting at an angle as if waiting. A glass sat in front of each chair and in front of his. It looked like someone else was going to join them. She didn't know for sure who. She knew who she wanted it to be but turned her thoughts away so she wouldn't give anything away. She watched as Heyusser stood motionless. The silence moved, filling the room as she waited for him to speak.

"Can I have a drink?" she asked.

"Before our guest arrives? Come now, it would be rude wouldn't it?" Heyusser continued to face the window as if in place like a sculpture. "We can wait. There are more important things to consider."

Maria wondered what they could be. Heyusser did like to leave her wondering. She saw it was his motif to keep people off their game. He wanted them guessing so they couldn't see what he was up to behind the smile. Confusion and disorder were his strategies. He was hoping for her to fall for it. She decided to sit and wait and see who the doors would open for next. She didn't wait for long.

The elevator doors opened and Jesus stepped out into the room and swept his eyes around. He looked at Maria, stopped, moved into the room, taking everything in as best he could. The doors hummed closed, leaving them alone.

Maria watched him, a smile tilting the corners of her mouth. She hadn't expected he would enter Heyusser's lair. She hadn't known he was close or they had taken him. What was he doing, what was his game? She wondered where the others were, what they were doing. She looked at the man she had thought lost, like her parents. He was thinner, the skin had shrunk around his cheekbones and a growth of beard softened the outline of his chin. His face was grave. In it she saw he had made a decision. Her heart sank to a depth she hadn't known for years. He had put himself here. And then she knew she would leave here without him, if she was to leave at all.

She knew Heyusser wasn't the winner here, he was the loser and he didn't even know it. Amid the depth her heart sang with relief. She looked at him again; saw his eyes. They were sunken and shadowed but clear and full of a purpose nothing would push aside. It would come to pass as inexorable as the tide. He seemed to fill the room as he stepped forward and came towards her. His eyes settled on her and he smiled. "Maria." He tilted his head, recognizing her as a woman and a comrade and she felt relief.

Heyusser had turned around but stayed where he was. "Good to see you." Jesus didn't respond. Heyusser took no notice of it. "Please sit down, you know the lady of course so don't insult me by claiming otherwise."

Jesus nodded as he sat down. He knew better than to argue until he had his feet under him and felt more certain of his position. and what the man opposite knew and wanted from them. He waited for Heyusser to say more. He needed the time to learn more about the situation before making his demands. Heyusser picked up a decanter of golden amber liquid. "Brandy?" he asked. Jesus said nothing and Maria followed his cue. He filled up the glasses and picked his up. "Salut."

Jesus and Maria picked theirs up and sipped, still silent. Maria wanted to speak but she followed the lead of the man she followed. His manner and silence gave her strength she didn't know she had. Calmness came from him and she let it cover her. She bathed in it, letting it fill her with warmth that didn't diminish, only grew. Heyusser had to see how she felt. She kept her eyes down so he wouldn't.

Heyusser didn't see the emotion spiraling through her. Having the two of them under his thumb was all he could think of. The knowledge he had the two people he needed most of all, ran through his mind on a circular track with no end. They were his playthings now, to do with as he pleased. He felt like a god. He pulled a folder out from a drawer and laid it on the table. It was blank faced and bulged in the middle. He wanted to keep the contents secret until he needed them. Jesus let him and kept his eyes from the folder to watch Heyusser's face to get a read on him.

He knew people like Heyusser often felt they were in a stronger position than they were. Insecurity lay behind everything they did. Being calm would help put him off his guard. A secure man off his guard would make mistakes. He wouldn't think to look for the traps. Jesus saw a thin man, sallow from too much time indoors, high on ego and assumed power. A man confident in the hold he has on people never knew how weak the hold really was. Jesus wanted to see how he would react when he realized his mistake and felt the power diminish. He wanted to find out and use it when it happened. He waited for Heyusser to make his move.

Heyusser played with the folder on the desk. Jesus knew it was one of the aces Heyusser thought he held. He wondered what was inside. Jesus watched Heyusser toy with it, tapping it with a bony forefinger and waited for him to speak. Maria knew each was assessing each other, using their minds to probe for weaknesses. There was a crackle in the air as if presaging an oncoming storm.

"You led us quite a dance until today," Heyusser said to Jesus. "Your arrival surprised me. I never thought you would give yourself up. I congratulate you for your bravery but not for your foolishness. You know I thought I had you once but I was mistaken. But those we managed to get were worthwhile for adding to our workforce. We go through so many workers with our attrition rate. I know there are others of course. The two of you wouldn't make it here by yourselves. The others don't matter they're extras to the grand plan. We'll sweep them up but don't worry we'll make good use of them." He sniffed then sipped the brandy. "I hope you like the brandy; it's a good vintage. They can still do something right over there despite their problems." Heyusser eyed his glass. "We can be grateful at least. Some things change for the worse, some for the better but good brandy never does. It remains perfect."

"I wouldn't know," Jesus said, knowing the game now. "I've had enough problems of my own to worry me without looking for those of others."

"I understand," Heyusser said. "Living as you have for so long in a dead city without hope of anything getting better, making do and surviving. You've craved for more, you must have." He watched Jesus for a reaction. Jesus gave him none even as the words struck home like darts. "Although things always change at some point in our lives. What we all want is a change for the better, an end to uncertainty. Isn't that right Jesus, an end to not knowing what will happen next, is what you came for? The certainty we all crave in our lives?"

"Or we want a different kind of certainty. The uncertainty of change is preferable to the certainty of no change." Jesus said.

Heyusser inclined his head. "You want us to change what is happening. We can you know." Heyusser put the decanter on the desk. He waved a hand over the decanter. "Help yourselves, I don't want it said I'm a bad host."

"Too early to tell." Jesus wanted to see his opponent. He knew what mattered was who bested the other in this flurry of mental combat. How they saw each other was the key. His mind smiled, may the best reader win.

"It is." Heyusser watched them both over the rim of his glass. "How was it in LA by the way? I haven't seen too many people from there."

"It's tough," Maria responded. "But you won't understand how much so from where you sit."

Heyusser nodded, smiling. "I agree it does depend on one's perspective. Yours is much different than mine and much smaller. We can debate the point for hours but we do not have the time to indulge ourselves." He pushed the folder around on the table like a chess piece, first here, then there, waiting for a question about it.

Jesus knew that Heyusser knew more about L.A. than he was showing. He would soon show them what it was. Men like him have to show off. "You didn't ask us up here for brandy, did you?" Jesus asked as the gloaming turned into night outside.

"Indeed not," Heyusser replied. "I do have good reasons for doing so. Not the least of which is wanting to know why you're here in my city. And it is my city." He filled his glass, halfway, no further. Jesus realized he was a man of order and repetition. Habit ruled his manner and his reaction. He wanted to know what habit drove him to this point and keep his secrets. Power? The desire to keep it can be hard to break. "You know a man by his motives not by what he does. I have my reasons for being where I am today and you have yours in turn. I know Maria's; it's the desire to know about her parents. I would like to know yours." Heyusser paused. "Motive has a purity action doesn't have. Many claim to be good and do good things but only out of selfishness. They want to get something in return and so reveal their character."

"Not everyone does things out of selfishness," Jesus stated.

"You can say so for yourself but would it be true?"

Jesus wondered at Heyusser. "What do you mean?"

"You didn't leave for selfish reasons did you?" Heyusser pointed out. "It's hard for a man to get any followers when they are thinking only of themselves. People will see through them unless they are good at hiding their real motive. Such a man could say it's for the people but you would have to have some desire for recognition underlying it. To have the selfish and unselfish in one man is quite an interesting dichotomy."

"How do you explain your hold here?" Jesus wanted to know and to dodge the point. "You're powerful. You hold it and have it. Isn't getting hold of power a form of selfishness? And does everyone who lives here see the selfishness of your own motives? Like you say you are good at hiding things."

"Point taken," Heyusser raised his glass. "And often you'd be right but not this time I assure you. My people have more things, personal things, to occupy their minds. Who holds the power is irrelevant to them, so is whether I am hiding things. They don't care and I make sure they never do."

Maria watched them like she was at a tennis match, wondering who was going to hold the advantage at the end. Words shot back and forth like a baseline rally.

Heyusser turned his chair to face the window. Maria noticed a bald spot on the back of his head and stifled a giggle. "I'll get to that later but first you, Mr. Contreras. May I call you Jesus?" Jesus assented with a wave of his hand. "I want to know why you left the city you lived in to come out here. What did you hope to achieve? Your companion," he waved over the back of the chair, "told me a little but she can only know so much. You can tell me so much more."

"And in return?" Jesus thought about how much he could reveal. He decided it couldn't be a lot.

"I will tell you my motives in return. Or not, you're in no position to demand or expect I will tell you." The chair swung round again. "Or I can let you live a little longer, the desire for life is a strong reason to tell me things."

"We all die at some point," Jesus said. "Everything passes in its own time. It holds no fear for me, *aceptar*."

"And if someone like me decides when the time will come?"

"We only think we intervene. Fate has its own way of doing things and of bringing death." Jesus sat placid in the chair.

"Another good point my friend." Heyusser opened the folder, a few pictures spilled out onto the desk. "But fate is a poor substitute for action. You would like to see these?" He pushed them across the desk.

"Why?" Maria wanted to know.

"Curiosity, and to know leaving might not have been a bad idea, no matter what your motives were." Heyusser smiled like a death's head.

Jesus and Maria picked up the photos and stared at them for long moments. They showed the ring of mountains locking LA into place, only able to spread north and south. In one they could see a large crowd in front of The Cathedral. In another a ring of steel was under the trees, concentrated in areas where roads led down to the city.

Other images were close up, they could see faces. Jesus thought he could see Wilton's bar. Wolves and bobcats scrounged among the trash and the rubble. A mountain lion was chewing on a corpse of a woman lying in the street. Jesus was happy she couldn't feel it. Death does have its benefits, he thought.

The images had a date stamp on them. Most were three hours old. Some were less. They showed how they would wipe LA off the map. There was nothing they could do to prevent it. They saw Humvees, tanks, and soldiers in numbers they couldn't count. They knew Heyusser was the only thing holding them in place. They were the only ones who could make him pull them back. Heyusser looked like a man who would need a lot of convincing.

It was full night and the sky had clouded over, keeping in the heat the sun had brought with it. Ishmael, Andrew, and Nancy had returned to the edge of the vast clearing beaming with light. It cast deep shadows in the forest that they crouched in, trying not to move. In the middle of the clearing and concrete sat the base of the support column. The massive structure that angled up until lost where the lights shone no further. Other lights ranged across the clearing. Getting close would be the hardest part.

Andrew opened his pack and pulled out the explosive and some detonators. Ishmael did the same and Nancy watched like a weasel watches a rabbit. Her eyes were intent and blazed blue in the light as it caught her. There were no soldiers around. They had scouted around and found themselves alone. Ishmael hoped they would be alone long enough. He told Andrew his fears in a low voice.

"No point in worrying about it," Andrew whispered. "We're here to do a job and we're going to do it or die trying."

"I'm not sure I like the last option." Ishmael said as he pulled the same material from his pack.

"I don't either, I like living too much but there's no other choice." Andrew sat on his haunches. "Daylight will get crowded and we don't want to be around when it arrives. When we set the charge we'll have to move fast and quick, and we don't want to be under it when it comes down. I'm aiming to get it to fall east of us but it could go anywhere." he grinned. "If it does land on us it will be a quick death at least."

"How high is it?" Ishmael asked.

"No idea, miles."

The idea made Ishmael shudder. "I saw on a computer that it could be hundreds of miles high."

"It will make one hell of a bang, won't it?" Andrew was not fazed.

Ishmael realized they were going to die no matter what happened. "It doesn't matter."

"You want to go out with a bang preacher man?" Andrew's grin was devilish in the dark and his eyes gleamed.

Ishmael stayed quiet there was nothing to say. Nancy broke the silence. "There's no wire around the spire. What does that mean? Seems strange that whoever built it would let anyone get close."

Andrew grunted. "Never expected anyone to try I suppose. Bad mistake on their part." He busied himself attaching the detonators to the explosives. He took Ishmael's and finished the job in less than an hour.

Then they were ready. "Let's make one more check to make sure no one's around," he said. "Then we move."

"Those lights worry me," Ishmael said an hour later when they had circled the clearing. "There has to be someone around or why have them covering the clearing."

"In the past people used fake security cameras," Andrew said. "They never took any images, but people thought they did and so they worked. I guess this is the same. Cheap too since you need to keep guards here all the time." He stood up and his face was set with the knowledge of what needed doing. He started towards the support. Ishmael and Nancy followed.

TWENTY-SIX

HEYUSSER spread more photos out on the desk. The images showed a dwindling crowd taken over a period of thirty minutes. Ishmael wasn't among them but others had taken his place; dressed in rags, arms stretched out. The last image was of an empty space. The crowd had vanished like smoke among the destroyed buildings. Only a few stragglers remained. In the hills among the trees and along the roads they saw men with guns along with parked Humvees and trucks. Even in the images they had menace. Jesus felt they would find little to amuse them when they reached the city. A more complete disappearance he hadn't seen.

"Interesting aren't they?" Heyusser asked.

"What do they mean?" Maria asked as Heyusser swept them back up and put them away with finality.

"They mean what your friend Jesus said earlier." Heyusser sat like a smug frog on a lily pad. "Everything has an ending, LA's time is due. It will disappear and be reborn like all the other cities along the coast. And don't insult me by saying you didn't know about the people in the image, their fate drove you here and I know it. And the men in those images know it as well. They show a remarkable prescience. I'm guessing they told the people to leave. And most of them did."

"At least they'll be safe," Maria said.

"That depends on your definition. If you mean not dying then yes, they're safe. But the only place they can go is into the mountains or along the coast and if they do we will collect them like fish in a net. They'll live but will they be safe? You decide."

"And those who stay?" Jesus asked.

"My men will clean them from the city. We will take as many alive as we can; unnecessary death bothers me. Then we will raze it and when it's over all you have known will vanish like bad dream."

"Do they all deserve to be prisoners?" Jesus pressed home the point.

"Does anyone? I wouldn't say life will be better for them here but I doubt the alternative is all it's cracked up to be."

"No one deserves to die like rats." Maria flashed anger at Heyusser. He ignored it.

"People die all the time." Heyusser tried to be the calm amid her storm. "This is power and this is my motive. The power to change the world as I see fit and do as I wish to the people who cross me and who would stop progress. Is it selfish to crave power when its use can help society keep itself structured? No. I keep this society running and the people are happy with their lives. I need no purer a motive than to keep others happy. Hardly selfish is it?"

Jesus breathed in. "To what end?" Jesus asked. "If society needs anything it's a goal, the structure helps the people to achieve it and do these people have a goal? Living and being happy isn't a goal, it's robotic, it breeds zombies. Where is the free will?"

"Is this why you left LA?" Heyusser asked. "To argue with those in charge of life? To argue about free will? It may surprise you but people always put free will behind being safe and secure. If rulers meet their needs they desire nothing else. That's what governing is about."

Jesus shrugged his shoulders. "You say I left to argue but the arguments solve nothing. I only came to find out why and to stop this. If you are the cause, I ask you to end things, *desinencia*. This is the reason we are here. To find out why the city is as it is, why you would destroy it and ask you leave us in peace. The only ones I could think of to ask were on the other side of the mountains, and so we left. You were the reason I left. Maria and the others had their own reasons, they came with me. I couldn't stop them. Now we are face to face as I hoped we would be and I ask you this. To stop."

"Ah yes, Maria and her reasons. She told me she wanted to find her parents, or what happened to them. They disappeared somewhere over the mountains. She believes I can tell her what happened and where they may be." Heyusser relaxed in his chair, not taking his eyes off them. "But there's nothing I can do to help." He aimed the words at her and she tried hard not to flinch.

"You said you'd tell me." Her reply was almost inaudible.

"Yes I did, and I will tell you what I know. Very little." Heyusser frowned at the words but it looked fake like he was acting a role. "People left LA a lot, always have. Most died. Either shot, or in the desert. We took the survivors to the camps. One of those possibilities happened to your parents Maria." He pursed his lips in thought. "I don't know which and I couldn't care less. They are two people who vanished out of thousands more. I'm afraid I can't say anymore."

"Can't or won't?" she wanted to know.

"Take your pick. It's none of my concern."

"It is to me," Jesus said. "What concerns her, concerns us both. She grieves for her parents and you can help."

Heyusser chuckled, it sounded like gravel in a bucket. "You can believe me or not, it's your choice but I have no reason to lie. Yet I can offer you the chance to watch the future of as it happens to make up for it. I can let you watch as the dogs of war are set on the city." He chuckled again. "I like that phrase, it has a nice ring to it. You should feel honored, not everyone gets to see the future unfold. It comes about through little things we never notice, a decision changes a life forever and so it goes. This is not one of those moments, this is the Pearl Harbor of your lives, nothing less. From this point everything has changed."

Heyusser picked up the phone next to him. "Go ahead." He sat back again and opened up some doors by remote control. Behind them were several monitors and they flickered into life. "It might take a while so be comfortable, drink up my friends and watch the future take place in front of your eyes. Be grateful, you might never get this chance again. Call it my gift to you both."

Jesus felt his gut churn at the casual inevitability of Heyusser's manner. "What if we don't want to?"

Heyusser felt like someone had poured cold water on a precious dream he'd held for months. He tried not to let it show. "You don't want to see history made?"

"You asked us earlier what we were here for and I told you." Jesus waved toward the screens, the silent accusers of his silence. "Now I will speak again for those who cannot. I came for a simple reason, to find you and stop you. Or to argue for life, the life in the city you want to destroy. I can speak to your morality if you have any."

"Stop me?" Heyusser felt almost sorry for the man sitting opposite him. "You do jest of course. You can't stop me if you tried and I do not destroy as you think. I only change things for the better and when change comes there are always winners and losers."

Jesus didn't let the words show on his face. "Why? Why do this? What did we do to you to treat us like garbage, trash, *bazofia*." He shook his head. "We do nothing to you. For living you would destroy us, wipe us out like you did to those other places, San Francisco all the others."

"You knew about them like I said. I'm not surprised but I'm curious about how you found out. It matters little of course; the death of LA was inevitable. The only uncertainty was when and even that has gone."

Jesus nodded. "We saw them before we left."

"Then you know what we can do, correct?"

Jesus nodded an assent.

"Then you know nothing and no one can stop us." Heyusser swung back to the screens. Blurred shapes were moving. Jesus felt unease, like he was staring at a ravening beast driven by nothing more than the need to feed, prey to its instincts. He knew he couldn't reason with it but he had to try.

Maria appraised the two men. She sat mute. Something told her she needed to listen. It was important. She continued to watch.

Heyusser was watching Jesus with the intent of a man watching for the dice to roll the right numbers. "Why do you want to try, Jesus. It isn't as if you will succeed, you've seen you cannot. Already the apocalypse rolls forward, unstoppable. I or rather we hold absolute power here and everywhere. We are as near as you can come," he smiled like a snake, no humor touched his face, "to being God. We control your lives in more ways than you can ever conceive and this is our will and no one will stand in its way."

Jesus narrowed his eyes at Heyusser. "You are a man, not God. Only He can hold such power and only His will matters, not yours."

"Not true," said Heyusser with finality. "We have it, I have it. Your god gave it to us after getting tired of doing it himself." He turned to look at the screens. The headlights of vehicles scoured the night and flickered among the trees. "Yet this is not the time and the place for a theology discussion. Soon the place where you lived will no longer exist, the people scattered or dead. You will have achieved nothing despite what you promised. None of them will thank you, especially those waiting for you outside."

Jesus and Mary both flinched. "How..." She started to ask. Heyusser cut her off mid-sentence.

"Did you think I wouldn't know your companions were here too? I said someone had to bring you here Jesus so there was no reason to even think of denying it. We have cameras everywhere. We saw you everywhere, we saw you come here, your companion leaving you here after bringing you to us. We were watching you everywhere you went. And we know where they are."

Heyusser picked up a remote control from the desk and eyed it close. He pushed a button and on the screens the image flicked and shifted. On it they saw the truck Jesus and the others had come in to Vegas. The truck was in the car park across the street. Their friends were watching the building. "What we will do with them," Heyusser wondered aloud. "I wanted to show you this so you'd learn how much we know and how much you don't." Heyusser turned to watch them. "You have no secrets, and we have many."

The screen stayed on. The truck sat under lights that made the night disappear. They saw their friends silhouetted against the glass, sitting like statues. Jesus and Maria watched them, helpless. Jesse was behind the wheel, Nathaniel next to him. In the back Jesus and Maria saw Wilton, Adeline, Jeremiah, and Arturo. "You want to mock us? Is this why you do this?"

Heyusser grinned again. Like before it was mirthless. "No mockery I assure you. It's only to show how insignificant you all are to us, to me. Despite that I like you. I admire your courage, misplaced as it may be, which is why I allowed you to watch what's about to happen. I don't usually do such things you know. It's almost an honor for you to see this. It's something your friends will never get to see. They are safe but they won't stay that way. We will take them, when is not your concern. After that, it's up to you what will happen." He noticed the look on Maria and Jesus' faces. "I can send them to the camps and you will never see them again. With one call they will disappear like ice in hot water." Heyusser watched Jesus. "Or I can set them free. All except you."

It took a moment for Jesus to understand, the ramifications grew like an excrescence in his soul. In his hands lay the lives of people he knew, who came with him across the mountains and the desert. In LA the people came and went from his life, he saw them pass in front of him. Saw them slink away into the buildings, afraid to face the sun and the reality. He didn't know them and had still come out to try and save them if he could. He had failed. He had faced the forces capable of ending the world as they had come to know it, in the man who sat across the desk. And lost.

The disgust rose in him like bile, stinging his eyes and burning his throat. The taste made him want to pour out the poison in the office of a man who controlled the fate of those he didn't know. And he still wanted to fight for them all. He faced the man who had their fates twined around his fingers like threads of cotton as strong as steel. He vowed to break them in any way he could. "You are going to make me an offer? Is this what matters to you, playing games with people's lives?"

"Only in passing, I want you to know where the real power lies and what real power can do." He gestured at the room. "It lies here, and I will give you the options you can choose from. They are not yours and no matter which one you choose it will still be my choice."

Jesus tilted his head sideways. Maria felt the mood in the room change. It was as if someone had let a current flow through the air and hung around to see what would happen next. Heyusser swung around to the window, the chair tilting as he did. "Your choice is simple Jesus, choose the people with you here or the people in Los Angeles. You care about them but you can't help them all so who is it to be, who will you save?" Heyusser tapped a button on his desk. "Hold and wait for further orders," he said. "I don't have all day Jesus. You have one hour so use your time well and make the right decision. People are depending on you more than you might think."

TWENTY-SEVEN

OUTSIDE, the companions sat in the truck. The windows were open to let what cool breeze there was come through to take the heat with it. Jesse was in the driver's' seat. Through the windshield they could see the building that held Jesus and Maria. The companions felt the void they had left. Spotlights lit the forecourt and played across the front of the building. "Well I can't think of any way to get them out," Jesse said finally. "Any suggestions other than using force, something I hope won't get us killed?" The response was a shrug, felt and not seen. There were no answers and Jesse hadn't expected any.

They were in limbo, unable to move in an alien place. Their thoughts swirled like mist, drifting through their fingers. Decisions made had led them here and could not be unmade. There was only the certainty of the truck and themselves. Even Jesus and Maria had an air of unreality. They grouped together in the truck, afraid to move outside and wary of staying inside. They shrank way from the windows hoping to lessen any attention. Only here could they know anything. So they stayed and watched as the people walked past under the gaze of security cameras.

"It's possible they've taken Jesus and Maria elsewhere." Wilton broke the enervating silence.

"Yep," Jesse spoke as short as he felt.

"So we could be sitting here for no reason?" Wilton pushed the issue.

"Could be the case," Jesse stated in a flat voice. "But what else can we do?"

The air grew heavy and dense. Wilton exhaled louder than he needed to. The building opposite looked ominous in the floodlights. They waited and watched as the moon arced across the sky. Stars lit the firmament in a fitful manner against the glow of the city. Their skins tingled as the cooler air touched them where the sun had left them red. For a moment Wilton wondered whether they would feel it worse the next morning. Then he wondered if they would see the next morning.

"I would like to try and do something, we can't leave them there." Arturo spoke from the back of the truck. Everyone knew how he felt.

"We all would like to do something," said Jesse, his eyes not moving from the front of the building. "There doesn't seem to be anything we can do except wait and see what happens."

"You sound defeatist," Wilton said.

"It would be if there was something we could do and didn't give a fuck about doing it so we didn't try." Jesse took his eyes from the building and closed them. "Sometimes when I was out hunting there'd be times when a deer or a rabbit would be in the wrong place. I'd have to wait. No point in fretting about what you can't control. It stops you from seeing what you can and acting when you need to. This is the same, so let's keep focused on what we can do and ignore what we can't. It's a waste of energy otherwise."

"Not the best of analogies," Wilton said.

"It'll do because it's good advice." Jesse kept his eyes closed. "You better listen to it."

"I suppose if I must, then I must." Wilton feigned an air of exasperated patience.

"Yep," Jesse put an end to the conversation. Outside, the night passed in silent hours and their thoughts moved with the moon.

The clearing around the support was more dangerous close up. It was brighter than day and Ishmael was grateful there seemed to be no one around as they neared their target. They never saw the small security camera tracking them across the expanse.

None of them knew that underground lay a bunker, hidden from view. In the bunker sat two men with crew-cut hair and black uniforms. They looked at each other and one picked up a phone and spoke into it. He put the handset down and nodded to the other. They were serious about their job. The safety of the spire was their responsibility. So were the lives of those who lived in the gondola at the end of it.

Ishmael, Andrew, and Nancy didn't know the men were there. Days before, Ishmael had talked with Jesus about where a man dies is less important than the manner of his dying. Ishmael lived by it, was clear headed about it. He never heard the small whir of an electric motor raising the guns from under the ground.

He never heard the small click of the firing mechanism. But he heard the first shots and felt the rush as several passed close by him and hit Andrew, taking away most of his face. He heard the grunt from Nancy as she collapsed forward and he felt the impact of bullets in the chest and stomach. He fell and in the dark where his thoughts stopped, he died.

In the bunker the two men saw the results. They would have work to do in the morning if the scavengers had left enough for them to bury. Coffee brewed on a hotplate. Above the ground the bodies lay waiting.

"How do you sleep at night?" Jesus asked the man at the window.

"What makes you ask?" Heyusser turned to face him. "Not simple curiosity I'm sure."

"You are about to kill many people and destroy their homes." Jesus pondered Heyusser's motives. "How many is not the point, *exacto?* But how you can do what you do and sleep I cannot understand."

"Nor me," Maria put in.

"It's not difficult. Decisions have to be made and I make them. The consequences are for others to bear, not me. LA is dead and I am the one to make sure it is reborn, like a phoenix out of the ashes of the past. Call it development or politics." He sat in his chair. "And to be honest much of the time the people care little for and never complain about these things. None who live here do and they are my only concern."

"Do you listen to hear if they do?" Maria asked.

"No, I don't have to, look at them. They are happy and why shouldn't they be? They have food, shelter, jobs for the most part, the feeling of security. They have everything anyone needs. They are safe, and safe people have no need to complain, they don't like it. It disturbs their comfort." Heyusser smiled again. "And their comfort is so important to them they will avoid doing anything to disrupt it. What they will do to anyone who does is anyone's guess." He looked at his watch. "Your time is running out Jesus, I wouldn't put off the answer or you may lose everything."

Jesus bowed in agreement. "I haven't forgotten."

The ring of steel around LA had stopped moving and waited for the order to proceed. In the remains of the city Ishmael had done his work well. Others had sounded the alarm after him as much as they could. Those who'd wanted to risk getting out did, going over the mountains and along the coast. The camps waited for many. The people who fled knew the risks and accepted them. Those who stayed knew their risks in turn. They feared the end and vanished, finding whatever hole they could use to wait it out in the hope of survival.

The night was long. Shadows touched and clung to themselves in the hills and on the roads with LA at their terminus. Looking up from the city, those who stayed saw the lights knowing death was coming. They watched the lights from their burrows and holes and sat down to wait. Their thoughts offered no comfort.

Jesus sat with his thoughts in the room where the windows opened onto a night lit by fluorescent tubes. Maria had gone back to her cell and Heyusser had left the room, "urgent business" was all he'd said. Time was running out and he measured it by the throb of blood in his temples. Images of people and places ran through his mind. The battered buildings. Deer and wolves roaming the streets. People trying to live. He saw Gabriel and the people who'd left to seek their own way and he knew Heyusser was right. They were dead or taken prisoner. He saw the lucky few who had made it.

But he still wanted to know one thing. Why things were this way and no other. What was the alternative? He wanted to know; no, needed to know. The answer would decide his choice. Who he could save if he could save anyone. No, it was more, he knew it in his bones, the surety of it lodged deep inside him. He knew whatever he decided Heyusser would set loose the dogs of destruction on the city he called home. In a corner of his mind he realized at least he could save someone. He could do no more. He made his choice and, closing his eyes, waited for Heyusser to return.

An unknown time later, shot through with his imaginings and fears, the door opened. Heyusser entered the room with Maria. "You've made your choice?" he stated as he sat down. "I hope so, our patience is not infinite."

"Yes I have," Jesus said. Then he stayed silent for several minutes. By accident of birth he was sitting where he was and across the table was Heyusser. They were both victims of fate. "How and where we are born is funny isn't it?" he asked Heyusser. "You are sitting there forcing me to make this choice and I am here making it. Yet if things had been different it could be me sitting where you are and the world would be different for both of us." He shrugged his shoulders. "Call it fate or destiny but here we are. Could it have been different, who can say."

"Odd time to get existential and wonder about the vagaries of life," Heyusser said.

"It's the right time," said Jesus. "With decisions like this it is right to consider bigger issues. It's hard to do when you don't know if you'll survive another day."

"Your decision please?" Heyusser waved a hand to cut the conversation short.

"In a moment," said Jesus. "*Momento* please, I have a few questions for you before I tell you. They will not take long, *menudos* only. A few minutes won't matter much *eh*?"

Heyusser looked at the ragged man in front of him as if seeing him for the first time. He was dirty, his clothes were rags, there was a hole in his left knee and his shoes had seen better days. Still there was something in his manner which baffled Heyusser. He should have been pleading but his manner was calm. He had shown little fear and others Heyusser had seen had shown a lot. This man was different, it was as if he had expected to be here and in doing so had something others did not. Heyusser wondered if he would ever find out. His eyes glinted and were clear. Behind them was a sharp mind Heyusser hadn't noticed before. It was a mind he could have used if things were different.

He knew Jesus sat in the chair not as a prisoner but as an equal, ready for whatever happened next. He'd never seen that before. Heyusser saw equanimity and calmness in his opponent despite his position. It was almost refreshing and he wished it could have been different. But it wasn't. On his desk the light on the console pulsed, counting down the seconds of their lives. Heyusser smiled, the decision wouldn't be his to make. He allowed Jesus to ask his questions.

"You said the people here feel safe, why, and who from?"

"It doesn't matter who, as long as they feel safe. Enemies are much an invention as friends if you know the right buttons to push." Heyusser watched the pulsing light. "We live in a harsh world Jesus, you should know more than most. You've lived that harshness all your life. Here," Heyusser waved at the window, "there is little harshness people face like you did. They are happy, not free, but happy and secure. People will give up freedom to be happy and secure and safe from what's out there. The trick is to make people think they are free and it's an easy trick in any case."

Jesus shook his head. "Freedom is what people want and you know it, you can't fake it, people know when they don't have it."

"No. They want the illusion of it, no more and no less. Here I give them that illusion. Rulers need not give the ruled anything more. To do so is foolish. You can't rule a free people they need to be in check. Those in power have always known it. It's a harsh world, threats abound and there are people out there who want what we have. I protect my people from those threats whether real or imagined. You can see the results, happy people going about their happy and safe lives. No fear, no worry, live as they please. They believe they are safe and they give up freedom because of it."

"But it isn't as they please, it's as you please. It's the same as you will do to my city. You will do as you please whether I like it or not, no matter the consequences are for the people who live there."

Heyusser snorted. "As I please? As far as that goes you're quite right. And as for the consequences, the only ones that matter are the consequences for the people that I rule. The only consequence people here worry about is they feel safe. And if a few have to suffer for that, then so be it. "

"It is of consequence to them." Jesus felt his temper rising in his gut.

"Ah Jesus how little you know when you count the few over the many." Heyusser strode to the window. "Come and look with me." Jesus walked over. "Look out there, you see these people going about their lives in peace. They like things this way. They like others making decisions for them, showing true leadership. I and my predecessors did the same when it was most needed. They are grateful and in return for what I provide, they keep to the rules."

Jesus didn't understand. "When was this and what did you do to keep them like robots, with no thought of a better world?"

"It was many years ago Jesus, after the world as it was then collapsed. It was before our time but as the climate changed, the sea started to rise and people left the coasts. It was too late by the time people finally got the will they needed to do something about it. Governments around the world collapsed and everywhere was war, famine, disease, anarchy." Heyusser stood facing the night. The lights were bright along The Strip. Images of women, cards, and gaming tables flickered and changed colors. In the distance a top hat glowed. "They were harsh times."

The lights shone bright and gaudy in a place where Jesus thought they didn't belong. For a few long moments he wondered about them shining over his dead city. He pushed the thought from his mind. It didn't belong. LA didn't belong anymore, like the others along the coast north and south. Cities were the playthings of the people who lived here, not knowing the price they paid to be happy.

"I know the people who left first, they have places to live where they are safe. Up there, above us in the clouds, they watch us every day like watchmen, *veladors*. They watch you too *eh?*"

Heyusser snorted a denial. "Ah yes, you can see one of the spires from where you lived."

"They left us to rot as they always did." Jesus felt bitterness in him he hadn't felt before. Bitterness for the power lying in the hands of evil people. He forced himself to stay calm. "You rule a fiefdom I've heard it said."

Heyusser barked out a quick laugh. "Oh I do but it's more than you know. I can see you need to learn what's going on and I'm not sure if I am the one to teach you. But I do know who can." Heyusser pressed a button on the console. "You've been listening?"

A voice responded, tinny and thin but there was a feeling of depth to it that make Jesus' skin crawl. "Yes we have."

"What do you think?"

There was a silence unbroken by the hiss of white noise. "Interesting. He is intelligent and he may be quite useful. Send him but not the others, they don't matter. Deal with them as you wish." The voice clicked off into silence.

"Deal with them as you wish?" Jesus asked.

"Depending on your choice." Heyusser sat. "Speaking of which, you have made it?"

Jesus nodded. "I came to ask you to stop and save my city."

Heyusser smiled like a winner who thought he'd lost. "What's done cannot be undone Jesus. All you can do is reduce the casualties."

"So I will only save those I can, those who left the city with me and who are waiting outside. And Maria of course." Maria gasped at the words, knowing what they meant.

Jesus rested his hand on her arm. "This is how it must be, Maria. Be strong, the future lies in your hands. Do I have your word, Heyusser?"

"Wise choice and yes you do have my word. They will be free and safe." Heyusser demurred. "Of course they will have to leave the city and my fiefdom and find another place to live. But the alternative is worse. I'll give the order." Heyusser picked up the phone. "Take the girl to the others, tell them to leave by the morning or we'll arrest them. Make sure they have food and water, they have a long trip ahead. And tell them Jesus will be staying a little longer, our business isn't over. Tell them he'll be safe if they do as they're told."

A voice came through affirming the order.

"There," Heyusser told Jesus. "As per your choice they are free to go. LA will be less fortunate." He picked up the phone again. "Proceed as planned." He hung up. "I didn't want to do that you know. I'm not without feelings."

"You don't let them get in the way."

"Like I said, politics." Heyusser averred. He pressed a button and a guard entered. "Take the woman and let her go." He watched Maria. "And don't try to come back, or it will not go well for you and for him. Make sure your friends leave with you. If they don't, I will cancel the deal with the obvious results." He spoke again to the guard. "Then take our guest downstairs and make sure he's comfortable. You'd like a shower and a change of clothes?" He looked at Jesus, eyebrows raised. Behind them, Marias was taken out. She didn't look back. She didn't want to. It was over.

Jesus looked at his ragged clothes and at his grimed hands. "I hadn't thought of it."

Heyusser told the guard to make sure Jesus had a shower and a change of clothes. "You have a trip coming up and I don't want you dirty. It looks bad on me." It was silent in the room then. All talk was over and the ending of things loomed. When the guard returned after freeing Maria, Heyusser guided Jesus to the elevator. He watched until the doors closed then turned back to his desk, Jesus and the others forgotten.

TWENTY-EIGHT

A T the top of the spire Jesus waited for his ears to return to normal. The trip had been a long one. At least he'd been comfortable. The pod had a toilet as well as food and water. Nothing fancy but he had been in worse. He avoided the windows after passing out from vertigo watching the planet disappear. It was hard going until the push under his feet stopped and zero-G kicked in. He stopped feeling like a bug on a windshield and enjoyed floating in the air. Until he threw up and spent hours trying to scoop up the mess. He wondered how the old astronauts managed without leaving their stomach behind.

He watched as the sky darkened from blue to turquoise and then black. He couldn't see the stars. He wondered why but put it from his mind. He had more important things to think about. On the second day he felt a slow but gradual slowing of the pod, he was reaching the end of the ascent. He remembered getting in after the drive to the spire. It had taken most of the day. He'd spent it in silence, watching the smoke rise from a city too long in dying and fighting its own burial. He grieved at the loss, made worse by the knowledge he couldn't have done anything to stop it. For all his intentions he had done little more than tilted at windmills of his own creation. Fighting sadness, he'd entered the pod and the door closed behind him. He tried to console himself by knowing he'd saved some lives and it was the best he could have asked for. It didn't help.

And himself, had he run to save his skin? He didn't think so but the notion he had nagged him. A quote Ishmael liked came to his mind. *"I know not all that may be coming, but be it what it will, I'll go to it laughing."* It seemed fitting but as he waited in the pod for what came next, he didn't feel like laughing.

A voice came over a speaker by the door. It told Jesus to strap in for the pod to dock with the gondola. He had five minutes. He was at the end of a journey that had seemed to last weeks but had only been several days. The shuttle started to slow. He waited, looking out of the window but couldn't see anything. A vibration ran through the pod and a green light shone by the door told him something was happening. The door opened into a small room and he entered as it closed behind him. He heard the hum and felt the slight rumble of the pod returning to Earth. He sat on a small stool and after a minute another green light shone and a door opened onto another corridor. He walked down the corridor to a circular door. It opened like an eye. He stepped through. He had arrived. "Welcome Jesus." The speaker was a small man, dapper in appearance, who looked like a butler. His face shone and his hands were pink. He gestured for Jesus to follow him. "I'm sure you have lots of questions for us and we will do our best to answer them." He showed Jesus into a small cubicle. "I'm sure you'd like to freshen up first, two days in the same clothes has a distinct, fragrant effect on people. You'll find clothes in there. They should fit." He looked Jesus up and down. "I'm sure they will." The dapper man bowed and left. Jesus entered and the door closed behind him.

He came out ten minutes later. Another man in a uniform was waiting opposite. He gestured Jesus to follow him. The corridor bent in a very slight, almost imperceptible curve to the left as they walked. Wherever he was it was large, magnitudes larger than the pod. Along both walls were doors with keyless entry locks. On the right wall the occasional window opened out onto the blackness of space. Paintings hung on the left wall. They were real. One was a Picasso. The man led him through a door into a large room on the right. A man was standing by the large windows, another stood to one side, watching as Jesus came in. The uniformed man bowed Jesus in and left. The door closed behind him. The man at the window turned and smiled. It didn't look real and Jesus was on alert.

"Ah the man cometh along with the hour," he said. "A somewhat mangled saying I know but what of it? Please sit, Jesus, it's a pleasure to meet you. I've been counting the hours until your arrival." Jesus sat in the most comfortable chair he could remember sitting in. The leather was soft and the cushion yielded so far to accommodate him then no further. "My name is Fleming, Woodhull Fleming."

Jesus remained silent, wanting the man to keep speaking until he felt he had his bearings again. He felt disoriented. Fleming seemed to know what he was going through. "Don't worry, you'll get your space legs soon enough. It always takes time to settle into the reality of where you are up here."

The sky remained black outside the window. "Why are there no stars?" Jesus asked.

"I asked myself the same question when I first got here. Something to do with the sun being too bright or so the experts tell us. Come look, the view is excellent." Fleming stood to one side and Jesus decided to see for himself.

Below him the planet lay stark against the deep inkiness of space. The continents and islands were brown and green, the seas blue. Clouds came and went in slow spirals and the bright white of snow flashed when the sun hit it. There in the window, under his feet sat the only place he called home. Somewhere on the surface his home, was being wiped from the planet, making way for others to enjoy a theme park.

"Makes the old saying of location, location, location seem trite doesn't it." Woodhull spoke with pride.

"Who are you?" Jesus asked.

"Myself, or everyone?" Fleming asked in turn.

"Everyone, you aren't the only ones here."

Fleming nodded. "Indeed we're not." He looked at the planet like it was a plaything and Jesus realized it was to them. "There are a lot of us up here, watching our planet and we've been here for some time. But you want to know more, am I correct?" Jesus nodded. "Have a drink. It's the finest brandy on board. Only the best you know, we have it sent up on a regular basis. Being distant like we are doesn't mean we have to suffer any privation."

Jesus wondered if the man next to him would understand what true privation meant. Not having his favorite drink to boast about would be the worst thing in his life. "No, I do not know, and you speak of privation like a joke. But from where I come from it's a way of life and death, something we must endure. There is nothing else for us." Jesus said.

"Then you must be grateful for us for removing the people and erasing it from existence. There is no more privation there, correct?" Fleming said with finality.

Jesus didn't feel grateful.

"To answer your question about who we are I will go back some years if I may." Fleming's face reflected the blue of the planet they were standing over.

Jesus stayed silent watching the planet below them, waiting for him to speak. He glanced askance at the man by his side. He had gray hair, smooth skin, and eyes that appraised him like a falcon assessing a pigeon. They lived well here, the carpet was plush, not thick but expensive and high quality. The furnishing looked hand-made. The living quarters would be the same he knew. Woodhull Fleming was one of the ones Jeremiah had told him about. The ones above the planet who left to live there years ago. One of the overlords. Jesus felt a sudden chill tickle his spine. He was in the presence of a man who knew he was God.

"Many years ago world leaders bickered about climate change like children in a playground. They wanted to blame someone else and do nothing. So we decided to take our leave and live up here, away from the trouble we knew was coming." Jesus knew the man was leaving something out. He remained quiet, letting the overlord talk. "We used ruses, and political sleight of hand as well as bribery to hide what we were up to. We came here to live where we were out of reach of the concerns of others and where they were of no concern to us. We were, alas, wrong in that assumption. For reasons I shall come to."

"But you couldn't do all that without people working for you down there." Jesus asked.

"You are right. We did have people working for us. They kept our secret about what we did to leave. If they didn't they were killed. We allowed nothing to get in our way. So we left but when we did we forgot one important thing. The certainty you get when people think someone is in control. The people thought their political leaders were, they never knew it wasn't them, it was us, the tech billionaires, industry magnates, oil tycoons, media moguls, all of them. Although some did suspect the truth it was easy to have them labeled as cranks. People living out a paranoid fantasy." Fleming looked out of the window and sipped his brandy

"You know if you look hard you can sometimes see the sunlight glinting off the other gondolas. We call them gondolas but houseboats would be more apt. I'm going to change that. So when the certainty left the countries collapsed. There were wars, bad ones, over water, food, resources and for the power to have either or both. It was the end times for civilization until we took a hand in things. That was the time we realized what happened down there was a concern to us. We couldn't allow it to continue."

"Why take a hand, why not leave it to die? You sound as though you would have welcomed it once."

"Stability Jesus. We wouldn't have survived ourselves if everything collapsed. We would have no sources of supplies or people. We intervened for our own survival, nothing more." Fleming pointed to the planet. "Look there, a storm is brewing in the Caribbean. Some things never change. So to make the planet stable we installed people here and there over areas of the planet such as Heyusser. We made the planet evolve to suit us."

"The man, Heyusser, is one of those who rule like puppets. What happened to the countries? Where did they go?"

"Countries were never real. They were legal fictions separated by imaginary boundaries to give people a sense of belonging. Do you notice anything?" Fleming waited a minute for Jesus to look. "There are no boundaries down there, between the fiefdoms as you call them. There never was. People created countries for their own amusement. They conquered what they didn't have and increased their control over what they did. People accepted these fictions and so the world went on for millennia until the temperature hit the tipping point the scientists said it would."

Fleming sipped his brandy, poured another. "You're sure you won't have one?" Jesus declined the offer. "People started to run out of food and water and those who lacked either fought others to get it. There was chaos. People died by the millions. The usual human verities fell underfoot. Governments collapsed and in the vacuums others rose to take their place. With our help as I said. People like Heyusser who do our bidding whether they like it or not."

"And all this time you have supported some and not others?"

"Well asked Jesus. Yes we did. Each of us laid claim to a patch of the world where we built our spires. We made it worthwhile for certain people to allow us the land you see. We made our own alliances here and there to reflect the reality. We built a peace on the ruins of the old. We made sure the resources were equal as best we could of course." Fleming shrugged. "There are some little spats from time to time but we have peace, better than before you know."

"But the price."

"Is one we are willing to pay. Heyusser told you people only want to be safe and happy and whatever the price is it doesn't matter to them. After all they don't need to pay it and don't care who does. It's simple human nature." He offered Jesus another drink. Jesus accepted. He had no reason not to. "But you asked where the countries went. They went back into the nothing that spawned them. From nothing they came and to nothing they returned."

"Why are you telling me all this, didn't the people notice there were no countries anymore?"

"Did you? Weren't you more concerned with surviving every day in the city you came from? No longer is it a city but a collection of derelict buildings and derelict people. It was a wonderful city once but now it is nothing until we rebuild it. I was born there did you know?"

"Then as it was your home as well as it was ours, even if it was no longer somewhere you saw as one." Jesus slammed his glass on the table. "It was my home and the home of others like me, you had no right to take it from us!" His eyes blazed.

Fleming seemed unperturbed. The man by the wall took a step forward but Fleming stopped him with a glance. "I have every right. The area around the spire is mine to do with as I see fit, you lived there as long as I alone allowed it. And I no longer allow it." Fleming turned back to the window. "The coastlines have no use anymore. Most of them are unlivable and so we make use of them as best we can and if there are costs so be it. Progress will always win in the end."

"Progress? You call what you do progress? Was it progress when the seas rose and the wars began?"

Fleming pursed his lips and his brow drew deep furrows in the smooth skin. "No, none of us wanted it but it happened. We all have to make the best of it; us and the rest down on the planet. And be honest, where would you rather be now, safe here? Or eking out an existence down there, never knowing if the sunrise you see will be the last one?"

"I would rather be there than with you. Living here separate from humanity for so long you no longer have any. You pretend to be Gods but you are not, you are less than human." He stared into the cold eyes of Fleming. "You still take from us, you always will. You didn't escape, you ran like cowards, *cobarde!*" He spat on the carpet under his feet. "*Bastardo*, take me back. I prefer to die there than live here."

Fleming smiled and the coldness of it made Jesus shiver. "I'm afraid you misunderstand, you have no choice. You will stay here since we cannot let you return with what you know. I'd much rather you stay out of choice but stay you will."

Jesus felt a chill in his gut, replaced as quick as it came by a calm implacability of purpose. "I am to be a prisoner?"

"No of course not," Fleming was trying to find the right words. Jesus saw the thoughts run like fleas across his face. "More of an honored guest. Permanent but honored."

Jesus smiled and shook his head like a man knowing he was being lied to. "Words pah! You use them like honey to lure and then trap. An honored guest who cannot leave is still a prisoner. I have no intention of staying here, no matter what you say. You will not be able to keep me."

"And we cannot let you leave to tell others about us and what we are doing." Fleming put his glass down on the table with finality. "If you do, you might foment an uprising, which would upset the balance we have in place. The people are happy and comfortable and we cannot allow you to interfere. It would," he stared at Jesus, "upset the status quo."

"You fear what I can do," Jesus said.

"We don't fear anything. We don't like disturbances in our lives. Not after all we have done."

"You are wrong. Fear rules your lives more than ours, you fear change. You want things to remain as they are but they will not and you know it and what can happen scares you. I came out of the city to change something and I know what it is. I do not fear change as you do. I am leaving and your world will crumble and take you with it." He looked at the man by the wall and the door leading outside and his course crystallized into certainty. "I wish I could see it happen. Would you take me to my cell now?"

"Your room? Of course." Jesus noticed the emphasis on the different word. Cell or room it didn't matter. He was a prisoner regardless of the word used. Jesus led the way into the corridor, the man following a few feet behind. Fleming was the last. Jesus saw the number on the door, remembered how many rooms he'd passed after leaving the airlock. He knew where he was going and what he was going to do. He walked on hoping they would reach his destination before they put him into the room he would die in. He was going to die and it would be on his terms not theirs. He remembered telling Ishmael the way a man died was important. He hadn't known how important until now. The way included the choice and he made it.

They came up alongside the airlock and he made a sudden move left. Then he snapped back to the right and hit the button to open the door. The man closed his hands on Jesus' jacket but it didn't hold. Jesus slipped free and began ripping the wiring from the control panel on the inside. The door slammed shut before they could follow. They could fix it he knew but not soon enough.

"Come out Jesus, there's nowhere else for you to go from there." Fleming spoke as the man pushed the outside button in vain before pounding on the door. "We can get in there soon enough you know."

Jesus smiled to himself. He looked around in a state of peace he hadn't felt before and saw the airlock release. So it came to this, would his death make a difference? He didn't know. It would come to mean something to the overlords. They might realize some people desired freedom enough to die for it. Would it change what they did in the future? He had no way of knowing. It would be their choice. Outside in the hall Fleming realized what was going to happen and sagged against the wall. Jesus waited for a long moment then pushed the button to open the door. As the air rushed out taking him with it he closed his eyes. He saw the stars.

TWENTY-NINE

A SMALL truck made its way along a road east of Las Vegas, heading for the Rockies. They saw them standing in front of them like a jagged wall. Wilton, Jeremiah, Arturo, Nathaniel, and Adeline were sitting in the back. Jesse was driving with Maria sitting beside him. Her eyes still held the tears she had been shedding since the guard put her in the truck and told them all to leave. They streaked the dust clinging to her face. The road blurred as it passed by on both sides. They had left Vegas for the flatlands and the communities over the mountains. They didn't know if Jesus was still alive, only had Maria's word he was when she left him. The thought kept them going as they drove east.

"What do we do now?" Jesse asked Maria.

"We carry on. We finish what we started when we left to follow his dream. It is ours now." Maria looked out at the disappearing desert and the approaching mountains. "We bring those bastards down. Jesus would want us to."

www.ingramcontent.com/pod-product-compliance
Lightning Source LLC
Chambersburg PA
CBHW051134020726
47501CB00005B/1500